THE ROSE GARDEN

(THE ROSE SISTERS, #4)

SIENNA CARR

AUTHOR'S NOTE:

THE ROSE GARDEN is the fourth book in THE ROSE SISTERS series, about three sisters, Ashleigh, Eloise and Ginny who live in the small town of Whisper Falls.

There are four books. The first three are based on each of the sisters, and the fourth book brings all their stories to a conclusion.

While they can be read standalone, your reading experience will be richer if you read the books in the following order:

The Bridal Shop
The Summer House
The Winter Beach
The Rose Garden

CHAPTER 1

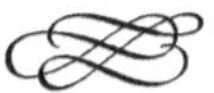

ASHLEIGH

The mood was dark and somber; a gathering of people in dark clothes talked in hushed whispers.

Ashleigh looked around and felt out of place more than ever. The last time she'd come here had been to see Patricia, Ford's mother, not so long ago.

At noon today they'd buried her.

"Why don't you eat something?" Eloise whispered. "I see quiche. It looks good."

"You're not dieting today?" Ashleigh asked. Not that her sister needed to diet at all, but Eloise seemed to be more concerned with her appearance lately. It had something to do with her having a younger beau.

"I haven't had breakfast," her sister retorted. Ginny appeared, with a plate of food which Eloise eyed hungrily. "You should get some," she told them.

Ashleigh huffed. "Thanks for waiting for us."

"I'll go up with you," Eloise offered, but Ashleigh was busy watching Kayla, the woman who had once looked after Benjy and Ginny, hover around the buffet table as if she were queen of the castle. Kayla seemed to have taken it upon herself to make sure there was enough food on the table. The house was filled to the brim. A testament to the number of lives Pamela Ford had touched in her ninety plus years.

"Hey," Eloise nudged her in the ribs gently. "Shall we go and get something to eat?"

"She's waiting for Kayla to move, I think," Ginny whispered as all three sisters gawked in Kayla's direction.

"It's like she owns the house," Ashleigh mumbled.

"Thank you for coming." Ford's rich voice made her heart jolt. She prayed he hadn't heard what she'd said. Eloise and Ginny greeted him warmly, and expressed their condolences, again. They had all managed to talk to him at the funeral, but he was so overrun with so many people coming up to him to pay their respects, that they'd stayed in the background.

"I'm sorry for your loss, Ford," she said. After all, what else could she say? Losing a mother, no matter how old or how long and fruitful a life she had lived, was always tough.

Ford shrugged. "I appreciate you all coming."

Eloise chuckled, making a noise that was so weirdly out of context in the setting. "We're family, Ford. Sort of." She side-eyed Ashleigh. "You don't have to keep thanking us. We're here for you."

"Yes, we are." Ginny touched his arm. "Whatever you need, just say. We can drop some food off for you, if that helps?"

This brought a smile to his lips. "I appreciate the gesture, Ginny, but I just need to keep myself busy." He jerked a chin in the direction of his ex-wife and daughter who were over by the food table. "Susan, Maddie and Kayla have made enough food to last me through next winter."

Ashleigh glanced once more in that direction. The sight of Kayla made her insides harden. She and her sisters had visited Ford at the home he shared with his mother soon after he called Ashleigh to tell her of his mother's passing. Because he'd called her, Ashleigh had assumed, wrongly, that he needed her, and now was her time to step up and be there for him, to comfort and console him and to help him plan for the funeral.

It had therefore been a cruel slap in the face to find Kayla already there when she'd rushed over. Ashleigh ground down on her molars just thinking about it. Any help or comfort Ford needed, he obviously wasn't looking to get it from her. She had known all along that Kayla was muscling her way into Ford's life. It was from Ginny and Ryan she'd heard the news that Kayla had been helping Ford to take care of his mother, and in return he was helping her with her driving.

Watching them now, they seemed friendly enough, if a bit mismatched. Ford, *her Ford*, was tall and big, broad-shouldered and strong, and still as handsome as the day she first met him, even if he was somewhat weathered by the years. Kayla, on the other hand, was like a school mistress from the Victorian times.

Ashleigh winced, annoyed at herself for thinking nasty thoughts about a woman she barely knew.

Ford looked at her expectantly, and now she was worried that he'd asked her a question, but her mind had drifted. "Just ... just let me know if you need anything," she said, erring on the side of being vague. "I'm always here for you, you know that."

"You must be Ashleigh." Susan appeared by Ford's side, with her daughter.

"Hi, Susan." Ashleigh knew who Ford's ex-wife was. She'd passed her a few times in the street when Ford had come home over the years. Ford introduced them properly.

"Congratulations, we heard you were getting married soon." Eloise was never one to read the room. Susan seemed a little taken back by the comment. "Thank you. I wasn't aware that the news had reached all over town."

"This is a small town," Ginny reminded her.

"But I don't even live here!" Susan exclaimed, tucking a lock of hair behind her ear. Her short brown bob gave her a neat and professional appearance. If Ashleigh hadn't known who she was, she'd have mistaken her for a lawyer not a doctor.

Eloise chuckled. "You don't have to live here; you just need a connection to someone in the town and guaranteed we'll know all about you."

"Thank goodness I'm going back to Boston," Susan replied, good naturedly.

"Sorry to interrupt, but could I grab you both?" Ashleigh didn't miss the way Kayla's hand rested on Ford's arm. "I'm not sure what to do with all the extra food we've got in the kitchen."

"Sure." Ford excused himself then disappeared and Susan followed on his heels.

"I didn't realize Kayla was so familiar with them," Ginny noted.

Eloise sniffed. "She seems like part of the family."

"Doesn't she just," Ashleigh muttered under her breath.

CHAPTER 2

ELOISE

"*U*ghhhhhhhh!" Eloise let out a high-pitched scream at the sight of the long skinny tail that vanished out of sight as quickly as it had appeared.

She jumped onto the chair, shivers scurrying all over her skin. Liam came running, wearing his toolbelt and gloves. She pointed at the floor and screamed. "There! Behind the sofa!" She felt icky, as if the mouse was crawling down her shirt. "There!" she cried, half-hysterical. The darned thing had scampered to the other side of the room. "Get it out, Liam! Get it out, NOW!"

"I'm trying!" Liam raced around as the mouse disappeared behind the sofa. Eloise screamed again. It didn't matter that the creature was on the floor. It might as well be crawling up her back. There was no way she could stay here. She'd have to move back to the main house with her sisters for a few days.

Or stay at Liam's place.

She could not, would not sleep here. She shivered, standing on the chair, rubbing her arms as she watched Liam corner the rodent who had scurried under the table.

She felt sick in her stomach. How had that thing gotten inside the house? "We need a mouse trap. Buy a mouse trap!"

"And kill the poor thing?" Liam had his back to her.

"Whatever it takes! It can't live here."

Liam crouched down and reached over. Eloise held her breath, waiting. Then he got up slowly and turned around, still cupping the small mouse. She screamed again. The sight of the scrawny little thing, the sight of that tail, made her feel itchy all over. She shielded her face with her hands, her body tensing. Liam smiled as he walked towards her. He showed her the mouse, even though he was holding it securely in his hands.

"Don't you dare!" She jolted back in terror. "Liam, DON'T!"

Thankfully, he changed direction, then calmly strode towards the door, opened it and disappeared outside. A few moments later he sauntered back in and she was still standing on the chair, her hands up in front of her, protecting her chest, like a boxer ready for a fight.

"Elle, calm down," he said, calling her by the nickname he'd given her. "It's okay. It's gone. I made sure to throw him in the field away from here." She tried to do calm down, but it was impossible. She was still in shock. Her body tense. She could stand spiders. Could deal with them herself, but mice? She shivered again just thinking about it.

Liam walked towards her, a big grin on his rugged, bearded face. "That little thing scared you that much?" He took his gloves off and wrapped his arms around her, which prompted her to wrap her legs around his waist. She shivered as the image of the long scrawny tail flashed through her mind. "Mice give me the creeps." She buried her face in his soft, warm neck.

She was lucky to have this man. And not only because he was good at catching mice. "Will you check around the house?" she begged, not feeling safe until a military-level inspection of the house had been made.

"In a while."

He carried her up the stairs.

"What are you doing?" She didn't want to let go; didn't want to be put back on the floor until the inspection had been done.

"Taking care of you. You looked scared. I'm going to make you relax." He carried her into the bedroom and laid her down gently on the bed. Then he pulled off his gloves, before lying down next to her, a cheeky grin on his face.

"Will you check the rest of the house?" she pleaded.

He turned on his side and propped himself up on an elbow. "Later." His eyes danced with mischief. Then he lowered his head and kissed her.

"A thorough inspection," she said, when their lips broke apart. "Under the tables and beds and every nook and cranny."

"In a while, I promise." He cupped her face, then moved in for another kiss.

CHAPTER 3

GINNY

"I wanna have pancakes," Daisy announced as they headed towards the diner.

Ginny tapped her gently on the head. "Then you shall have pancakes." Ryan continued to push the stroller as they walked down Main Street.

Benjy gurgled happily, reaching out and playing with the toys hanging on his stroller. Six months old now he'd only just started on solids and was also starting to sit up with a little help. Daisy with her hand on the stroller, kept slowing it down as she bent down and made Benjy giggle.

He loved Daisy. He truly adored her. His little face would light up every time he heard her voice, and laughter would erupt from him like a volcano. She would race to him and shower him with kisses whenever she could. She played with him and would chatter away to him, as if they understood one another perfectly.

They were inseparable. Like brother and sister, and now that school had finished for the summer, Benjy saw Daisy more than usual. When the little girl wasn't going to summer camp, Ginny and Kayla took it in turns to look after her. For Ginny, it simply meant that Ryan would drop her off to the house, and she and the two children would spend the day together, making cupcakes or doing artwork or going to the park or the mall. Things would get a little tricky when Ginny started work at the shop again but Kayla, being a teacher, had the summer free and was able to look after Daisy more. They would manage.

Ryan stopped pushing the stroller and came to a standstill. "I wish we could put you inside the stroller, Dee. It would make pushing this thing a heck of a lot easier."

"Want some, Benjy? Want some pancakes?" Daisy asked the baby, completely oblivious to what her dad had said.

"We can feed him little pieces of fruit once we sit down, sweetie," Ginny told her. Benjy was filling out nicely. He was getting heavier, chunkier, and easier to hold and was no longer a fragile little baby, but a robust little boy. Ginny's heart filled with joy every time she woke up and saw him in his crib. She loved this tiny being with every fiber of her being and she couldn't imagine her life without him. He was the center of her universe. The sun around which her world revolved.

"You'd climb inside and sit with Benjy if you could, wouldn't you?" Ryan teased his daughter.

"Can I?" Daisy cried.

He raised an eyebrow. "You wouldn't fit now, would you, sweetie?"

"If I shrink myself I will." Daisy gave him a cheeky grin.

"And how do you propose to do that?"

Daisy shrugged. "I'm hungry," she stated, as if suddenly remembering where they were going.

"We're almost there. You can order as many pancakes as

you like, sweetie," Ginny told her. They'd had a lovely long walk this morning. The town was only a half an hour away by foot.

Ryan had recently rented a beautiful and spacious four-bedroom house overlooking a lake. The owner was looking to sell in a few months' time and Ryan had the first option to buy. Having a place of his own had been good for them all. For Ginny it meant more privacy away from the house she shared with her older sister, Ashleigh, and for Ryan it meant finally leaving his sister Kayla's place.

It also meant that Daisy had a big room to herself. With Ryan in the master bedroom, there were two spare rooms. Ryan kept telling her he would get one of them ready for her and Benjy; she just had to tell him which one she liked more, but Ginny kept putting him off. She didn't want to rush things.

They'd recently gone for a day trip to Starling Bay. Leaving Whisper Falls and having a change of scenery had done them all good. Especially after the recent upheavals in all their lives. Daisy going missing had scared them all to death. Then Vanessa had turned up and caused chaos. Thankfully she hadn't stayed on and had found a job in Seattle and had decided to settle there. A day trip to a different town had been just the thing they needed and they'd come back enthused by their experience. So much so that they were now talking about going away for a long weekend.

As a couple wanting to spend time together, being at Ryan's new place was easier. Privacy had been difficult to come by. In her own house Ashleigh seemed quieter than usual. Her sister was convinced that Ford and Kayla were together, although neither of them had confessed to such a thing, or been asked about it outright. Ginny wasn't so sure that they were a couple, and Ryan maintained that Ford and his sister had an arrangement to help one another, and that it was nothing more than that. Still, a change had come over Ashleigh recently, and Ginny was relieved to be out of the house more.

"Hey, Ginny."

Ginny blinked, as they came to a stop in front of a woman she didn't instantly recognize.

"It's Rhonda. Remember me?"

"Oh, hi." Ginny would never forget the woman who, unknown to Ginny at the time, had started seeing Benjy's father. Rhonda's eyes bounced around the group, and Ginny felt obliged to make introductions. "This is Ryan," she said, threading her arm through Ryan's possessively. "And this little angel is Daisy."

"Who are you?" Daisy asked the woman innocently.

"I'm ... I'm a ..." Rhonda hesitated. Ginny didn't rush to help her out. "I'm a ... a friend of ..."

"She's someone we know," said Ginny, relenting.

"Is she your friend?" Daisy asked, with the simplicity of a child. Ginny remained silent as Rhonda peeked at Benjy. "He's so cute. He looks ..." The woman pressed her lips together, leaving unsaid words hanging in the air.

"He looks like Ben," Ginny finished for her.

Rhonda swallowed, and nodded. "Yes, he does. It was nice to see you again." Ginny smiled, and nodded and they continued on their way. She had managed to get through that unscathed. There had once been a time where she couldn't be in that woman's presence. She watched Daisy bend down and mess around with Benjy, flicking one of the hanging toys on the stroller. Ryan pressed Ginny's arm which was still entwined with his. "You okay?" His eyes bore into hers, filled with concern. He was always so alert and watchful. Always keeping an eye on her. He could always gauge her mood and read her thoughts.

He *knew* her. It was such a comfort to be so understood. To have a man who loved her so completely. They hadn't even been together for that long, and yet it felt like they'd known each other for years. "I'm absolutely fine," she answered, staring back at him and finding strength, like she always did when she was with him.

She was fine. Seeing Rhonda Moore hadn't fazed her at all. Going out for brunch at the Sunnyside diner with her family on a Sunday morning was a normal family day out and no one and nothing from her past could put a dampener on it.

CHAPTER 4

ASHLEIGH

She was expecting a new client today. Someone who had travelled a few hours to get here.

Angelina McBride.

Twenty-one years old and extremely pretty, judging by the photo of hers in the emails they'd been sending back and forth, she also had an unlimited budget. Or so she said. She was in a hurry to find the perfect wedding dress having been so disastrously let down by a previous wedding dress designer.

Ashleigh liked the sound of that. After a slight downturn in the business in recent months, she and her sisters needed to turn things around. A client with an 'unlimited budget' would most definitely help.

Though the sisters advertised their business in bridal magazines, most of their customers came from word-of-mouth recommendations made from happy brides. Indeed, these women made the best customers.

Ashleigh intended to give Angelina her utmost attention. Primping her hair, she checked her face in the mirror, then smiled to make sure she didn't have any of the peanut butter bagel caught between her teeth.

The main door of the shop opened. She turned around to see a tall, slim and beautiful girl walk in. She immediately recognized Angelina who was followed by a few more girls of roughly the same age. A tall man, older and distinguished looking, entered last.

Ashleigh walked over to greet them. "You must be Angelina. I'm Ashleigh, we've been emailing each other." Up close the girl was even more stunning. Ashleigh wondered if her mother was the same.

"Oh, hi! It's great to finally meet you," the girl replied. Her friends had wandered off to look around, and were making loud exclamations as they ran their hands over the dresses on the mannequins dotted around the boutique. "Would you mind if I had a quick look around first?" Angelina's eyes fixed on a mannequin. She looked like a child in a candy store. "These dresses are gorgeous."

"Go ahead, take as long as you like, and then we can—" She was about to tell Angelina how they could help her to choose a dress, but the girl had rushed off to swoon over a dress.

"I'm Patrick, Angelina's father." With his salt and pepper hair and his handsome, chiseled face, he made for an arresting figure. Ashleigh's breath hitched in her throat as she shook hands with him. Her heart did a little jumpstart. "It's uh—it's lovely to meet you."

Angelina's father cast his eye all around, surveying the shop slowly. "This is very nice. Very intimate and classy. I felt the difference as soon as I stepped inside."

"Thank you."

"Who's the owner?"

She felt affronted by the question. That he couldn't see or it didn't cross his mind that she could be the owner. "I am."

Dimples formed in his cheek when he smiled, looking apologetic. "That's remiss of me. I'm sorry. It wasn't meant to be disparaging in any way, though ..." He scratched his brow, "I don't see how you could take it any other way. I apologize."

She smiled. "Apology accepted."

"How long have you had this?"

She hadn't expected such a long and personal conversation. Usually brides-to-be and their entourages were focused on the dress, and the shop talk came later.

"It's a family business. My parents owned it and ... well, now my two sisters and I run it."

"Your parents retired and passed it down to the next generation. That's the way these things go." He nodded as if he understood. As if he had any idea. She was puzzled. This was unusual, but no more unusual than her being drawn towards this enigmatic man that she'd only just met. He was charming. And a charmer.

"I wish they were retired. They ... they passed away when we were young. It was a car accident and they were taken from us too soon." Her voice wavered, and she steeled herself to pull herself together.

The man looked shocked. "I'm sorry. I'm so sorry for your loss, and for asking you." His expression turned apologetic. "I'm sorry. This isn't how I usually start a conversation with someone I don't know. You must think me very forward and nosy. Irritating, probably."

She laughed, wanting to ease the tension and because he was right on all those accounts. He glanced over to where his daughter was, giving Ashleigh the chance to study his chiselled face. Even with fine lines and wrinkles, he was still incredibly good looking. He must have been drop-dead handsome when younger. She placed him at being in his late forties, maybe early fifties.

"Let's start again." He held out his hand. "I'm Patrick McBride, father of Angelina, over there." He waved in his daughter's direction. "She's looking for her dream dress and we are in a hurry. I believe the two of you have been emailing one another?"

"Yes, we have. I'm sorry for the problems you've encountered. Angelina briefly explained. I'm confident that we can get her the wedding dress of her dreams."

Angelina reappeared. "Daddy, I'm so glad we came here." She tugged her father's hand. "But I can't make up my mind. Come and see." She walked him over to one of the mannequins.

Ashleigh patted her hair, and wished she'd worn some under eye concealer, instead of rushing to get here so that she wasn't late for this client. She walked over, then followed them around the shop as Angelina and her friends excitedly admired various dresses. "I want them all," Angelina cried. "I like the skirt on that one, and the bodice on that one. I really like the beads on that one. I wants bits of them in one dress."

Ashleigh's insides felt light, as if they'd emptied. She wasn't sure if it was because of the way Angelina's father smiled at her, or because of the dollar signs she saw springing up in the virtual cash register in her head. "That's something we can do for you. Absolutely not a problem."

Patrick grinned again, making the dimples in his cheek more pronounced. "That's good to hear. We've been all over the place. All around New York, she's even looked in Paris and Milan and she almost settled on a dream dress in Paris, but the designer didn't seem to understand exactly what Angie wanted, so …" He shrugged. "Besides, we had to get back to New York for a wedding, and couldn't spend any more time there, so here we are. We hope you can help."

Ashleigh's jaw fell open. "Oh, we absolutely can help." In the emails they had exchanged, Angelina had mentioned the problems with the dress she'd set her heart on, but she hadn't said anything about going all the way to Paris or Milan. Who went to those cities and couldn't find a wedding dress there? "We have twenty years of experience in this business," she said, determined not to let this slip by, "and my sisters and I provide the most—"

"I'm not doubting you, Ashleigh." Patrick McBride's light blue eyes pierced through her, sending a shiver down her spine. She felt her heart starting to thump and worried that if it continued getting louder he might hear. So she forced herself to look away. As if that would change anything.

"Eleanor, my daughter's friend, recommended this place. We were blown away by her wedding dress. It had quite the 'wow' factor, you might say," Patrick told her.

"Oh, yes, Eleanor's dress was beautiful," Angelina joined in. "And now I want something that will have an even bigger impact. Something similar, but different. Something *uniquely* me."

"Eleanor de Freitas?" Ashleigh asked.

"You remember her?" Patrick sounded impressed.

"I do." Funnily enough, she remembered most of their brides and their dresses; their stories stayed with her. Also, it helped that Eleanor's wedding hadn't been so long ago.

"She's a very good friend of mine," Angelina replied. Ashleigh recalled that Eleanor was the daughter of an investment banker from New York. The girl had been quite demanding, with parents who fussed and fretted over her. But in the end, Ashleigh and her sisters had created a gorgeous wedding dress for her and the family were extremely grateful. And now Ashleigh was extremely grateful that their good work had prompted another word-of-mouth recommendation and brought them another customer. "Her dress was indeed unforgettable. We can help you, Angelina. We can do the same for you. Something uniquely you." Ashleigh reassured the girl with a smile.

"Why did we even bother going abroad, Daddy?"

Angelina's father shrugged. "Because your mother insisted we do."

"I don't know why we wasted so much time and effort." Angelina smoothed down her tulle skirt. "They have everything we need here, Daddy. Eleanor said this boutique was unique." She gave Ashleigh a dazzling smile.

Patrick beamed at Ashleigh, causing her heart to beat faster than usual.

"Where dreams begin." One of Angelina's friends pointed to the wall. Ashleigh pursed her lips together. She had come to dislike that tagline over the years, and especially more so now because life for the Rose sisters had been anything but dreamlike, although Eloise and Ginny seemed to be making their dreams come true, which was wonderful for them. Ashleigh wanted her sisters to be happy.

Life just didn't seem to have an opening for her own happiness.

"Why don't you go around the store and point out all the dresses you'd like to try on? I'll have one of my assistants help you," Ashleigh suggested. "We have a designer in-house, it's my sister, Eloise, but she's away for a few days. We can also look at some pictures if you give me some ideas of what you have in mind. When Eloise returns, she can sketch these more fully, perhaps on your next visit. This is how we work."

Angelina clasped her hands together and looked deliriously happy. "I told you, Daddy. I told you this was the place to go to."

"How about you go and try some dresses on?" Ashleigh suggested. "Get a feel for what you like regarding the fabric and the way the dress hangs and fits. Whatever you like, be it pearls or beads or Swarovski crystals, we can design your dress to have that. I'll make some notes and you can tell me what you'd like to put together into your dream dress. I'll get Rachel, my assistant to help you." She waved Rachel over. "You can talk to Eloise next week or we can do a video call if that might help."

"We can come back again, can't we, Daddy?"

Patrick smiled at his daughter. "We can do whatever you want."

Ashleigh summoned her assistant over. "Rachel, will you help Angelina? She's found a few dresses to try on. I'll be over in a moment."

She left them by the red velvet chaise lounges. The sparkling chandeliers above the fitting room area gave this part of the shop a very upscale touch.

"Where dreams begin. That's a clever tagline."

Ashleigh spun around quickly, hearing Patrick's praise. "Thank you." She didn't understand why he'd followed her back to the desk area. Surely he'd want to see how his daughter looked in the dresses she'd chosen? She smiled at him, and when he smiled back but said nothing, she said, "You went all the way to Paris and Milan, to look for wedding dresses? We are indeed honored to be on your list of places for wedding dresses."

"Your reputation is what made us come."

She blushed. "We're proud of what we've achieved."

"How long have you had this?"

"Twenty years," Ashleigh replied, a hot flush creeping up her skin.

"Twenty years?" Patrick exclaimed. You don't look old enough to have run this business for that long."

"Well … I am and I have been." She wished she had a superpower that would turn her into an ice queen on demand, so that she wouldn't feel hot and bothered while this man was looking at her. The effect he had on her was palpable in her voice. How she couldn't quite moderate her pitch, and had to work harder to keep her voice level. She tried to think of something to talk about. Something that would deflect from the hurricane of emotions swirling inside her. "I was in Europe a few months ago, actually." She heard her voice, but it didn't sound like her, and all the while little butterflies skirted along the lining of her belly.

"You were?"

She nodded. "I went on a little trip."

"With …?" He nodded, then waited for her to elaborate.

"By myself."

"By yourself?" There was an inflection at the second word.

Heat warmed her cheeks and the back of her neck start to get clammy. This was not the time to get heated up or start sweating under this customer's gaze. She caught him looking at her ring finger.

"I never married." She felt as if she owed him an explanation. Either that or she wasn't thinking straight. Those pesky butterflies in her belly were making her feel unsettled.

"Never married? I find that hard to believe." His eyes widened in surprise. They looked at each other and a rash of goosebumps scampered across her arms.

This was too much.

Too much talking about non-wedding related things.

Too much flirting.

"Mrs. McBride, did she not want to come along?" She spluttered the words out before thinking. The woman might have died or been ill or ... *something*. There was likely a reason, a *sad* reason, for a mother not accompanying her daughter on such a trip.

"The ex-Mrs. McBride, is taking care of all the wedding arrangements. I'm paying for everything, and she's in Monte Carlo as we speak, attending a society wedding there. Otherwise she would have come with Angie, but I'm glad, on this occasion, that I got to come instead."

Ashleigh opened her mouth to say something, but from the corner of her eye, she saw Ginny struggling to get through the door with the stroller, a rucksack on her back, as well as another small bag dangling from the stroller handle.

This was so *not* the look Ashleigh wanted for the shop. She rushed over to hold the door open, glad to get away from the charming Mr. McBride.

"Sorry I'm late, Ash. It's been a nightmare trying to leave the house on time." Something fell out of the stroller. A rattle from the sounds of it.

Patrick McBride picked it up. He'd only gone and followed her.

"Thank you," said Ginny. "I never realized how difficult it was to leave the house with a baby in tow. I should have practiced. I wanted to make a good first impression."

"Why don't you head over to the office?" Ashleigh suggested, her voice tight. A good first impression? Her sister had completely failed there. Ashleigh had forgotten that this was Ginny's first day back. She should have told her to stay at home, especially because of the McBrides' visit.

"I will, I'm going to. Phew." Ginny stopped to take a breath. Her face was flushed, and she was oblivious to the annoyance that simmered under Ashleigh's skin. "I thought I could push the stroller with one arm and carry Benjy in the other, but then I had to carry the bag and—"

"It's fine," Ashleigh said, gritting her teeth together and finding it difficult to suffer Ginny's complaining any longer. "Why don't you go through to the office?" She wished Ginny had stayed at home. What was she doing thinking about returning to work when Benjy wasn't even a year old?

"I wasn't sure I needed the stroller. Maybe I should have bought a travel crib for him? But then I thought he could—"

"Just *go*, Ginny." Ashleigh forced a smile, and when Ginny disappeared, she apologized to Patrick. "I'm sorry about that."

"About what?"

"This is not the ambiance we want for the shop."

"Understandable, but it gives the place a nice touch."

"A baby in a stroller? Thank goodness Benjy didn't start crying." She walked back to the changing room area. Gasps and giggles were to be heard.

"Was that your sister?" he asked, following her. "I see a slight resemblance."

"It is. That's Genevieve, the youngest one. She's just had a baby."

Angelina walked out of the fitting room looking resplendent in a stylish white satin dress. Her friends gasped and stood around her, admiring with awe-stricken faces. Patrick's eyes turned glassy, a bittersweet expression on his face. "Beautiful."

"Daddy, I love this."

"You look stunning, Angie."

"Please excuse me for a few moments. I'll be back. I need to take care of a few things." Ashleigh stepped away, knowing that this was an emotional moment, for parents especially. Also, her heart was beating fast, as if she'd run a mile. She charged into the office, her heart having palpitations. Her face was red. This was something different. Like a high school crush; like the first time she'd set eyes on Ford.

Patrick McBride was having quite an effect on her.

Ginny was settling Benjy onto a playmat on the floor. She propped him up into a seated position and had scattered cushions around him to support him. Ginny and Ryan had come in at the weekend and made a little area in the corner of the large room for Benjy. It wasn't ideal him being at work here with Ginny, and Ashleigh wasn't too happy about it but her stubborn sister was insistent on spending a few hours at the shop.

"Ginny, really?" Ashleigh cried in despair. "We're running an upscale business. Or trying to. You can't just come in with a stroller and all your things hanging off your arm and falling onto the floor."

Ginny looked horrified. "How else am I supposed to get inside?"

Ashleigh fanned her face and didn't answer.

"I was a little late and I'm sorry. Next time I'll get here sooner. I didn't know there was so much involved in trying to leave a house with a baby. I had to take a zillion things with me."

"Try to be a bit more refined when you walk in. Try not to drop things. Try not to make a commotion."

"What are you complaining about?" Ginny looked vexed.

"We have an important client." She'd told her sisters about her emails with Angelina.

"Have we lost her?"

"No."

"Then why are you so angry?" Ginny snapped. Your face is redder than a tomato."

Ashleigh's jaw tensed. "Because we have a great customer,

who loves our dresses, and is willing to spend a good amount here. There's no limit on the cost."

"Oh." Ginny's eyes turned round. "*That* customer." Ashleigh had mentioned the McBrides to her sisters, and the interesting detail that they were being driven by a chauffeur all the way from Boston.

"That customer."

CHAPTER 5

LIAM

"You want shelves along here, here and here?" Liam gestured at the wall of Ford's new office.

"Yeah." Ford let out a sigh. "It seems strange getting back to normal life."

"I know." He patted Ford on the shoulder, understanding the man's pain. He'd lost his girlfriend to a rare form of cancer years ago, and the experience had broken him. Losing someone young and in the prime of their life made him appreciate life more, and with Elle, he'd been able to find love again. Ford seemed lost and lonely and Liam was determined to be there for him. "You have to get on with life. It's what your mom would have wanted."

Ford coughed lightly and looked away for a few quiet moments. "I need shelves and some filing cabinets. I ordered them before all hell broke loose, and they'll be here within the week. Will you be able to fit me in some time soon?"

Liam took off his ball cap and put it back on again back to front, the way he often did when he was thinking things over. He had to rejig some of his workload, to accommodate Ford, but he could do it. Of course he could. The most important thing after losing a loved one and grieving their loss was to continue living. He would do whatever it took to make sure Ford came out on top. "I sure can. It's not a problem. This is a good office space. I like it."

Ford cupped his chin, looking pensive. "It's been neglected for too long. I should have had the office ready months ago."

"You would have been, but life got in the way. It's not your fault." Having someone you love die was nothing light or easy to get over. Ford had been good taking care of his mom, and now the guy needed help, and Liam was more than happy to step in and be that guy. Now that his mother had passed, the man was focusing on the accountancy practice which he'd put on hold when his mom got sick.

Ford let out a loud sigh. "I need to be up and running soon. The business has been on hold too long, as it is."

Liam patted him on the shoulder. "I'm not going to let you sit around or wallow." He'd seen the guy go through some rough times, and he'd now realized that Ford hid his emotions from most people. It was only lately, after his mother's funeral that the guy had started opening up more. Days after his mother's funeral, Liam had convinced Ford to go out for a few beers, and then he listened as the guy talked for hours, reminiscing about his childhood, and his life back here growing up in this small town. He seemed lonely, like he had no one, with his ex-wife getting married, and his daughter away at college, and now his mom gone, too. Ford and Ashleigh, Elle's sister, had been an item once, but now those two had broken up and Liam wasn't sure if Ford was involved with Ryan's sister, Kayla. The guy seemed quite dependant on Kayla on the day of his mom's funeral, but Liam didn't feel ready to poke around in that business just yet and ask him outright.

"How long will it take to complete the work? It's not just the shelves, it's all the other stuff left undone. " Ford looked around and let out a heavy sigh.

Liam scratched his chin. Remembered that he needed to shave because Elle complained that his beard was getting not too long and she liked him with a five o'clock shadow more than anything else. "There's not that much to do. I'll get some of my guys to help me and we'll have it done within the week, but we're going away for a few days, and I'll get to it as soon as I get back. Is that okay with you?"

"That works for me." Ford raised a half-smile. "Remind me where you two lovebirds are going again?" Liam couldn't stop the grin that was spreading from ear to ear. "Cape Cod. Elle's friend, Beth, has moved and they're having a party."

"Ah. Beth." Ford nodded to himself.

"It's her husband's fortieth birthday, so they're having a big birthday celebration. Why?" He wanted advice from Ford, and the man would know more about Beth than Liam currently did.

"She's always throwing parties and Eloise was always going to them. She spent more time there than here."

Liam shifted uneasily. "She hasn't been there in all the time we've been together."

"That's because her world spins around your axis." Ford chuckled. "You got a tux?"

"A what?" Liam wasn't sure he heard right.

"A tuxedo?"

He had heard right. Wear a tux? Liam hadn't considered that. "Elle didn't say anything about a tux."

"Beth comes from old money. The whole family's rolling in it. You might want to make an impression."

He shrugged. He wanted to make an impression, but it

wasn't for people he didn't know and didn't care about. "They'll have to take me as I am. Elle does."

"It's a big celebration, right? You gotta look the part."

Liam balked at the suggestion of him wearing a tux. No way. He was at home wearing wifebeaters and jeans, white tees mostly, with a shirt thrown over were his trademark. Toolbelt optional. The last time he'd worn something like a tux was when he'd gone to prom, back in high school.

"You need to get one," Ford told him.

"You're kidding me, right?"

"I'm not kidding you. Did Eloise not tell you anything? Beth's family are seriously, disgustingly wealthy. The last thing you want to do is look out of place."

He couldn't work out if Ford was joking with him or being serious. "You mean a smart shirt and jeans won't cut it?"

"For a fortieth birthday?" Ford folded his arms. "I don't know. I could be wrong but from the impression I got about that place, from Eloise, I wouldn't turn up to a party wearing casual clothes."

Liam scratched his chin again. "She hasn't said much about the party. She doesn't talk about Beth much." He wondered why she hadn't. It was surprising given what he was hearing from Elle's sisters, and now Ford; that she used to go there whenever she got the chance.

"You're staying at the house?"

"No. I booked us a room in a pretty cool hotel nearby."

"She usually stays there. I guess it makes sense if you're both going, though I've heard her friend has an enormous house."

"She's since moved—"

"It'll still be a stinking big mansion. Just you wait and see."

He didn't relish the idea of staying at someone's house. Didn't matter if they were Elle's friends. He didn't know these people and from what Ford had told him, he wasn't sure he would like them much, though he was going to do his best to not be so judgement. "Elle said it would be better for us to stay someplace else, and I prefer to stay in my own place. I'm not so sure I want to go now."

"Go! Don't let an old fool like me put you off. Like I said, I could be wrong. What do I know?"

"You really think I need to get a tux?"

"I wouldn't show up there dressed like that." Ford jerked his chin at Liam's attire.

Liam scratched his jaw again, the shine of his and Elle's special few days away were now dulled by what he'd heard. But it wouldn't change his plan. "I ..." He sucked in a breath. "I'm going to do it. I'm going to propose to her." He'd booked a nice restaurant for Sunday evening, and had planned to go for a walk with Elle after dinner on this pretty little scenic route he'd found by the beach. There, with the sun setting, he was going to ask her to be his wife.

Ford blinked fast a few times. "You're going to ask her to marry you?"

"That's right. I am."

Ford's jaw fell open. "Wow. Awesome. You finally got her to settle down."

Liam took in a breath. He hoped he could. "Hasn't happened yet." But that's what the extra days after the party were for. When he planned to whisk Elle away to another little town nearby, where they'd spend a few days together, before he proposed. "I want to spend the rest of my life with that woman, if she'll have me."

"I'm pretty sure she will."

"You ready?" Ford eyed him.

"I'm ready. I've been ready for a while. I want to marry her, and I'm hoping she'll want to marry me." Elle was the one for him. The one and only.

Ford was by Liam's side in an instant, slapping him on the back and shaking his hand heartily. "Good on you, buddy. This news makes me real happy. Congrats."

"She hasn't said 'yes' yet." Liam pulled the ring box out of his pocket and opened it. He'd spent two months wages on buying the type of ring he thought Elle might like.

Ford chuckled. "You carry that around with you all the time?"

Liam shook his head. "I wanted to show you. Wanted to run my plan by you."

Ford looked at the ring in fascination. "That must have cost a fortune."

"She's worth it."

"That's awesome news, Liam. Just awesome."

"I'm hoping she'll say 'yes'."

"She will. She knows you're the real deal. She knows a good thing when she sees it."

He grinned, closed the box and put it back into his pocket. "I hope so."

"I know so," Ford told him. "She's smitten by you. I've not seen her be like that with anyone."

"She's the one for me. She's my everything. This past year, this time we've been together, it's … it's been the best time of my life." He couldn't put into words as succinctly as he wanted, but life with Elle by his side was more of everything he wanted. It wasn't about the fantasy coming true; about him ending up with the beautiful high school cheerleader. No. There was something fateful about him and Elle being together. How in fixing up her home, she'd helped to fix his heart.

It would make for a pretty cool story to tell their grandchildren one day.

He hoped.

"Good luck, dude." Ford slapped him on the back again. "Not that you need it. That girl is going to say yes before you've even finished asking her."

He hoped so. He certainly hoped so.

CHAPTER 6

GINNY

Ginny moaned with delight. Every time Ryan kissed her, goosebumps scuttled along her skin and her insides felt light and airy.

His hands trailed down and rested on her lower back, then, with his eyes pinned on hers, his hand trailed lower until it rested on her bottom.

He kissed her again, the kiss deepening, and stretching out for seconds. Longing melded with lust as his lips, warm and soft, claimed her mouth. Her insides were on fire. She moaned against his lips, her body pressing harder against him, and then she squealed when he squeezed her bottom. Every cell in her body vibrated as tingling sensations rippled outwards from her belly.

Soon it would be impossible for her to hold back.

When they broke apart, their gazes locked, and raw passion flickered across his hooded eyes. Lifting a hand to his face, she stroked his cheek. So far in their relationship they had kissed and nothing more. Ryan was patient and understanding; qualities that lifted him way above what she had known before, with Ben.

"Now that I'm back at work, the weekends are more precious than ever," she said, her voice raspy as she thumbed his moist lower lip. "How about we go away for a long weekend soon. If that's something you might want." She was sick of interruptions and how busy life had become. A short break seemed so appealing.

"Yes." He nodded. "Yes. But ..." His eyes searched hers carefully. "We don't have to rush into anything. We have all the time in the world, Ginny ."

She pressed her lips against his, thankful for him. "I feel like I'm ready." She was filled to bursting with desire, and he was a better man for being so chivalrous.

He groaned and lowered his forehead to hers. "You are impossible to resist, Ginny."

"We could have a weekend away this time, not just a day trip like we did when we went to Starling Bay. It was great, wasn't it?" she asked him. Vanessa's departure had given them some peace, and they'd visited the quaint little town for a day trip, leaving early in the morning and coming back late at night. It felt like one complete family, walking around, her and Ryan with the children. She wanted more days like that.

Ryan's face turned soft. "It was the best. Daisy still talks about it.

"Benjy's ready for an overnight stay," she added.

He smiled. "Then it would be great to go on a small family vacation."

Small family vacation. She loved the way he'd said it. Their lips sealed again in another kiss, and the intensity heightened. She would follow this man to the ends of the earth, be with him for an eternity, because she had finally found her soulmate.

"Daddy! Ewww!" Daisy giggled, and covered her eyes with her hand.

They sprang apart. Ginny was disappointed. It was impossible to find time alone. They snatched quiet moments when they could, but she'd never stayed the night at Ryan's place, and he would never entertain the thought of staying with her at her house.

Which was why a trip out of town, an overnight stay, would be the way to have that first special night together.

Daisy advanced towards them and held out Ryan's cell phone. "Mommy wants to say 'hi'."

Ginny's insides hardened. So did Ryan's judging by the thunderous look on his face. He stiffly took the phone from his daughter. Ginny stepped back, out of view, but not before she'd caught a glimpse of Vanessa's fully made-up face on the screen. "Ryan, how are you? Daisy says you have company?"

"I'm busy, Vanessa," he growled, then as if he'd realized Daisy's presence, schooled himself to politeness. "You look well."

"I am well. I feel great!"

"I'm happy for you."

"The job is working out well," Vanessa continued, even though he hadn't asked. She was blissfully ignorant of how irritating she was.

"That's good."

"And how are *you*, Ryan?"

He scratched his jaw, looking as perplexed as Ginny felt. Vanessa had a habit of doing this. It wasn't the first time she'd called and demanded to talk to Ryan. It just happened that lately Ginny was with him for most of the weekend. She was beginning to see through Vanessa's ploy. Ryan's ex-wife was determined to be a thorn in Ginny's side for as long as possible.

"I'm great. I have to go. Here, Dee." Ryan cut the call short and handed the phone back to Daisy. Then he grabbed Ginny's hand and pulled her out of the study, and into the hallway. "Sorry about that." He wrapped his arms around her.

She snuggled against him. "She's been doing that more and more, have you noticed?"

"I've noticed."

Ginny pulled back and gazed into his eyes. "It's okay. I have something she doesn't." His lips curved up in that smile she'd come to love so much and he kissed her again. But Daisy was once again at their side. "Mommy wants to ask you something." She held the phone out; Vanessa's face filled the screen and she would have seen that Ginny and Ryan were standing extremely close together. Ryan took the phone from Daisy, the muscles along this face flexing. "What now?"

"Oh, hi, Ginny. Was that Ginny? Say 'hi' to her for me."

"What do you want, Vanessa?" Ryan's face turned to steel.

"It's my birthday soon."

Ginny tried to skulk away, not wanting to overhear their conversation, but Ryan grabbed her hand.

"And?" Ryan asked.

"How old are you, Mommy?" Daisy wanted to know. Ryan groaned, but it was barely audible, not loud enough for Vanessa to hear, but Ginny heard.

"Always twenty-one, pumpkin."

"Twenty-one?!" Daisy giggled.

"She's lying," Ryan snapped. "Why are you telling me this, Vanessa? What does that have to do with me?"

"I might do something to celebrate. I'll keep you posted."

"Sure." He handed back the phone to Daisy, and tugged at Ginny's hand, pulling her into the living room. Benjy was in his baby bouncer, watching a baby program on TV. "Hey, buddy," Ryan said softly.

Benjy kicked his legs in excitement and his face turned into one big, cheeky smile as soon as he saw Ginny. She crouched down on the floor, beside him. "Hey, baby. How are you?" Benjy kicked his legs and bounced against the bouncer even more. "Wanna go for a walk? Shall we take you out of here?" she asked, taking him out anyway. But he squirmed out of her arms and wriggled onto the floor where he lay on his stomach, trying to push up with his bottom.

Ryan crouched down beside her. "I'm sorry about that."

She ground down on her teeth, then reminded herself that Vanessa interfering and trying to elbow her way into their lives wasn't Ryan's fault. "It's not your fault. You don't have to be sorry."

"She does this on purpose. More ever since I moved into this new place."

Ginny had thought as much. Vanessa's intrusion was bordering on stalking. "Maybe it's because she knows I'm here more?"

"You should just move in," Ryan said.

"It's too soon to move in," she whispered.

"Then at least let me do up one of the spare rooms in case you ever need to stay." He looked at her with hope in his eyes. He'd said the same to her when he'd moved in. He'd told her then that he could easily put a bed and a crib in and have the room ready, 'just in case' she ever needed to stay over. She'd dismissed it casually then.

But now they were in a different place. Now, spending so much time here, snatching precious moments whenever they could, their relationship had deepened. She wanted to be with him more, and where at first she'd declined his offer because she'd promised herself not to rush into anything, she now felt the time was right.

She wanted more with this man, and even though she'd known him for less time than Benjy had been alive, it felt as if they'd known one another all their lives.

"Not yet, Ryan. You've only just moved in. Let's take things slow." She glanced at the door, half-expecting Daisy to come in with another question from her mother. "Let's go on our mini vacation away first, and then … then we'll see."

His lips twisted, and he shrugged his shoulders. "Okay. Let's go on a short break first."

CHAPTER 7

ASHLEIGH

Ashleigh walked out of the gardening center with pots of red, pink, yellow and white rose bushes in the oversized trolley.

Their mother loved roses, and on her birthdays, their father would always buy her a beautiful bunch. Tears formed in Ashleigh's eyes at the memory, so old and tattered and cherished.

She tried to arrange them in the back of her car, and wished she'd asked Liam to come with her as he could easily have transported these pots and plants in his truck.

She could have asked Ford, because he had a truck, too. She could have asked him *once upon a time*. Not now. Turning around to lift another pot out of the trolley, she was startled when the hulking frame of a man stood before her. She jerked back with shock, then relaxed when she saw who it was.

"Hey." Ford's easy grin confused her momentarily. "Since when did you take up gardening?"

Her heart started to pitter patter. Damn it. "I've always loved nature." Not the answer to his question but, whatever. He raised an eyebrow, and for a fleeting moment suspended in time, it brought back memories of when they were together.

"Come on, Ash. I know you don't have a green finger on you. What you're doing with all of these flowers and shrubs?"

Folding her arms and lifting her chin, she surveyed him with a cautious stare. This Ford was a stark contrast to the surly and distant man from recent months. He was back to being 'normal Ford', but even this, so close after his mother's passing, was too big of a change and she wasn't sure she trusted herself to be around him.

And then it hit her.

The man was in love.

Ah.

That's what had gotten into him.

That's what had softened him.

"My mom loved roses, and I was going to plant some in our back yard."

"Sweet."

She had to do something to keep busy.

As if the shop wasn't enough.

Lately, she'd been feeling more nostalgic and introspective than ever and, after Ford's mother's funeral, found herself thinking more of her parents, and their passing, and with those thoughts came the dread she herself faced; of getting older, and being lonely, and having no one else to share her life with. She would be forgotten within a few generations. She had no children of her own, and never would. Who would remember her a hundred years from now?

Remembering her parents, their memories so frayed and

faint, she was afraid of letting their memory die. They were always in her heart, but it was only the funeral of Patricia Montgomery that had brought her cherished memories back stronger. Determined to be more mindful of them, she decided to fill her backyard with roses, as well as other plants and shrubs which had taken her fancy.

His expression turned somber. "I can help you out. I'm pretty good with gardening."

"Thanks, but I've already got someone in mind." Ford had nailed it correctly. She didn't have any green fingers and she'd asked Darcie's gardener to help her.

"Yeah?" He didn't seem to like the sound of that.

"Yes. Someone Darcie uses."

The expression on his face told her that he didn't like her answer. "Ash. I know things have been difficult lately, for both of us, but I don't want us to be distant with one another."

It ruffled her feathers him calling her Ash, and now casually throwing in that he wanted them to be on better talking terms; now that it suited him. It hadn't mattered when she'd tried to make up with him in the past. Now that he had Kayla, he was filled with good cheer, was he?"

"Susan must be getting married soon?" she asked, deflecting his comment.

"In a couple of weeks." He lifted his hand to the back of his neck. "Maddie and I are making our way there a few days before the wedding."

"You're invited?"

He seemed surprised by the question. "Susan and I parted amicably. We're not mortal enemies. Yes, I'm invited."

"That's nice, and healthy, for everyone." They had a daughter together, so it made sense.

Ford was friends with everyone, and it shouldn't have come as a surprise to her that he was on such good terms with his ex-wife. It seemed that he was on good terms with everyone but her, until now. And that was only because he was no doubt happy with Kayla.

Seeing him and Kayla at his mother's funeral had been difficult, but she had come to terms with it. Ashleigh understood that there was no future for her and Ford, and she also had to move on, but it was harder for her when everyone around her seemed to be blissfully happy with their love lives.

Eloise and Liam were going away to visit Beth for her husband's big birthday celebration soon, and were taking a few extra days 'doing their own thing,' according to what Liam had told them.

Ginny and Ryan were madly in love. With Ryan moving into his own place, Ashleigh saw less of Ginny, who preferred to go there with Benjy for dinner, and then she would return home late at night. Ashleigh didn't understand why her sister didn't just sleep over. Maybe because of the crib and Benjy being used to the home environment.

With Ginny busy at work, and not at home at the weekend as much, Eloise and Liam didn't visit often because they'd mostly come to see the baby. Increasingly, Ashleigh found herself becoming more isolated and left on her own. Seeing Ford moving on with his life so easily was a big blow to her. Seeing them together at the funeral had been difficult.

When the two of them got married—because surely it was inevitable—she'd have to go away again; leave the country because seeing Ford marry someone else was something she would never be able to stomach. Maybe now that all was well back in her own family, it was time to start planning another trip to Europe, to make up for the one she'd cut short.

"How are you doing?" she asked, because she still cared for him and would always care for him. He looked away. "It's hard being in my mom's house and her not being there. She was a part of that place for all my life, and now she's gone."

"It can't be easy," she agreed, "but you have memories to last you a lifetime. Your mom lived out her life."

He surveyed her thoughtfully, his gaze searching her face as if he was waiting for something. "I am grateful for that. I need to get on with my life now. It's what my mom would have wanted. I hit the pause button on the accountancy practice but it's time to go full speed ahead with that."

"You're sure that this is where you intend to stay, in Whisper Falls, for the rest of your life?"

"Of course." His brows pushed together as if he didn't understand why she was asking him such a thing. "This is where I plan to be. There's nothing for me in Boston, and Maddie is traveling this summer, and after college who knows where she might go next? Whisper Falls is home to me, and always will be."

"I would have helped, with your mom, I would have come to see her and help you take care of her."

He tilted his head at the words which seemed to have come from nowhere, words she'd had to suppress when visiting him that time she paid her respects soon after his mom died because it hadn't been the right time, and neither was the day of the funeral.

"You were busy with Ginny, and the shop, and you had so much going on in your own life, Ash."

She gritted her teeth and wished he'd stop calling her by that nickname. "I would have made time for you, for your mom."

He straightened up, stood taller. "I was thinking of you and I didn't want to burden you."

She scoffed. "Burden me?" She found his choice of word surprising. There was a time when they shared things, good times and problems, and talked and were there for one another. "It felt more like you were pushing me away."

He let out a sigh. "If I've been distant, it's because I couldn't focus on anything but my mom. It was difficult dealing with her after her fall. She went downhill quickly, and I had to stop everything, including setting up the accountancy practice. I had to take care of my mom and block everything out, including you."

She smoothed down her hair, and wished he would come out and say it. The truth. The real reason he had excluded her. But he didn't. "I would have helped you with her. I could have. I wanted to."

He put his hands together, imploring her. "And again, I was thinking of you, Ash. I saw the state Ginny was in. I used to come and check in on you all. You girls had so much to handle. I couldn't do that to you, Ash, burden you with even more. I couldn't expect you to help me with my mom on top of all the responsibility you already had. I could see what you were going through with your own family."

"It's okay for you to check in on me, on my family, not allow me to do the same for you?" she cried indignantly. She didn't fully believe him. He had Kayla, and Ashleigh knew he no longer felt that way about her. She just wished he would come out and be truthful about it.

"You've always been that person, Ash. You've always been the father and mother to your sisters, and you didn't need to be the carer to my mom, too."

She pressed her lips together, hating that she'd wandered into that territory, keeping her at bay because he was mad at her for the trip, for not letting him come over to Europe to surprise her that time. "You didn't have to punish me."

"Punishing you?" He looked perplexed. "I wasn't. Why would I punish you? Kayla offered to help, and she could easily do it. She has no family, bar Ryan and Daisy, and they seemed to be doing just fine. She wasn't working then, and she had time on her hands. She needed help getting behind the wheel of a car again. It made sense for both of us to help one another. She helped me, and I helped her."

Ashleigh's jaw tightened. "I'm sure you did."

"What's that supposed to mean?" he cried, his eyes narrowing, causing the fine lines to fan out along his temples.

Ashleigh didn't like this new prickliness between them. Seemed like the days when she and Ford could be politely civil were long gone. "Kayla's been a great help, I'm sure. We can all see how great she's been." She slammed the last rose bush into her car and prayed she hadn't broken the pot. She turned to go. "It's been good seeing you, Ford. Good luck."

CHAPTER 8

GINNY

She was watching Daisy spoon the cake mixture into the cupcakes when Kayla walked into the kitchen. Ryan must have let her in.

"We're making chocolate chip cupcakes, Aunt Kayla," Daisy proudly announced.

"I can see that." Kayla looked around. "You've settled in well."

Ginny closed her eyes and tried to inhale a deep breath. She'd been enjoying her day until she saw Kayla. Ryan's sister had never liked her, and Ginny hadn't forgotten the way she'd spoken to her, telling Ginny that she had a lot of problems to deal with and not to take advantage of Ryan's kindness or attention. Those words had imprinted on Ginny's memory.

Back then, knowing that Kayla had offered Ryan a lifeline in his time of need by allowing him to stay at her place when he'd moved to Whisper Falls, following the breakup of his marriage. Ginny tolerated the woman but she was going to play it cool and keep her distance. She had to be careful not to let the history between her and Kayla affect the relationship between brother and sister.

"I haven't settled in. I don't live here," she corrected Kayla, avoiding her gaze as she focussed her attention on Daisy. "I've come over for a little while."

Kayla moved closer and watched what they were doing. "I'm sorry, if I've offended you, but that's not what I meant."

Ginny looked up, startled by Kayla's soft voice. She looked apologetic. She looked *different*. Younger. Happier. Not the Kayla she was used to. "Where are your glasses, Aunt Kayla?" Daisy asked.

"I'm wearing contact lenses."

So, that's what it was. Having no glasses made a huge difference to Kayla's appearance.

"What are they?" Daisy squinted at her aunt.

"Contact lenses. They're like little pieces of plastic, polymers really, that you put into your eyes so that you can see."

Daisy looked pained. "Plastic? Does it hurt?"

Kayla smiled. "Not plastic, not hard plastic, but something soft, and no, they don't hurt."

She looked at least five years younger, and she wore jeans. *Jeans.* Ginny did a double take at them. Dark, but they were jeans. She'd paired them with a nice buttoned up blouse. Her hair was different too. And, goodness. Ginny tried not to stare too much, but was that a hint of eyeliner and mascara?

Daisy giggled. "You look real pretty."

"Why, thank you." Kayla's face softened even more. "We can go shopping at the mall one day when you're over."

"Can we watch a movie instead?" Daisy asked.

"We can do whatever you want, honey."

"Can I bring my friends?"

"Of course. We can go for a picnic in the park, or by the beach, afterwards. Whatever you want to do."

"Yay!"

Kayla grinned and looked at Ginny. "It's a full-time job, isn't it, looking after children?"

"I love it," Ginny replied. "Just one more, sweetie." She watched Daisy fill the last remaining paper case with the cake mixture.

"Can I lick it?" the little girl asked, a wooden spoon in one hand and the fingers of her other hand wiping the mixing bowl clean of the cake mixture.

"Go ahead." Ginny shook her head; this had been the fun part of cooking when she was younger. "These are ready to bake now." She lifted the baking tray and popped it in the oven. "Can you read the instructions, sweetie, and tell me how long we have to bake these for?"

Daisy narrowed her eyes as she read the back of the packet. "Fifteen minutes."

"Could you set the timer, please?" Ginny asked.

"To where it says fifteen?" Daisy lifted the yellow egg-shaped timer.

"What do you think?"

"I think ... yes?"

"Good girl. Set it and keep an eye on it."

Daisy grabbed the egg timer and made to run off. "Where are you going with that?" Ginny cried.

"I wanna show Benjy!" She ran off before Ginny could say another word.

Ginny busied herself with clearing up, wishing that Daisy would rush back so that she didn't have to be stuck with her aunt.

"You're very good with her," Kayla remarked.

Ginny glanced at her and forced an appreciative smile, while wondering when the jab would come. Kayla had an opinion about Ginny, and she had never been keen on her and Ryan being together. Even though Ryan had told her to ignore his sister, it wasn't easy, especially not now, with Kayla cornering her the way she was. "Thanks," she mumbled. With her back to Kayla, and she made a face at these unexpected words.

"I … I'd like to say something, if I may."

Ginny's insides suddenly turned to lead. She continued to clear up, and was grateful that she had something to keep her busy.

"I'm sorry for everything I said to you that time, about staying away from my brother."

Ginny couldn't believe her ears. She wiped the table, feeling relieved that she had her back to Kayla.

"Ginny, please. Could you turn around?"

Ginny's body sagged, as if the air had been sucked out of it. Reluctantly, she did as she was told.

"I've been so nasty to you, and I want to apologize. It was unacceptable, and you must hate me for it. I just want you to know that at the time I was only thinking of Ryan. I didn't want him to get into something when his head wasn't clear, but it wasn't my call to make. It was wrong of me to say such horrible things to you, especially given all that you have gone through and suffered. I can't tell you how awful I've felt, how much I've wanted to apologize to you before but I couldn't seem to find the right opportunity. Please, Ginny, please forgive me."

The apology sounded heartfelt. Ginny wiped her hands on the dishcloth, unsure of what to say. "You've caught be by surprise, Kayla. I never expected this from you."

Guilt swept over Kayla's face and she sat down on the stool near the kitchen island. "That says a lot about me; the fact that me being nice is a shock, but me being that vindictive nasty person wasn't."

Ginny joined her, sitting down. "I wouldn't say you were nasty. I sort of see where you were coming from. If Benjy was in a similar situation, when he grows up and falls in love with someone who I might not think is suitable, I'd probably tell him to be cautious, too. We want to protect those we love," she said softly, "But I don't think I'd ever stand in the way of his happiness. I don't think I'd have it in me to warn his girlfriend off." There. She'd gone and said it. The simmering anger which had festered inside her like a boil, had now slowly released.

Kayla stared at her hands. Her lips twisted, and Ginny wondered if she'd hit another point home. She looked up slowly. "My brother ... you saved him. You were what he needed. You helped him heal, Ginny, and for that I can't thank you enough."

Ginny shook her head. "Ryan helped me heal. He was everything I needed but I couldn't see that at the time. Ryan made me see."

They stared at one another, an easiness blossoming between them. "I appreciate you saying this, Kayla." Because suddenly, the tension between them had vanished. Pulverized into the air. "It means a lot."

"I've wanted to have this conversation with you weeks ago, but you're always busy, understandably, with the little one, and then Daisy." Kayla let out a sigh, nodding to herself as she fiddled with the cuffs of her shirt. "You're so good with Daisy. You're like ... you're the mother she deserves and needs. That child adores you."

Ginny wasn't ready for the praise which was coming thick and fast. "I love that girl as if she were my own." She laughed just thinking about it. "Sometimes, it feels as if Daisy is Benjy's older sister. She dotes over him, and plays with him, and it makes me so happy that he has someone like that."

She didn't want Benjy to be an only child, and she hoped for a large family in years to come. But, knowing how suddenly life could change made her cautious, so she tried to tamp down her dreams and not allow herself to get carried away, because her life with Ryan was so perfectly idyllic and she was scared that something would come along to change it.

"I'd be more than happy to look after Benjy, if you ever need a break," Kayla offered. "You maybe didn't consider me as a childminder for him, with me being so nasty to you, but I hope we can put that behind us. I see how you are with your sisters, Ginny, and I ... I just wish I could have that kind of something ..."

She looked almost uncomfortable saying that, and the Kayla of old would never have let down her guard so much.

But this before her, wasn't the Kayla of old. This was someone else. Softer, approachable. Nice.

"What's this?" Ryan asked, walking in with Benjy in his arms. He looked apprehensive as his gaze bounced between the two women.

"Nothing. We're just catching up," Ginny said casually, getting up and grinning at Benjy. "Hey, Benjy."

Kayla stood up. "Can I have him?"

The little boy bobbed in Ryan's arms, as if he wanted to be let loose on the floor. "Come here you gorgeous little thing." Kayla scooped Benjy into her arms and hugged him. He stared up at her, making baby noises. She baby-talked him back, holding his hand and making funny face. He kicked his legs and waved his arms.

A ringing sound went off, and Daisy ran in holding the timer. "It's gone off!" she cried.

"The cakes must be ready, come over and I'll show you how to check them."

As she got busy doing that, she heard Ryan comment on Kayla's new attire. "Where are you going?" he asked.

"I'm meeting Ford."

"Are you still taking driving lessons? Because I'd be happy to take you now that I'm all moved in."

"I'm driving. I'm fine."

"The cakes are done," Ginny announced. "Now we just have to wait for them to cool down and we'll decorate them with chocolate icing," she told Daisy who scrambled onto a stool and looked at them greedily.

"I must go," said Kayla, kissing Benjy on the cheek.

"Stay a while," Ginny said. "Stay and have some cupcakes with us."

"Are you sure?" Kayla seemed genuinely surprised by the invite.

"I insist."

CHAPTER 9

ELOISE

L iam opened the door to the hotel room he'd booked. "What do you think?"

Eloise gasped in delight. "Oh my goodness!" Her jaw fell open as she stepped inside the large room with her luggage trolley. "This is gorgeous!" She put her arms around Liam's neck, rewarding him with a kiss.

"You like it?"

"I love it." How and where had he found this little gem? It was on the outskirts of Cape Cod and near to the new mansion that Beth and her husband had moved into recently. Kicking off her shoes, Eloise rushed to the super king-sized bed and dove onto it. "I love it! I LOVE it." She sounded like a teenager let loose on spring break. Liam grinned, then slowly took off his shirt, standing in front of her in his white tee.

She surveyed him with greedy eyes, then hooked her finger, beckoning him. "Come over," she said in her silkiest and most

52

seductive voice. "Let me reward you for booking such an amazing place." She expected him to join her on the bed, but instead he bent down and opened his suitcase, then started taking the clothes out and hanging them in the closet.

Perplexed, she lifted her head and propped herself up on her elbows. "Can't that wait?"

Liam glanced at her, without a hint of a smile. "Let me hang these up before they crease. Wait for me."

He was tired, having just taken on a big job, with his team of guys. On top of which he'd promised Ford to work on his new office. She understood, and of course, she would wait. She had no intention of doing anything else. He had chosen an amazing little place to stay. She was impressed, especially because he'd insisted on making the booking. Usually, she stayed with Beth whenever she visited, but that option didn't appeal this time around, even though Beth had offered. She seemed very excited to show off her new home.

Eloise preferred having Liam to herself so that they could go and do their own thing instead of being stuck at Beth's house. She couldn't put a finger on her reluctance, where at one time Beth had been her only escape and she'd rush to see her, these days she was content to stay at her new home and be with Liam.

"This is such an amazing place. How did you find it?" She lay back, her hands behind her head and surveying the room slowly.

"You don't think I'm capable of finding something classy?"

"I'm aware that you're a man of many hidden talents."

"It wasn't too difficult to find. I looked around online and checked out all the photos and videos on the websites. I just wanted you to have somewhere that's more your taste."

"That's very thoughtful of you. I'm the luckiest girl on the planet to have a guy like you." She stared at his back and wished he would hurry up and come to her. "What do you mean by more my taste?"

"Just, ya know. A motel would have done me but I wanted this trip to be special."

"I would have stayed with you in a motel." She sat up and kneeled on the bed, her hands resting on her thighs. She was excited for this mini break, having time alone with Liam; time away from work and the humdrum of normal life. Being away from Whisper Falls and The Bridal Shop and her sisters, and being with the man she loved.

While she was looking forward to seeing her friend Beth and the other people she'd gotten to know through her, she was more excited about those few days after, when Liam told her he'd booked another quaint hotel in another town close by. She couldn't wait for that.

Before that though they had to get through Griffin's fortieth birthday celebrations which were tomorrow, and Beth had invited them over for pre-birthday drinks tonight. On Sunday they'd been invited over for the usual post-party brunch. Beth's parties were never just a one evening affair, and for the first time, Eloise was slightly irritated by it. "Why are you doing this now?" she asked, growing impatient.

"I like unpacking straightaway."

She couldn't tell if there was a tight edge to his voice. It almost felt as if something was off but she couldn't put her finger on what.

Liam was in an odd mood. A little snarky and somber. Not quite the Liam she knew. She'd had slight misgivings about coming to this party anyway, but Griffin's fortieth wasn't something she could easily miss without Beth getting suspicious and their relationship had been distant enough as it was. She and Beth had drifted apart; Eloise was to blame for most of it because there had been so much to deal with this past year in her own life, with Ginny, but also, *this* wasn't her world. She no longer needed the hedonistic escape that Beth provided, or her friends—the champagne and oysters crowd—the ones who had no worries in the world. These weren't people she felt comfortable around. She hadn't wanted to be around them when her own life, and that of the people she loved, had been a wreck.

"What time do we have to be there?" Liam asked.

"Beth said the pre-birthday drinks start at seven, so we have plenty of time."

"Pre-birthday drinks, huh? The guy's turning forty and they're having a three-day event?"

"It's a milestone," Eloise explained. "Their celebrations always tend to be larger than life."

"You can say that again," he muttered.

He still had his back to her, so she got up silently and tiptoed towards him, putting her arms around him from behind. "They come from old money and they are quite showy. They like to do things with a bang."

"Remind me what they do again?"

"Beth flies around the world. She's always on vacation or throwing parties, or going to parties."

"No kids?"

"No."

"Why?"

Eloise shrugged, stepping away from him gingerly since he hadn't responded to her hug. "I don't know why."

He sniffed. "Imagine having all that money and I would have thought they'd want kids, all that generational wealth and inherited money's gotta flow somewhere, surely?"

"I don't know, Liam. Beth was never keen to have kids. Maybe they've been trying. Who knows? What's the matter with you lately?"

He didn't answer. She glanced away from him and noticed something hanging in the closet. "What's that?" She pointed to the hanging suit carrier.

"A tux." He turned around, arms folded, looking defensive.

"You have a tux?"

"Why are you so surprised?"

She froze at his tone and at the hardened look on his face which was so alien to her. "I didn't … I didn't mean anything by it."

"Don't you think I could own a tux?" His voice was oddly different, and his words were cold.

"No, no, no. I don't, I mean, I *do*. I've never thought about it."

"You're shocked I have a tux."

She struggled to save the moment, to deflect the point, because he wasn't wrong. "I'm shocked at the way we're being with one another right now. It feels like you don't want to be here. I'm sorry for dragging you all this way."

"You don't want me here?"

"That's not what I said." He was putting words in her mouth.

"Then what did you mean to say?" He was acting so out of character that it startled her. She tried to rack her brains for what it could be. Was he sick? Hiding something from her? Did he want to confess something? Or did he want to break up? It hadn't helped seeing those big sprawling mansions they'd driven past in the taxi. She was scared. Afraid of this new side to Liam. A side to him she'd never seen before and which now left her plagued by self-doubt. The romance which had filled her world with happiness now seemed to wither and die before her eyes. "I … I don't think you need to wear a tux, if you don't want to. I don't think it's that kind of party."

"You never told me much about it."

"There wasn't much to tell you." She wrung her hands together. What she really wanted to do was to close the distance between them, to cup his face and look into his eyes, the way she could so easily do in the past when everything was so nice and wonderful, and amazing between them. When she'd taken it for granted, not thinking for one moment how things could change, how men, and relationships and circumstances could drive a wedge between two people in love. She was completely in the dark. Something was going on with Liam and she had no idea what it was. "I've been to these parties, and I guess you can wear a tux."

"Why didn't you tell me before?"

"Because I didn't think you would want to. I didn't want you to be someone you're not. There's something else going on here, Liam. What is it? What's the matter?"

"Are you ashamed of me?"

His words caught her off guard. Shone a light into what was going on in the that head of his. "What?"

"Are you ashamed of me?"

"Of course not! What is wrong with you?"

"Nothing. Just … let's just get this over with."

"We have plenty of time. The drinks aren't until this evening." The desire burning low in her belly now turned cold as ice.

"I'm going to take a shower." He started rifling through his clothes again, presumably to get some fresh ones.

She went back to the bed, her shoulders hunched, and feeling down. All the shiny hopes she'd had for this weekend turned to dust. She'd been looking forward to having a few days away, especially after the party, but now it felt like she was with a completely different man. Someone she felt uneasy with.

~

They got a taxi to Beth's house. Eloise had almost suggested that they walk there because it would have made for a scenic route, but she wanted this over and done with fast.

With Liam being so changeable, she was wary about the evening ahead, especially as they passed some more beautiful and opulent mansions along the way. She was overcome by dread at what Liam would think when he walked into Beth and Griffin's home. She was used to Beth's level of grandeur, and expected her friend's new house to be amazing. Being used to it, she wouldn't be so fazed by the opulence and size of their new mansion, but having Liam by her side made her nervous. She didn't want to guess what was going through his head, or what he might think when he saw the servers and Beth's housekeeper. Clearly, something about Beth and coming here had made him grouchy.

While they were getting dressed, their conversation had been minimal. If only she'd listened to her gut and not come. Ashleigh had been going on about a very important bridal client coming to the shop and Eloise could have stayed back. She could have made an excuse to Beth and her friend would have believed it. The business had taken a back seat and they had to work harder than usual to get things back on track.

Liam looked so handsome in his dark blue button-up shirt and trousers. With his height, he turned heads as they walked into the house. Unease mixed with anxiety as Eloise reached for his hand, grateful when he didn't flinch or let go.

"Eloise!" Beth rushed up to her looking effortlessly elegant in her long purple printed halter neck. Eloise felt inferior in her short green A-line dress. They hugged and Beth held onto her for a moment longer. "It's been *soooo* long, Eloise. I was beginning to think you were avoiding me."

Eloise feigned a laugh. "No, never. It's been so busy, what with Ginny and the baby."

"I'm so glad you came. You look amazing." Her gaze drifted to Liam. "Is this the handsome man you've been keeping a secret?"

Eloise wasn't sure if she heard a grunt from Liam. Her nerves frazzled even more. "This is Liam, and I've not been hiding him." Beth leaned in and wrapped her arms around Liam as if she'd known him since childhood. "At last, we meet!"

"Hey. Good to meet you," he said, if a little gruffly.

Beth flashed a Hollywood smile, then waggled her finger. "She's been hiding you. Naughty Eloise."

"I wonder why," Liam said, dryly.

Beth's forehead puckered as if she didn't understand. Her gaze bounced between them and she smiled as her husband, Griffin, joined them. He gave Eloise a warm hug. "Long time no see, stranger. Where have you been?"

"Hey, Griff. I've just been busy with life and stuff. This is Liam, my better half."

They shook hands. Griffin nodded at Liam. "Good to meet you."

Liam managed a smile. "Likewise."

"How's Ginny, and the baby?" Beth asked her, just as she heard Griffin ask Liam what he'd like to drink; a bourbon or whiskey? Eloise tried to listen in on their conversation, her belly churning. She hoped Liam wouldn't act moody with her friends. Only half-listening to Beth, she watched from her periphery as Liam scratched his jaw. "I'm a beer kind of guy."

"Beer it is." Griffin waved a server over. An uncomfortable moment of silence spread out, until Beth asked, "Why didn't you come for a visit sooner? Easter or at any time? I can't believe you've been hiding this hunk from me."

"I've been busy," Eloise told her again.

Beth fixed her with a stare. "How is little Benjy? Is Ginny okay now? You said she had a traumatic birth."

"He is *so* cute. I'll show you some pictures later once the party is over. I have hundreds of photos. He's so adorable." Eloise laughed, but she could sense that same disquiet from Liam. He was usually good with people, especially strangers. He was good at putting people at ease, but now his mood set her on edge.

She and Beth talked some more, about Ashleigh and Ginny and what Eloise had been doing for the past few months, and she caught up with her friend's news. The men talked, polite chit-chat about nothing important. Eloise kept one ear on their conversation, and one on hers. Liam ran his fingers around his collar, loosening it, as if he were getting too hot, or too uncomfortable. She put her arm around his waist but he stiffened at her touch.

"Well, this is ... nice," Beth said, as a server appeared. Liam grabbed his bottle of beer, and Griffin handed her and Beth a glass of champagne each. "To finally meeting up." Beth raised her glass and they all touched glasses.

"What do you do, Liam?" Griffin asked. Eloise's insides hardened at the question.

"Do?" Liam blinked.

"Are you in real estate, finance, oil? Or are crypto and fungibles your jam?"

Liam appeared confused. As if the question had been asked in Russian. "Uh ... I'm a handyman."

"A what?"

"I'm a handyman. I fix up houses, do some construction work, work on projects as and when."

"Oh ... interesting." Griffin seemed a little lost for words. "By yourself?"

"I have a team of guys I use when needed for bigger projects, but pretty much I can handle most things by myself, minor works on houses and stuff. We all need houses to live in, right?" Liam took a swig of his beer.

"Yeah, I guess." Griffin raised his beer bottle to his lips, his brow puckering. The two men looked at one another for a silent moment and the air turned hard and prickly. Eloise stared at the ground and wished it would open up and swallow her.

"What about you?" Liam asked. "I bet you have your fingers in a lot of pies."

Griffin nodded. "I sure do."

They laughed, Eloise out of sheer desperation to gloss over the awkward moment.

"Hey, why don't I introduce you to some people, seeing that the ladies probably want to talk and get all caught up?" Griffin was about to pull Liam away, but Eloise saw the flashing warning signs as she reached for Liam's hand. "I was going to introduce him to everyone." Worried about Liam causing a scene, which would be disastrous, she decided it would be best if she and Liam worked the room. But Liam moved his hand away from her. "Don't worry about me, Elle. I'll be fine." His voice turned tender, and he even smiled.

"Sure?" she asked, bracing a smile back.

"Yeah."

When the men left, Beth squeezed her arm. *"Elle.* Is that what he calls you? He's *so* gorgeous. So ... so ... down to earth and big and strong. So *rough,* I mean *rugged.* Sexy and rugged, as a man ought to be. Where did you find him?"

Eloise looked at the men and her heart sank as Griffin led Liam to a group of men. With their slicked back hair, Oxford cloth button downs and khakis, she knew instantly that Liam would feel uncomfortable.

She didn't like this at all. This situation, this stranger, this new Liam. Her eyes were still on him when she felt a gentle poke in her ribs. "You can't even take your eyes off him!" Beth exclaimed. "Where did you find him?"

"He helped fix up my house."

Beth hooked her arm through Eloise's and walked with her away from the crowd, over to a quiet corner.

"Seems to me like he fixed up more than your house. Will you quit staring at him?"

Eloise pulled her gaze away from where Liam was and tried to regulate her breathing. "Huh?"

"You're so lovestruck. You're like a teen, look at you. You're completely wrapped up in him, and I don't blame you. Oh, Eloise." Her friend hugged her. "I'm so happy for you. He seems so nice."

Eloise's gaze drifted to Liam again. She was trying to gauge his mood as he was surrounded by guys he would never ordinarily hang out with. "He's really good. He's everything I need." Eloise's heart thundered inside her ribcage. She wished her words could be true in this moment, because right now what she'd said felt like a lie.

Beth leaned towards her. "I have some news of my own."

Eloise turned back to her friend.

Beth grinned, her shoulders lifting as she clasped her hands together, looking as if she could barely contain her excitement. "We're having twins. I've been wanting to tell you for a long time but I—"

"*Twins?*" Surprise hit her for six. Eloise stared at her super thin friend's flat belly. And she was drinking champagne.

"Twins. Through a surrogate. I wanted to tell you in person."

The news on all fronts floored Eloise.

Twins.

A surrogate.

Beth being a mother.

She threw her arms around her friend, careful not to spill her champagne. "Oh my goodness! How wonderful! I'm so happy for you, Beth. When?"

"They're going to be delivered in just under three months' time."

"Oh my goodness, Beth. You waited six months to tell me?"

"You've been so busy. You didn't return my calls, and you haven't visited as much, not like you normally do. I understand why, now." She giggled, her face lighting up like a beacon of happiness. "I'm so happy that you're happy. You and Liam make a beautiful couple."

Beth was talking about aesthetics, obviously, because she didn't know Liam, and hadn't seen her and him interact as a couple. And, until today, Eloise would have agreed, because she believed that they were great together. They fit together like the pieces of a jigsaw puzzle, yet the shock of how this visit was turning out, with Liam being so different, made her have second thoughts.

She suddenly wasn't so sure anymore. Wasn't sure she knew this man as well as she'd let herself believe she did. This new Jekyll and Hyde side to him scared the living daylights out of her. "Thanks," she said, hiding her misery well, smiling and looking across the room at her boyfriend as if he were the best thing to have happened to her.

Yet inside she was slowly dying. Now she had an added worry. A new fear. What if she'd rushed into this and made another mistake?

"I'm so happy for you, Beth." She didn't want to dwell on her problems, not here, not now. "Twins. Who would have thought?" She hugged her friend again.

"I know, right?"

"I can't wait to come back and see them, and to see you as a mother." They both stared at one another, and a montage of images flew through Eloises's head, of all the parties, vacations and good times she'd had with her friend. Beth had been adamant for as long as Eloise had known her that she didn't want children.

"We'd like you to be a godmother to them," Beth told her.

Eloise held Beth's hands. "You would?"

Beth nodded, excitedly.

"Then I would be honored."

"I'm so glad we're back to normal. Come early tomorrow, so we can talk some more. I'm going to have to mingle with the guests for now, but we have to catch up," Beth said.

"What's the dress code for tomorrow? Are people coming in tuxes and stuff?"

"We didn't say. But it's the big four-O, so it's a big year for Griff. He's just done a multi-million-dollar deal in the Far East and he wants to celebrate in style. Tux's, cocktail dresses, whatever. Come how you want, you know what it's like. Why are you asking?"

"I'm just curious. I'm so happy for you, Beth. Soon-to-be mother of twins. Who would have thought?"

CHAPTER 10

GINNY

Benjy lay on the floor trying to roll over and failing. Daisy watched over him, and found his struggle hilarious. That little baby provided such entertainment for Daisy. It was amusing to see. Toys lay strewn around, and every once in a while something would catch her son's attention, and he would grab it and start playing with it.

Even though she didn't live here, Ryan had childproofed his new place. Even though Benjy hadn't yet started crawling, there were safety gates blocking access to the stairs, and all sharp table edges had been covered by soft plastic tabs. Even the plug sockets had protective covers on them. She hadn't asked him to do any of this; he'd just done it. He poked his head through the door. "Dinner's almost ready."

Ginny nodded. "We'll be there in two. Almost done."

"Wow, Dee." Ryan walked in and inspected his daughter's new hairdo. "That's amazing."

"Can I see?" Daisy cried.

"It's incredible." Ryan nodded at Ginny. "Where did you learn to do this?" He seemed in awe of the fishtail braids she'd done for Daisy.

"Lemme see!" Daisy cried.

"Just one minute. I'm almost done." Ginny weaved the hair between her fingers. Ryan shook his head. "I'm *never* going to be able to do that. What have you done, Ginny? You keep raising the bar and I can't keep up."

Ginny grinned, seeing him looking so worried about what she considered to be a minor thing. Admittedly, it was a girlie thing, but Daisy had such lovely long hair and Ginny wanted to see what French Fishtail Braids would look like on her. Having often done them on herself, she was adept at plaiting. Ryan wouldn't know how to do these but he could learn, and being the sort of man and father he was, it wouldn't surprise her if he did learn. "I'll teach you."

"It looks complicated."

"It's really not."

He folded his arms and watched her finish off the second plait. "Easy for you to say. Putting wax through my hair is as complicated as I get."

"I'll teach you. Calm down, Ryan. It's only a different style of hair braid."

"I wanna see!" Daisy asked again. She was like a little windup toy, vibrating with energy and unable to keep still. Benjy wasn't far behind in that respect.

"Done. Go and take a look." Ginny sat back and rested her hands on her lap. Daisy shot off.

"We were doing just fine with the pigtails." Seeing that the coast was clear, Ryan grabbed his chance. Encircling her waist with his arms, he pressed his lips down on her mouth and giving her another toe-curling kiss.

She was breathless when he pulled away, just as Daisy ran in, looking as if she might burst with so much happiness. "I love it! I love it, Ginny. It's *soooooo* cool."

Ryan fake-groaned. "See. She's going to want this every day."

"You look so pretty, sweetie!" Ginny exclaimed, then watched as Daisy got down on her hands and knees to show Benjy first. He shrieked with excitement at the funny faces she made as she showed him her braids.

"It looks super cool, Dee. Super cool."

"You have to learn how to do them, Daddy."

Ryan gave Ginny a pointed stare. "I will. Don't you worry about that." He clapped his hands together. "Dinner's ready. Can we eat now, please, before it gets cold?"

Ginny picked Benjy up, surprised he hadn't nodded off for a nap. They'd been out to a children's soft play center earlier. She'd fed him there, and was now going to give him a little pureed fruit later on, just before setting off for home. That was the part she dreaded. She didn't like leaving because it felt like home here. Not because of the house, but because of the people who lived in it. Their little group of four. They fit together. Like a family. Like she'd known them for ever. Like they were hers and she and Benjy were theirs.

Ryan kept telling her about the spare rooms in which he was happy to put a crib and a bed for her—just so she didn't have to travel back, but she always dismissed his suggestion lightly. She was forcing herself to be cautious. To not rush into things the way she had with Ben, even though Ryan was nothing like Ben. Ryan would never hurt her, or cheat on her, or make her feel less. Every time she had to leave, it took every inch of willpower in her to not give in. Staying here would be so easy. It was what she wanted, yet a small part of her made her hold back.

They had dinner. Ryan had made pot roast. He was a great cook. He was a great dad. He was a great boyfriend. He was a great father figure for her son. She couldn't ask for anything more.

After dinner, they all cleared up and she fed Benjy. Daisy wanted them all to watch a family film. It was impossible to say 'no.' Ginny didn't want to go home or be away from Ryan and Daisy. She'd lived with her sisters in the family home her whole life, and had known nothing else, save for the place she'd bought with Ben, Benjy's father. They'd decorated it together, but had never lived there. It had been the plan to move in after the wedding, but that hadn't happened and everything related to her life with Ben soon fell apart.

How would her life have been had Ben not died? She shivered, not wanting to think about it. She would have gone back to him, stayed with him for Benjy's sake, but something would have happened. They weren't meant to be together. A knowing in the pit of her belly had told her that something didn't feel right.

She couldn't work out what it was about the home Ryan had recently moved into that gave her such a feeling of belonging, and grounding and happiness. This home was new to her, and not imprinted with any memories. If anything, every day was ripe for making new ones.

They watched the film, with Benjy sitting in his bouncer and Daisy curled up beside him on a bean bag with a blanket for them both. Ginny snuggled with Ryan on the sofa. It was perfect, pure bliss.

Then what was she waiting for? Why not just move in as Ryan had suggested? If life had taught her anything, it was that when things are going well, and life is too good, that the curveball wasn't far behind.

She was waiting for the curveball. Treading carefully. Going slow.

The credits were rolling when Ryan woke her up. "Hey," he whispered gently. "The film finished."

She yawned. "I fell asleep." She rubbed her eyes and sat up and sat forward, saw that Daisy had disappeared, and that Benjy was fast asleep. She groaned quietly, not wanting to get up to gather her things and put Benjy into the car then drive all the way home. Then at the other end take him back out, along with all her belongings, and get him to bed.

It seemed like too much hard work, when right now, this was all cosy and warm and just right.

"Stay," Ryan whispered.

She tried to summon what willpower she had left, waning as it was. "I should go."

"Stay. It makes sense to. It's so late."

"I can't stay, Ryan."

"Why can't you? I'm not suggesting anything inappropriate, Ginny. I don't want you driving back this late with Benjy fast asleep. I'd be happy to drive you there, but why disturb Benjy and ruin his sleep? You're both so comfortable here. You're comfortable aren't you?"

"A little too comfortable."

He raised an eyebrow. "What does that mean?"

"I'm trying not to get too comfortable, even though every time I'm with you, I just want to stay."

"Would that really be so wrong?" he asked.

She was trying to shake off her sleepiness. "It's not wrong." She lifted a hand to his face. "It's … it's the best thing. You're the best thing, you and Daisy, after Benjy. You're both just so … completing."

"Completing?"

"You make me feel whole again."

"Oh, Ginny." He went to wrap his arms around her but she stopped him, needing him to hear how much he meant to her. "You know how you make me feel, Ryan. How blessed I feel every day that Benjy and I have you and Daisy, but I just need to … go slow. I rushed into things before and it almost destroyed me."

"I will never hurt you. Never. You don't have to worry about us rushing into anything, or me leaving, because I'm not going anywhere." He kissed the back of her hand. "I can put a crib and a bed in one of the spare rooms. They're sitting there empty. Just say the word."

Ginny twisted her lips. It was tempting. She leaned towards him and kissed him. "I'll think about it, but tonight I really must go." She got up.

"Please have a sleepover!" Daisy cried, rushing inside wearing her pajamas. Ryan put a finger to his lips to shush her before she woke up the baby. He turned to Ginny. "Why not do what Dee said? Why don't you have a sleepover?"

She threw him a don't-pit-me-against-Daisy look and surveyed the floor and the toys and Benjy in the bouncer. It was going to take a Herculean effort for her to leave. "I should make a move. All our things are at the house. I don't even have my pajamas."

"You can have mine," Daisy offered.

Ginny bent down to Daisy's level. "They won't fit me," she whispered, "But thank you."

"I've told you plenty of times to bring some things over, Ginny, just to make it easier for you, so that you don't have to carry so much with you." Ryan wasn't going to let her off so easily.

"Why don't you bring your things, Ginny?" Daisy asked. "Then you can live here with us and me and Benjy can share a room."

"Oh, sweetie." Ginny crouched down and tapped Daisy on the nose gently. "Maybe one day, but tonight I have to go home."

Daisy pouted. "I wish you could stay." She touched her braids. "Can I sleep in these?"

"You certainly can."

"I want to go to summer camp in them on Monday."

Ginny ran her fingers tenderly across the girl's hair. "I don't know if they'll last two days, sweetie."

"But if you live here, you can do them for me every day."

She chortled in response because she didn't have the words to respond. "I'll stay over one day. I promise."

"When?" Excitement widened Daisy's eyes.

"One day." Ginny started gathering Benjy's belonging.

"I hate it when you go." Daisy sulked.

"She's not the only one." Ryan waded into the conversation. "Daisy's right. I don't like this. I don't like you leaving late at night. Let me drive you back."

Ginny stopped shoving Benjy's toys into his toy bag. "What would be the point of that? I'll still have to come back to get my car tomorrow."

He sighed in response.

He worried too much about her, and he wasn't making this easy on her. "What do you think's going to happen to me, Ryan?"

"Anything could happen. You could get a flat tire."

She laughed out loud. "I haven't had a flat tire, ever!"

"There's always a first time for everything."

"Ryan! You sound like a doom monger." She prised his hands away from his hips and hugged him. "I'm going to be fine."

"I still don't like it, Benjy's fast asleep. You're gonna have to take a sleeping baby, put him in the car, drive home. And then you're going to have to get him out at the other end."

She'd run the same sequence of steps through her head. "It's not that far."

"Stay. We have spare rooms, and they're yours."

She made a face.

"Promise me you'll think about it," he pleaded, softly, nuzzling her ear.

"I promise."

CHAPTER 11

ASHLEIGH

She was pleased.

The gardener had done a great job planting her rosebushes and making a beautiful rose garden in one big section of her yard.

"How wonderful," said Darcie. "Your whole back yard is transformed." Ashleigh had to agree. Planting those rosebushes and the shrubs and flowers she'd bought recently had changed her yard into something else completely. "I don't know why I didn't do it sooner."

Darcie fixed her with a look. "You've had a lot to deal with."

That was true. "We should have planted rosebushes a long time ago. I can't believe we didn't think to. They were my mom's favorite flowers."

"Though I guess, since you got Herb to plant everything for

you, and you didn't really have to lift a finger yourself, you could have done all this a while back. I wonder what made you do it now," Darcie mused, cryptically.

"Meaning what?" Ashleigh asked, though her friend had a point. Darcie's gardener had been brilliant.

"Sounds to me like you're keeping yourself busy and out of Ford's way."

"Ford?" Ashleigh scowled. "What's Ford got to do with anything?"

"I know you, Ashleigh Rose. You've been quiet and subdued lately."

"And you think any of this is to do with Ford? I don't care about Ford. He's living his own life and I'm living mine."

She still thought about him, though. That was the problem. Because he was no longer hers, was the main reason why she thought of him more now than ever.

"I saw Kayla in the diner last week," her friend remarked, a little too casually.

"With Ford?"

"See." Darcie pointed her fork at her. "You are interested in what he's up to." Ashleigh lifted her pizza slice and took a bite instead of denying the assumption. "She wasn't with Ford," said Darcie, stabbing a chunk of potato from her salad. "She was by herself. I almost didn't recognize her at first. She looks different. Like she's had a makeover. She wasn't even wearing her glasses either."

Ashleigh took a big gulp from her wine glass and continued to eat, letting Darcie twitter on. She'd heard the same from Ginny, who probably saw Kayla more than anyone even though Ryan had moved out. Ginny said Kayla sometimes popped over to see Daisy, and that she was becoming more friendly now. Ginny had mentioned the transformation, but had said nothing about Ford. Ashleigh took another bite of her pizza. "I invited you over to admire my garden, not to sit here and talk about Ford and Kayla."

"Your garden has been fully admired. I'll bring Tom over next time to take a look. I want something as pretty as this."

Darcie's husband was a good guy. Ashleigh was fond of him. "Bring him over, any time. This is so good, Darcie." Ashleigh helped herself to a second helping of Darcie's homemade pizza. "Thanks for bringing this over."

"You're welcome. Glad you're enjoying it. Tom and Matt wolfed it down but didn't say anything about it. They were more concerned about watching the game. It's nice when your cooking is appreciated."

"I certainly appreciate it." Ashleigh sat back, admiring her rose garden. "My mother loved roses. That's what I remember the most as time goes by. Isn't that silly? I don't remember birthdays, or Christmas, or big events and celebrations. I remember little moments, like when Dad would buy us roses to give Mom for Mother's day, or when he would give them to her on special occasions. Sometimes he'd just get them for no reason."

"No reason, huh?" Darcie lifted her wine glass. "That's true love, right there."

"They were so much in love. I just wish they were still here today." Ashleigh's voice wavered, and she regained her composure when she felt Darcie's warm, reassuring hand on her shoulder.

"I know," Darcie said, gently.

"I don't remember them ever bickering, but they must have," Ashleigh mused. "They must have. Surely they must have. All couples bicker, even you and Tom must bicker?"

"A little. He always gives in."

"He'd walk on fire for you," Ashleigh threw back. That man would do anything for Darcie. A tiny knot niggled in her chest. She wanted someone in her life like that. Ford had been that guy.

"Amen to that. I saw Ford walking down the street the other day."

Ashleigh groaned. "This is such a lovely evening; do we have to talk about him?"

"You keep avoiding the topic, but is there no repairing the rift?" Darcie asked, a hint of hope in her voice.

"There's no rift. We're just not together. In time I'm sure we'll get back to being on good terms with one another, but for now ..." For now she couldn't stomach the thought of him being with someone else. It hurt like a knife slowly slicing through her skin.

"She's not his type."

"Darcie." Ashleigh threw her a pained look. "Why, on a beautiful summer's evening when we can sit back, eat pizza, drink wine and admire my rose garden, why in the world would you keep going on about the man I'm trying to forget?"

Darcie almost spat out her pizza. "Trying to forget? There, I knew it. I *knew* it."

"Only because he's here, under my nose, and he came back."

"And because he was your first love."

"Stop it!"

Darcie wiped her mouth with a napkin. "She's not his type. She isn't. I can't see the chemistry. They're so different."

Ashleigh took another gulp from her wine glass, then sat back with her glass in her hands. "I'm not sure Ford has a type. Kayla, Susan and I are as different as chalk and cheese ... and ... and roses," she said, trying to find a fitting analogy. It was only at the funeral that she'd managed to talk a little with Susan, Ford's ex-wife.

"I've known Kayla for a long time and I've never known her to be romantically involved with anyone," Darcie retorted.

"Well, she met Ford. The End." Kayla had been on the sidelines and she and Ford had gotten to know one another. How could they not? The setting had been perfect. At Eloise's housewarming. The two of them mixed in similar circles. It was only a matter of time before the uptight and prim and proper schoolteacher realised that with the big, tall and handsome Ford she was onto a good thing. Not only had the man aged well, but he was handsome and charming and all the things a woman would want. "I wish them well," she said tightly. Her voice not at all reflecting her words.

"That's very *sweet* of you."

"I'm a nice person."

"I still think you're in love with him."

"He's moved on while I'm destined to spend the rest of my days here, living alone in the house I grew up in, while my sisters move out and have beautiful and full lives where they are loved. I'll be nothing more than a shriveled up spinster—"

Darcie slapped her hand playfully. "Don't say silly things like that."

"I will be. I'll be that sad old lady sitting in her garden, admiring the view."

"You won't be alone. Ginny and Eloise will always be here, and so will I."

"Figuratively. Not geographically," Ashleigh pointed out.

"Your sisters will move on, but in time you will, too. You're not even fifty."

Ashleigh groaned.

"You will meet someone, or ... Ford will come to his senses."

"I did meet someone." Ashleigh swirled the wine around in her glass.

"What?" Darcie jolted forward in her chair.

"I *think* he was flirting with me."

Darcie slammed down her wine glass, causing a splash of red liquid to slosh onto the table. "Who?"

"Patrick McBride."

"Who?"

She told Darcie all about the encounter with the handsome father of the bride-to-be. About the way he'd followed her around the store, and the searching questions he'd asked.

"You wait until the end of the evening to tell me this breaking news?"

"I'm not one hundred per cent sure he was."

"He was flirting with you alright. When's he coming back? He's coming back, right?" Darcie cried, her eyes lighting up.

"His daughter will need a few more visits to see us, but Eloise is in charge of the designs and alterations."

"He'll seek you out, I'm sure. Sounds to me already like he can't keep away from you."

Ashleigh waved her hand and dismissed her friend's comment. "They have a limitless budget, and Daddy wants to give her the best that daddy can buy."

"Daddy's rich?"

"Daddy is rich." Ashleigh turned up her nose. "I don't care for rich. I just want someone to sweep me off my feet."

Darcie patted her hand. "Someone will, Cinders. You shall go to the ball." A notification sounded on her cell phone so she was distracted and didn't see Ashleigh roll her eyes at the comment. "I need to go, it's getting late. Tom's in the car outside. He's just texted me. Ginny's still not back. Has she moved in with Ryan?"

"She'll be back, but it's probably only a matter of time

before she moves in with him, and then I will most definitely be left here alone. I should get a cat."

Darcie chugged down the last of her wine. "No. You are not getting a cat. You're getting a man."

Ashleigh groaned loudly and told her friend to leave.

CHAPTER 12

ELOISE

Breakfast turned out surprisingly fine.

Which was a relief given the tense silence which followed after they returned to the hotel last night after Griffin's pre-birthday drinks.

Eloise had an inkling as to why Liam was in such a mood. She was accustomed to Beth's wealth, having been to college with her, but to an outsider, visiting this world of jaw-dropping riches could be jarring. She hadn't expected Liam to be fazed by it; a man like him could easily hold his own, even against the Griffins of the world. Still, she didn't want to risk their mini vacation turning problematic and was eager to clear the air. She sat forward and stared into his eyes. "I love being here with you, Liam. I love having time away just for ourselves, but you're not your usual self. I feel like something's bothering you. You and I need to talk. I want you to tell me what it is."

The hardness was gone from his face. He leaned across the

table, looking sheepish. "I feel out of place here. I didn't think I would, but I do."

A heavy weight dislodged from her gut. Was that all it was? She reached for his hands. "It takes some getting used to, but don't let it worry you. We're only here for tonight and tomorrow. It shouldn't matter how the rich live."

He shook his head, "It seems like a different world. I can't help thinking that this is what you're used to. That this is what you want."

"Me?" She blinked in shock. "This isn't what I want. This isn't where I belong. Not anymore."

"Not anymore? Is it because of me?" There was an intensity in those green eyes.

"It's nothing to do with you." She pressed her fingers into his palms, hating that he felt that way. She had to erase those gremlins away. "I used to come here a lot before, to get away from the shop and my sisters, but once I met you that all changed. I love you, Liam. I love everything about you. I love the life we have. I love what we have, and that's the reason why Beth's world no longer appeals to me. I felt burdened by the business and feel chained to the shop. Before you came along. And I would try to get away whenever I could. I'd come here because Beth's world was an escape. It was fun, and hedonistic and at one time I contemplated living here."

"You were thinking of moving here?" His voice was deathly quiet, and it shook her.

"Well, not *here*, but in Boston. I'm not rich like Beth is. Some of us still need to work for a living." She intertwined her fingers in his, desperate to emphasize her point. She needed him to understand. Hoped he would. "But that changed when I met you. I didn't want any of this. I didn't need any of this, a reason to get away, the desperation to escape. Everything I had, everything I wanted was already there, under my nose." She searched his face for signs of understanding, but found none. He didn't seem convinced. "Say something. What are you not understanding?"

"I don't want you to settle. For me."

Her eyes flew wide open with stone cold shock. She couldn't believe her ears. Or follow his trail of thinking. This was new, the way he'd suddenly started questioning their relationship.

Was he getting bored with her? The extra few days tagged onto the end of this short and now disastrous break made her wonder if he was breaking up with her.

Was that what the extra days were about?

She let go of his hand, and then immediately took it again, not wanting to let go. She couldn't now imagine her life without this man in it. "Are you having doubts about us?" she whispered.

"Are you?"

"No." She shook her head vehemently. "I don't understand what's prompted this. I have no doubts, but it seems to me that maybe you do. Do you?"

"I'm not sure." He pulled away, sat back, making her aware of the physical distance between them.

"You're not sure?" she cried, feeling her insides hollow out.

"I love you, Elle, but I don't want to be with someone who's with me because I'm *convenient.*"

"Convenient? When have I ever said that?"

"How we met. I happened to turn up in your life during a dry spell—"

"What?" Elle cried. "What do you mean a dry spell?"

"Wrong word," he muttered. "A downturn ... a ... a ..." He looked at her helplessly, "I saw those guys, Griffin and his crew, and to know that this was the life you yearned for makes me wonder. It makes me think that maybe you settled for me."

She couldn't believe what she was hearing. Panic gripped her throat, made it harder for her to breathe. "No. No. That's not true. You keep using the word 'settled.' I haven't settled for anything. I don't '*settle*'. I'm in love with you and you're all I want." As if to press home the point, she got up and moved beside him, turning to him on the cushioned seat. "I loved partying. I was a party girl and maybe it's because all my life I've, *we've*—me, Ash and Ginny—have had this responsibility. Growing up with no parents and just Aunt Becky and Ashleigh; that was our world. It was harder for Ashleigh, so much harder, and I've been a selfish brat to her even in recent years, but having your own business ties you down in so many ways. And then, when my marriage didn't work out, I wanted to party and let my hair down. What's wrong with that?"

This time he squeezed her hand, as if to reassure her. "I'm not judging you, Elle. I'm sorry if that's what you think." He put his arm around her shoulder, then hugged her. Her body sank against his and the tension seeped away. His hug was like coming home. "I was scared that you were breaking up with me," she whispered.

"Is that what you thought?" He stared down at her, surprise widening his eyes.

She gaped up at him. "You've been so moody and strange lately."

"I feel like a fish out of water here, Elle. I can't hide it."

"We both feel the same. This isn't my world any longer, Liam. I love my world with you in it. I love you with your white tees and your toolbelt and your handyman gloves. That's my Liam. That's the man I want to be with forever."

The corners of his lips curved upwards. "Forever, huh?"

"Yeah. You're my man. Rough and rugged, even if you are three years younger than me."

He chortled, the way he always did when she brought up

their age difference. "It's just a number. It doesn't mean anything."

～

They visited a craft brewery, only because she thought Liam might like it.

And he did. But he still didn't seem to be his usual easy going self despite their earlier talk. They went for a long walk through the town, and had a light lunch later, after which they returned to the hotel and had a short nap before getting ready for the big party.

Liam disappeared into the bathroom saying he wanted to 'give her a surprise.' When he stepped out, wearing the tux, she clutched her chest. Inside her ribcage, her heart did the mamba. "Oh my *goodness*!" she squealed. "You look *so* hot."

His smile widened to his ears. "You think so?"

"I know so!" She whipped out her cell phone and snapped away. "I have to show my sisters." He chuckled, and she loved that he was in such a good mood. "You're not changed," he said slowly, his eyes staring down the length of her body. She was still wearing his t-shirt.

"I've done my make-up and I just need to slip on my dress." She walked up to him first, and pouted. "Kiss me, before I put on my lipstick otherwise I'll be thinking of kissing you all night." He obliged, giving her a deep and delicious kiss before scooping her up. She wrapped her legs around him, and they stumbled around, falling deeper into the kiss and not wanting to let go. She groaned in delight. "We could be late?" she suggested, naughtily.

"We could be." His eyes turned dark with promise and a hint of mischief. She nibbled the corner of her lower lip, wanting him, needing him, but loathe to mess up his clothes or her makeup. And she didn't want to rush. "Or we could go to the party and come back early."

His eyes lit up. "You really like me in the tux, huh?"

"I'll show you how much when we get you back tonight."

"Promise?"

~

Music and laughter spilled out into the air as they walked up to the house, the noise mixing with the chattering guests and the clink of glasses.

Eloise couldn't help but notice the way some women gawked at Liam as he walked through the crowd. Her heart swelled.

He was her man.

Her Liam.

She was relieved that the odd turn of character he'd shown was over, and that he'd opened up and told her what had been bothering him. Being with him was so different. He wasn't like most guys who kept their feelings bottled up. Liam talked and let it out, and she liked that. Communication was key in a relationship, and she felt so much more connected and closer to him because they talked things out.

They weaved through the crowds of people, dressed in their finest, and enjoying a warm summer evening against the backdrop of the ocean. If the house looked resplendent yesterday, today it was transformed with decorations and looked even more stunning in the dusky evening, with the fairy lights twinkling against the sky. Eloise didn't want to think about the cost of this party. The entire place, inside and outside, was richly decorated with balloons, candles, flowers and huge 'Happy Birthday' signs. A band played on a stage set up in the grounds outside. Platters of seafood on ice were laid out with bottles of champagne and fruit, and small kiosks serving freshly made food were dotted around.

"No burgers?" Liam asked, looking disappointed.

"They'll have some, I'm sure."

They saw Griffin and Beth, surrounded by a group of people over by the bar. Eloise tugged Liam's hand. "We should go over and say 'hi' and give him the birthday card." She stopped. "There's something I didn't tell you. I'm not sure if it's a secret, but they're having twins."

Liam looked surprised. "Twins? She doesn't look pregnant."

Eloise observed his confused reaction with interest. "Because she's not. Someone *else* is having the babies for her. A surrogate."

Liam blinked and she could see him processing this news, as strange and as surreal as it was. "That's great news." He seemed pensive. "Twins, huh? Double the excitement, double the happiness."

"Double the cost," she added. Children were expensive. She'd seen how much some of the things had cost for Benjy. She was happy for Beth. Having seen with her own nephew, Benjy, how much happiness a child brought to a family; she was overjoyed for her friend. Watching Liam's reaction made her wonder if he wanted kids, and that led to her considering what it might be like, if they had a child, but she was in her late thirties now and time was marching on. She quickly pushed the thought away.

"Yeah but ... kids. They're just so ... special." He looked at her. "Look at Benjy. Isn't he the coolest dude?"

Her insides bristled with anxiety. The way Liam spoke, the way his voice turned soft, there was no denying he wanted them. They hadn't discussed having children. They hadn't discussed anything more about themselves, or their relationship. It was still new, sort of, even though it felt as if he'd been in her life forever. Beth having babies made Eloise feel unsure of herself.

"You're here!" Beth appeared by her side and hugged them. "I kept looking out for you guys. I'm so glad you're here."

"This is amazing! The whole place is done up beautifully." Eloise hugged her.

"The decorators were here at six in the morning."

"It looks amazing," Liam told her. "That's a pretty cool band."

"Thank you. Griffin wanted a band so … that's what we had to get. Anyways, there's food and drink and we have a dance floor." Griffin joined them just then.

"Happy birthday, Griff." Eloise hugged him and handed him their birthday card. Then Liam shook hands. "Happy fortieth, dude."

"Thank you."

"We didn't know what to get you," Eloise explained. "I mean, what do you get a man who has everything?"

Griffin grinned appreciatively. "You both coming is enough."

"We got you *something*, and we hope you like it. All the details are in the card." Eloise didn't want to ruin the surprise by telling him. They'd bought him a monthly subscription to a wine club which meant he would receive wine from a French vineyard for the next year.

"Thank you, Eloise and Liam. I appreciate the gesture, but really, you two being here is more than enough."

They talked a while, and Beth reminded them about the post-birthday brunch tomorrow and she hoped they would come early and spend more time with them.

"Sure, we'd love to," Liam replied, surprising Eloise. Every now and then she caught flashes of the man she'd fallen in love with. Maybe this was just a phase he was going through. Some work-related problems on his mind, perhaps?

"Help yourselves to the food. We have someone making pizzas and burgers, there are tacos somewhere and we have an ice-cream van as well," Griffin said.

Liam nodded. "Cool."

"We have to mingle, but we'll speak later." Griffin left with Beth. Eloise held hands with Liam and stared up at him. He was so handsome in his casual clothes but him in a suit was something else altogether. She wanted to wrap her arms around his neck. He caught her looking, and the corner of his mouth curved upwards. Before she knew it he'd pulled her towards him and planted his lips on hers. They kissed under the stars studded in the inky purple-blue night sky.

This was what she wanted for their short vacation. Happiness coursed through her that things were finally working out. "We don't have to stay too long at the brunch tomorrow." Ideas flashed through her head about lying in bed with him until late tomorrow morning. Here, surrounded by people, enjoying a fabulous party in an amazing place, being with this man made her feel complete.

"I don't mind. Whatever you want, Elle."

She was deliriously, madly, utterly happy and in love. "Let's go and find the burger stand," she suggested. Liam wanted burgers, and she was determined that he would have his fill of them. But, to her surprise, he seemed reluctant to move. "I'd rather stay right here and kiss you all night."

She nibbled her lower lip, secretly overcome with joy. "We need to eat." She tip-toed up to his ear. "You're going to need your energy for later."

"Is that so?" He licked his lower lip, a wolfish smile breaking out. "Then we better go and find those burgers."

Making their way to where the food was being cooked took

a while because whenever Eloise bumped into people she'd met through the years, she would introduce Liam and they'd get talking.

Eventually, they made it to the food stands. The delicious aroma of wood-fired pizza and burgers wafted through the air. Eloise's mouth was already watering. She left Liam to get his food while she grabbed hers. At last, with something to eat, they sat at one of the many tables, decked with centrepieces of flickering candles and flowers.

"This is *soooo* good." Eloise sat back, enjoying her slice of pepperoni pizza. Liam tucked into his big, fat juicy burger. They ate quickly and quietly. Having ravenously finished her food, she looked around to see what else was being served. "I'm going to get some tacos," she announced, not caring about what she ate.

"Moving along the food stands one by one?" Liam asked, grinning.

"It has to be done. I'm not counting the calories today."

"Nor should you ever."

She smiled. "Want me to get you another burger?"

"I'll go up when my plate is empty."

Over by the taco stand she couldn't decide on which ones to get. The serving platters were labelled. There was Peruvian chicken, five spice cajun bean, hoisin peking duck, chipotle charred steak tacos. She took one of everything and was making her way back to the table where Liam was when she felt a hand on her arm. The touch was familiar and warm. "I was hoping you'd be here."

She knew that voice. She turned in shock, as her insides did a triple somersault in her stomach. Liam could see, she was sure, the way the guy was touching her arm. "Hey ... Alan." Sweat dampened the back of her neck.

"It's *Alex*. How could you forget?"

"Oh, right. Yeah … sorry, Alex." Her heart raced and goosebumps sprang up on her arms.

He stroked her skin. "You're obviously excited to see me."

She moved her arm away, conscious of searing, burning eyes on her. Of Liam watching.

Alex's eyes glistened as his gaze swept over her. "It's so good to see you. You look amazing."

"I'm … I... I came with … come and meet Liam." She moved to her table.

"Who?" he said after her. She sat down and saw Liam's face cloud over with apprehension.

He'd seen.

"This is …" Thud, thud, thud, went her beating heart. "This is Liam, my boyfriend."

"Uh..." Surprise washed over Alex's face. He tried to school his expression, tried to smile and look normal but he was a few seconds too late. "Hi." He held out his hand stiffly. Liam shook it hard.

"This is Alex," Eloise said to Liam, but all the while she was trying to gauge Liam's mood and trying to work out what he was thinking. Alex was so slick and polished. Ordinarily she wouldn't care much, but she was sure that Liam would notice such things. The atmosphere turned deathly silent. The band were taking a break, and the sound and laughter all around lowered. Eloise shifted in her chair while Alex stood there. Liam had stopped eating.

She stared at the tacos on her plate. "Are you here with anyone?" She struggled to think of safe questions, praying that he wouldn't bring up anything from their brief past together. She was very aware of Liam's thoughts. He didn't like this and he didn't look happy. She was sure he was wondering how long she and Alex had been together and why they'd broken up.

"No. I came alone."

More silence. It made the unspoken questions hang in the air like stalactites. Their sharp, icy points threatening to pierce the happy bubble she had Liam had shared.

"Beth and Griffin are over there, in case you haven't seen them yet." Eloise gestured in their direction.

"I'll go and see them. Thanks." Alex's gaze ping-ponged between her and Liam. "It was uh ... it was good to see you again. Nice to meet you." He nodded at Liam.

Eloise slouched back. Her appetite had vanished. She moved her plate away. Liam didn't look at her, but focussed instead on eating his burger. When he had finished eating, he got up silently and left the table, presumably to refill his plate.

Eloise hoped that's what he was doing. The sullen man had returned and when Liam was in this mood, she didn't know what to expect. To her relief, he came back a few moments later. He couldn't be too upset, she surmised, seeing his plate full of food. Maybe he was okay.

After all, what was the big deal? She'd told him about Alex when they'd shared their past relationships. "That was ... that was the guy I told you about. The one I briefly met at Beth's wedding."

"You told me."

"He's nice."

Liam grunted.

She moved her chair so that it was next to his instead of across the table from him. "But he's not you." She placed her hand on his lap, then felt the muscles stiffen. He didn't want her touching him. She wanted to talk, to have it out with him, but now was not the time. Picking up her taco, she took a bite but, as delicious as it was, she wasn't hungry and it felt like a chore to eat.

Liam ate in silence while she waited patiently, and uneasily, for him to finish. When he did, she suggested they get up and dance, but he told her he wasn't in the mood. She tried to mingle with the people she'd come to know, and introduced them to Liam, but the evening turned sour for her. The celebratory mood sucked out by Liam's brooding and heavy presence.

She wished she'd never come.

They left the party early and walked home. Back at the hotel, they undressed and got into bed, but this wasn't quite the ending she'd had in mind.

Liam told her that he was tired, then turned his back on her and went to sleep. Lying on her back she stared up at the ceiling in the darkness. "They've invited us over for brunch tomorrow," she reminded him, eager to hear what he would say.

He made a noise.

"It's a tradition with Beth and her family. They always have it after a party."

"I'd rather not go."

Why? She wanted to ask, but dared not for fear of causing a big row. He was being unreasonable again and difficult. Probing too deep might set him off. Eloise sighed, hating that they had become this; uncommunicative strangers. "Then I don't want to go either."

"You should go. Say 'hi' to Alex for me."

Eloise's jaw dropped. She sat up in bed and switched the lamp on. "You're behaving like a jealous teenager."

"I am younger than you."

"What?" she cried, her nostrils flaring. "That doesn't even make sense."

"It was a low blow. I'm sorry. That was me being a big jerk." He sat up and turned to face her.

"You were being a jerk. *Again.*"

"If it came down to me and Alex, who would you pick?"

"What kind of question is that?" It was as bad as she'd

feared. He was comparing himself to Alex, making a big mistake. They were different breeds. Alex was in her past, and her encounter with him had been but fleeting. Men like him were transitory entanglements. Men like Liam were steadfast, solid, and forever. Or so she hoped.

"Me or Alex?" he asked.

"You. Always you. Undeniably you. Why are you asking me this?" she cried, not believing her ears.

"Why me when you could have someone like him?"

She threw her hands into the air. "But I don't want someone like him. I told you. It was a little bit of fun. Nothing more. Nothing important. Nothing lasting. I'm with you. I choose *you*."

"Maybe you're with me because I was doing up your house and one thing led to another."

"Not that again." She rubbed her forehead in despair. "I've had handymen before, to fix little things, and one thing has *never* led to another with them. What point are you trying to make?" she snapped. She could understand women getting moody and irritable and irrational at certain times of the month, but what excuse did men have? "Why are we arguing like this? I met an ex. So what? I'm not with him now, am I?"

"Shouldn't you be?"

"You really do sound like a teen," she said, through gritted teeth.

"I imagine you being with someone like him."

"That's just sick." She stared at him, not recognizing this man anymore. "If you're going to be like this, I don't see the point of us spending the rest of our time here together."

His face dropped, and it confused her even more. What did he want? "If that's what you want."

It wasn't what she wanted, but Liam was irrational and he was annoying her. She hadn't come here to be riled up and to feel bad. She wanted a relaxing weekend away with the man she loved.

The problem was, this *wasn't* the man she loved.

This was someone else. "That is what I want." It was no good. It wasn't good for her health or her sanity to have Liam be hot and cold. She couldn't take it. All she wanted was to spend time with him away from their everyday environment, but witnessing this jealous and brooding side to him made her regret coming.

"Let's just go home." He got out of bed and sat on the two-seat sofa fiddling around on his cell phone.

"What are you doing now?" she cried in exasperation.

"Changing our flights."

CHAPTER 13

GINNY

"Shuush baby." Ginny tried to soothe the baby in her arms.

She had no idea why he was so upset. "Shush! Aunt Ashleigh will have my head if you don't be quiet." She bounced him around, tried to give him a little baby treat to nibble on. He'd been so hungry lately, and ate everything she gave him, which was good, but she didn't understand why he'd now turned into a fretfully crying baby.

Raising him with both arms to her face, she smelled his bottom. Nothing going on down there. She'd changed his diaper not so long ago, and he'd been fed so, what was the problem? He'd developed an annoying habit of chewing his fingers and she kept pulling his hand out of his mouth.

Ashleigh stormed into the room; her face twisted with hardness. It was too late now, and Ginny prepared herself for a telling off.

"Will you keep him quiet? I have someone in for a fitting," her sister hissed.

"I'm trying. I don't know what's wrong with him." Ginny was doing her best, she really was, and she had no idea why Benjy was playing up. It was pure bad luck for her especially since she'd managed to convince her sisters to let her start back at the shop now instead of waiting until he was a year old, which was the date Ashleigh was pushing for. With Eloise out of town for a few days, Ginny had managed to convince Ashleigh to give her a chance, but now she was scared of Ashleigh's 'I told you so' face.

"I'll take him out for some fresh air. I'll … I'll take him to the park and put him on the baby swings," she suggested. That would tire him out and then when she returned, he would hopefully fall asleep. Benjy had finished nibbling on the little baby biscuit she'd given him but he was crying again. "He's so hungry all the time," Ginny lamented. "I'll feed him some more while I'm out."

Ashleigh took one look at the crying baby who was now trying to gnaw on his fist. "He's teething."

"No he's not!" Ginny looked at her son who was chewing his fingers, and her jaw dropped. Could he be?

"He's teething," Ashleigh insisted with such conviction that Ginny believed her even though her sister had no experience of raising children.

"Are you sure?" Ginny asked, feeling relieved. She hoped this was the reason behind Benjy's behaviour and it gave her some comfort.

"I'm sure. Aren't you reading any baby books? Maybe spend less time with Ryan and more time reading up on what to expect in a baby's first year."

Ginny's brows lifted. "Ouch," she retorted at the below-the-belt comment and was about to throw back a remark when she stopped. It wouldn't help her case if she got into a row with Ashleigh.

Not now.

Not if she wanted to work at the shop for just a few hours every so often. It didn't need to be every day. She didn't want to be a stay-at-home mom, stuck at home. She wanted to make more of her life, and with her future uncertain, she wanted to start early to provide for both her and Benjy.

The office door flung open causing them both to turn their attention to it.

Ashleigh gasped as Eloise walked in. "What are you doing here? You're not supposed to be back until Wednesday."

"We got back early." Eloise looked miserable. As if she hadn't slept. As if she'd hadn't been away for the amazing short break she'd been looking forward to.

"What happened?" Ginny asked, letting Benjy suck his thumb, feeling grateful for his silence.

"Nothing." Eloise threw down her bag and took off her jacket, before sitting down at her desk and turning on her computer. Ashleigh walked towards her with her hands on her hips. "Something's happened? What is it?"

"I don't even know where to start." Eloise buried her face in her hands.

"Did you and Beth fall out?" Ginny asked, equally as clueless.

"Worse." Eloise's voice was muffled behind her hands.

"Spare me the story. I don't have time to listen to it yet," Ashleigh snapped. "We've already had some drama this morning."

"Someone's in a bad mood," Ginny mumbled, to no one in particular. She put Benjy into the stroller.

"That's because we're not running a baby day care center here," Ashleigh answered, standing by the door and looking impatient. Eloise stood up and grabbed her bag and her jacket again.

"Where are you going?" Ashleigh cried.

"I don't need this right now. I'm going to the diner to get breakfast."

"Great," Ashleigh snapped.

Ginny welcomed the idea. "Wait for me, I'll come with you. I need to go to the drugstore."

"Leave me to run the store all by myself, *again*, why don't you?" Ashleigh stomped out after Eloise.

Eloise was sitting at a table in the Sunnyside Diner by the time Ginny got there. She'd bought some teething gel and Benjy seemed to be responding well in such a short space of time. Ginny had checked his gums and there was something coming through.

Poor baby.

Teething already.

He was changing before her very eyes every day. Talking more, gibbering more, and he was expressive and beautiful and incredible. Her son was turning into a little boy right before her eyes.

This baby was her everything. Her life, despite the setbacks and tragedy she had experienced, was getting better. She had reunited with Benjy's parents, and had surprised them one day by agreeing to meet them at the mall. Ben's mother had burst into tears at the sight of her only grandchild and her husband had struggled not to break down. Ginny could see the poor man trying to keep his composure.

They held Benjy's hand as he sat in the stroller staring up at the people who were strangers to him. They talked to him lovingly, and stroked his cheek as they cried silent tears while gazing at Benjy with such love, longing and sadness, that Ginny felt even more awful for keeping them out of their grandson's life for so long. When Benjy's grandmother asked if she could pick her grandson up, Ginny agreed. That day there were a lot of tears as they grieved together and remembered Ben, and now celebrated Benjy.

Ginny felt good for meeting them. Her son had no maternal grandparents, and she could not deny Benjy the only grandparents he had. It would be the wrong thing to do by Ben, despite the wrongdoing he had inflicted on her. Ben's parents were innocent in all this, and she couldn't punish them for their son's transgressions. In time, she would take them up on their offer to visit them at their house one day.

With her own life now filled with joy and happiness, Eloise's anguish was clear to see. Her sister sat, stirring her cup of coffee absentmindedly. Ginny parked the stroller by the side of the table. Eloise instantly cheered up and stroked Benjy's cheek. "Hey, Benjy. What's he chewing on?"

"A teething toy. He's teething. I just found out," Ginny announced proudly.

"Teething? You're teething?" Eloise asked the baby, staring into his chubby face.

"He was making such a commotion this morning before you walked in. Ashleigh wasn't happy."

"I don't blame her, Gin. We're running an upscale establishment. Or trying to."

"He's usually very good. You know how good he is, but lately, he's been a nightmare. Maybe I shouldn't have gone into work today, but I didn't know he was teething. If I'd known I would have stayed at home."

"Ash let you start?" Eloise asked. "I didn't think she would so soon."

"I convinced her that you being away was the best time to let me start."

"You could come back after a few months, or a year, wait until he's older and more settled," Eloise suggested. Ginny took in a breath. Neither of her sisters were keen for her to help at the shop. They both complained about being chained to the store, and now that Ginny was stepping up and volunteering to help—showing more enthusiasm than ever—they didn't seem to appreciate it. Instead they were giving her reasons to stay at home and be a mom.

"I don't want to be a housewife. I want to be a working mother, and I don't see why I can't have the best of both worlds especially because we own the shop and we can make our own rules for work."

"You can't have a wailing, screaming baby disrupting the ambiance of our store. Customers don't want to feel like they're in a day care center when they're admiring tulle skirts and beaded bodices."

"I'll make it work. I'll figure it out," Ginny insisted. "Benjy's teething now, but once that's out of the way, I'll be back with a vengeance."

Eloise chortled. "He's not going to have just one tooth."

There it was again; the reluctance for her to return to work. She was going out of her mind being stuck at home all day. With Ryan at work and Daisy sometimes at summer camp, she felt like a spare arm. When Daisy was at school things were worse. She loved spending time with her baby, loved that she took care of him, but she was now able to bring him to work. It wasn't as if she would be working for an employer.

She also wanted to be independent and not rely on her sisters, or Ryan, for anything. She wanted to provide for herself. Benjy depended on her and while in the months following his birth she'd been plunged into a listlessness she found hard to shake, now she was pumped and motivated to better her life and that of her son's.

Maybe it was because she'd spent the least amount of time at the shop, that she was more enamoured with it. Ash and Eloise, she sensed, found it to be a burden, but Ginny saw new potential for her future and that of the business.

"Why are you back so early?" she asked. Clearly Eloise was going through something. Her sister sighed in response, then slumped back in her chair. Her face downcast; the happy, bubbly Eloise of recent months now seemed to be wilting before Ginny's eyes.

"I think we broke up."

Ginny gasped as she sat up straighter, shockwaves coursing through her at the words. "You think what?"

"We broke up."

"I don't believe you."

"I wouldn't joke about something like that. I think we did, but I'm not sure."

"What do you mean you're not sure?"

Ginny listened as Eloise told her about the trip and Beth's husband's party, of how Liam had been a little uneasy at first but then things got better. Then she told her how she'd run into someone she'd had a short fling with, and how this had riled Liam, and made him jealous. They'd come home early and had an argument after which they'd rashly decided to return home earlier.

"You couldn't resolve it?" Ginny asked, finding the way they dealt with this most peculiar and nothing like the happy couple she knew. Liam was the most laidback guy, easy going and fun and caring. She didn't know what to make of it.

"We did, at first, but then at the party on Saturday, when I ran into Alex, Liam got all funny again. Things went downhill after that."

"Alex?" Ginny asked. Eloise didn't say much about her visits to see Beth, and all she and Ashleigh knew was that she had a lot of fun partying over there.

"I've mentioned him before. He's no one special. It didn't last long."

"I can't believe you cut your trip short and you couldn't work things out. What a wasted opportunity." Ginny wiped the drool trickling out of Benjy's mouth.

"We could have salvaged it, but Liam was so difficult. So different."

"Salvaged?" Ginny didn't like that word. "Is it really over?" She was aghast at how quickly it had happened. This was what she feared. Even with Ryan. Love was so fragile, so nebulous, and so changeable. It had the ability to light up the soul, and also to break the spirit.

Eloise shrugged. "I'm not sure. We changed our flights, and got a taxi from the airport and got home yesterday evening. He went to his place and I went to mine. I haven't heard from him since."

This was most unheard of. Knowing how many curveballs she'd had in her own life, and how they'd knocked her back, Ginny suspected there was more than just jealousy going on. It sounded so out of character for Liam to behave in this way. "What are you going to do? You need to fix things. You and Liam are so perfect for one another. He makes you so happy. You make him happy."

"I know." Tears welled up in Eloises's eyes and Ginny reached forward and grabbed her arm. "You'll work it out, I know you both will. You're too good together, and too strong and you are both meant to be together. You'll work it out."

"I hope so."

"Are you going to call him?" Ginny asked.

"At some stage I will, but for now I have to get back to

work. If Ash is as angry as you say, we can't afford to be sitting here talking about our lives."

"You don't have to get back to work right now. It's your day off today. You're supposed to be on vacation still."

"But *you* can't go back," Eloise pointed out. "Not with Benjy crying and not feeling well. Ash will explode."

"She's like that most of the time these days." Ginny told her about Ashleigh's new project of transforming her garden and how she'd had so many rose bushes planted.

"Mom loved roses." Eloise's voice was close to breaking, whether from the sadness related to her parents, or from the breakup with Liam, or both, Ginny couldn't tell. "She loved them so much. We'd always give her a bunch."

A knot twisted in Ginny's chest. "I don't remember." Feeling wistful she gazed at her son who had miraculously fallen asleep. Being only a toddler when her parents died, Ginny had no real memories of them, apart for the ones her sisters brought to life and the things they told her.

Her sisters' memories formed *her* memories, and losing her parents so young that she had no real permanent impression of them made her even more determined to do more with Benjy and give him precious memories of her.

Ashleigh had been twenty-one years old and Eloise fifteen. They were so spread-out age wise. Ash couldn't leave to go and live her own life. Ginny understood that now. Saw it as clear as day, and now wanted to give back. Wanted her sister to have the life she never got to lead, because what Ashleigh had done was live a life of service. Not as a nun, but as an older sister who, along with Aunt Becky, had taken responsibility for them.

That wasn't fair on Ashleigh, and Ginny was determined to step up.

CHAPTER 14

ASHLEIGH

She felt his presence first.

Felt the hairs on the back of her neck shoot up in attention before she turned and looked at him.

Patrick McBride strode into the shop with his daughter in tow. He looked like a distinguished movie star from another era, with his swept back hair, his tall height, slim frame and a face that was chiselled to perfection. As if that wasn't enough, the light wrinkles on his forehead and around his eyes gave him an air of authority that added to his allure.

"Well, hello there." His voice turned her insides soft.

"H-hi." She fought for composure. "I didn't expect you to come back so quickly," she said, not liking the way her voice wavered. She wished she'd dressed better today; worn a more stylish blouse and skirt.

"As I mentioned before, we're under a lot of time pressure because of what happened the last time."

"Don't worry. We won't let you down."

"And it's nice to come back and see you."

"Oh, really?" Her heart dropped into her stomach. *Was he flirting with her?*

"Yes, really."

He *was* flirting. She tried to steady her breathing, to still her racing heartbeat, level her voice. "Okay. Mr. McBride … I don't know what to say to that."

"There's no need to say anything. Just accept the compliment." He wasn't being smarmy or slick. He had an air of good old-fashioned charm about him, which dispelled her any revulsion she might have felt had someone else, less debonair, made those same moves.

She pressed her lips together, resulting in a half-wince, half-smile and tried to think of a suitable answer to give him. But then her attention went to his daughter who was admiring a dress on a mannequin. Today she had come alone, without her friends. Ashleigh forced a laugh. "I … I just didn't expect you to turn up again so soon, that's all."

She'd only called him yesterday, when Eloise had unexpectedly returned. Clearing her throat, and tucking her hair behind her ear, she inhaled a breath as she stared down at her diary, not looking for anything in particular, just trying to look busy. Trying to forget the effect he was having on her, by apparently doing nothing except for standing in close proximity.

He placed his hands on the counter, squaring his wide shoulders, and giving her the most disarming look. "Angelina loved your dresses, and she is excited for you to create her dream dress. You called me, Ashleigh. That's why I'm here."

"Of course. I thought it best to contact you right away since my sister came back unexpectedly early from her trip."

"Sorry for your sister. I trust everything is okay? But I'm

glad you called." There it was again, the effortless smile, the easy charm. His full attention on her. Just by looking at her he made her feel as if she were the only one in the shop.

Over his shoulder, she could see that Eloise was on the shop floor, adjusting the veil on a mannequin. "My sister's here. Let me introduce her to your daughter." She walked towards them, with Patrick following, and made introductions. Eloise was already aware of Angelina McBride because Ashleigh had fully brought her up to date with the goings on.

Eloise gave Angelina her most dazzling, professional smile. "Why don't we sit down and talk about what you're looking for, and I'll sketch out exactly what you have in mind," she said, sounding business-like and a woman with a mission. This was good; the last thing Ashleigh needed was a heartbroken Eloise adding doom and gloom, especially here, the place where dreams were supposed to begin.

Eloise led Angelina away.

Ashleigh turned to Patrick. "They will have plenty to talk about. Can I get you anything? Iced tea? Tea or coffee?" She made to leave, wanting to get some distance between them, and the work she needed to get on with.

"No, nothing. Thank you."

"In that case, I'll leave you, I'm afraid, as I have plenty of work I need to get on with."

"You've been traveling, you said?" He followed her back to the counter again where she had been looking through the diary.

"Uh … yes. Yes, I did." Her heart was beginning to thump again.

He didn't seem to want to stop talking to her. It wasn't wedding dress related conversation, either. She felt a quivering in her stomach, then acute panic set in. Ginny wasn't coming in today, and Ashleigh had nothing to take her attention away from this man. She suddenly wished she could hear Benjy wailing in the office just so that she could excuse herself and disappear.

"Where to? You mentioned you went to Europe." He was pressing for more details.

"Europe. Portugal, then Spain and France and Italy. It all seems such a blur now."

"Fascinating."

"It was. It was amazing. I'll never forget it."

"You travelled alone?"

Was he trying to work out if she was single?

"I was looking for adventure, Mr. McBride. I needed a change from the small town I've lived in all my life." She couldn't believe the words that were coming out of her mouth. She hadn't intended to tell him this, but the words just somehow fell out.

"Adventure?" His eyes twinkled. "What sort of adventure."

"Not the sort of adventure you—"

"Daddy, what do you think of this?" Angelina asked, sashaying towards her father. Ashleigh was relieved for the interruption. She'd been about to get entangled in some dangerous conversation, not thinking through her words but reacting. She turned to Angelina who looked like a perfect porcelain doll with her slim figure, her cherry red lips, large doe-ish eyes, hair swept back and held in place by the veil. The dress was a V-necked gown with a beaded bodice.

"You look beautiful, darling. But isn't that the one you tried on the last time?" The girl's father looked puzzled.

"But with these changes." Angelina did a flourish with her hand, signalling for Eloise, with her clipboard, to explain. "Shall we sit down and I can show you, Mr. McBride?"

Patrick nodded. He glanced at Ashleigh. "Come," he commanded. "I'd like to hear your thoughts on the changes."

"I was going to ..." Ashleigh was about to protest but the

words petered out. This was an important client, and she would have ordinarily jumped at the request.

It doesn't matter what I think. But she reluctantly followed Patrick McBride. Something was going on. There was a charge in the air. Something electric. She felt an invisible connection to this man, something that made her giddy with delight, yet at the same time it felt reckless and dangerous. But here she was, following Patrick McBride and doing his bidding.

Even if it was only to give advice on his daughter's dream wedding dress.

"So, Angelina would like to have a full circle skirt, instead of this column," Eloise rifled through her sketches and plucked one out to show them. "We were thinking maybe fine gossamer tulle, and possibly a blush colored lining to give depth to the gown. What do you think?" she asked Ashleigh.

Ashleigh nodded. "Yes. Oh, yes. I can see how that would work."

"And a tiara," Angelina added.

"Your mother is taking care of that," Patrick said.

Angelina's smile was dazzling. "It's all coming together, Daddy."

"It seems to be, and very quickly, too, I might add."

"Are you happy with these changes?" Eloise asked the bride to be.

Angelina nodded. "That's exactly what I want. *Exactly.*"

"Is that something you can do given the time constraint?" Patrick asked.

"We certainly can," said Ashleigh. "We have designers who can create exactly what you would like, and any adjustments to be made, we will make here. We'll be able to get the dress ready in your time frame."

Eloise elaborated some more about the beading and design

of the dress, and Angelina's face lit up. "That's it! That's my dream dress!"

"Splendid." Patrick looked satisfied, and his daughter seemed ready to burst with excitement. "If that's what Angie wants, then that is what Angie shall get."

"Thanks, Daddy."

"Could you take some pictures for me?" She asked Eloise as she fished around in her bag and pulled out a cell phone. "So I can send some pictures to my mom?" Eloise happily obliged.

"Shall we talk finances?" Patrick asked Ashleigh.

"Of course." Ashleigh led him back to the counter.

"Money is no object," he reminded her.

Ashleigh smiled. "You've made that very clear." She scribbled away on her notepad, and told him that these were rough figures, but she would confirm everything with Eloise and give him an exact price later. "It all depends on the level of beading and the different materials needed for the dress."

"I understand. It's fine, whatever it costs."

"I will have a final price for you by this evening."

"Ashleigh." His smile dazzled her, partially blinding her to everything and everyone else in the room. With his hands on the counter, he leaned in again slightly, reminding her of his height, his scent, and his authority. Her dizzying attraction to him multiplied by a thousand. "This evening, tomorrow, next week. It doesn't matter. The price won't change my mind. Please go ahead and get started with Angie's dress. I trust you implicitly."

"Right. Sure." She tried to smile, and hoped he wouldn't notice that she was suddenly feeling very warm. And bothered, and not in control.

"How was your weekend?" he asked, casually, while adjusting the cuffs of his shirt sleeves.

"My weekend?"

"The days in the middle, since you and I last met." He gave her another disarming smile.

Since you and I last met.

He had a way of making the words sound sexier than they should have been.

"Oh, I … " She tried to think but thinking had suddenly become difficult.

"I ... I had a friend over to admire my garden."

"Your garden?"

Admire my garden. She cringed inside. That sounded so adventurous. So rock and roll.

Not.

"I … I wanted to have lots of rosebushes planted," she heard herself explain.

He opened his mouth, then closed it again. Then nodded. "How very fitting."

This was a man who flew around the world, in private jets, probably, who came here in a chauffeured car, and probably met worldly wise women. *Glamorous* women.

And her.

A lover of planted rosebushes.

She wished a tsunami would sweep her away.

"Daddy, it's mom. She wants to talk to you." Angelina held out her cell phone and, mercifully, the man disappeared.

CHAPTER 15

ELOISE

*E*loise scooped out another big spoonful from the supersized tub of chocolate fudge ice-cream, then passed it to her sister.

This beat sitting at home and brooding on her own. She'd had dinner with Ashleigh and Ginny this evening, grateful to have some company, and something to take her mind off her problems with Liam.

She hated being like this.

Without him.

Not talking.

Not being friends.

She missed him, and she couldn't figure out what had gone wrong. Now that she'd had time to think about it, she realized that he'd been in a sour mood before they'd met Beth and Griffin. Running into an old boyfriend—not that Alex fit that category—hadn't helped.

She was saddened breaking up with Liam, and his temperament scared her. She thought she knew him. Thought they were soulmates, but the change in his personality, the way he had been during their short vacation, this wasn't the man she loved. It made her question just how well she knew him. How well they were suited to one another.

And whether he really was 'the one.'

"Have you heard from him today?" Ashleigh asked.

She'd only briefed Ashleigh quickly yesterday, on what had happened, but Ginny was fully up to date with events, and now the poor girl had to sit through another explanation all over again. Eloise shook her head. "We texted. I asked him how he was and he asked me how I was."

"Texting is the coward's way. You both need to meet face to face and talk this out." Ashleigh passed the ice cream tub to Ginny.

"That's what I told her," said Ginny, accepting the tub and digging her spoon in.

"It's not like Liam to turn nasty and cut your weekend short," said Ashleigh, a hint of blame in her voice.

"That's what I said." Ginny licked her spoon.

Eloise surveyed her sisters with mild irritation. "You both think I'm the one who cut the trip short?"

"Yes." They replied in unison.

She scratched the back of her neck. "It might have been me," she said, sheepishly, trying to remember.

"What did you do?" Ashleigh asked.

There it was again. The insinuation by her sister that she'd been the one who'd done wrong. Everything happened so quickly. She was on edge at Griffin's party when Alex approached her, and she started to feel anxious knowing that Liam might see or hear. Turns out he did both.

It shouldn't have ruined their evening. She had a past, she'd had boyfriends. Liam had had a girlfriend he'd been pretty cut up about. They both had pasts. She didn't hold his against him. So why Alex reappearing had changed Liam's mood so badly was a mystery to her.

It wasn't jealousy. She sensed, but didn't understand, that he might have felt inadequate being around Beth's people. She was used to it, to the glamor and the glitz, but she could see how it would have been a big shock to Liam.

Now she wished she hadn't gone to Griffin's birthday, even though it had been great to see Beth. Unfortunately, they hadn't been able to spend much time together, and the next day she and Liam missed the post-party brunch. She'd already told Beth that Liam had planned a short break after the party, and she let Beth think that's where she and Liam had gone.

No point in confessing that they had a row at the party.

That night, they left early, and returned to the hotel room. Liam was sullen, and she, not wanting to pour fire over the gasoline of his anger, let things be, even though she wanted to discuss, analyze and dissect the evening in the hope of getting to the root of the problem.

But Liam, being a man, someone different, behaving in a manner she wasn't used to, didn't seem remotely interested in solving anything.

She'd woken up alone the next day and jolted with a start to see that he wasn't beside her. There was a note on his pillow.

Gone for a run.

Disappointed, but relieved, she clutched it to her chest and lay back down again. At least he was still here. At least he hadn't walked out on her. They changed their flight and flew back later that evening, after having a lunch that was more agony than pleasure. Conversations filled with long pregnant pauses.

This was not who they were. Liam and Elle, the happy

couple, had vanished, and it was tragic that this was what they had become.

"I met an old flame and Liam didn't like it."

"An old flame?" Ashleigh's brows shot north.

"She must have had a few of them, because she'd go to Beth's at any opportunity," Ginny quipped. Eloise smiled weakly. There was no use in bringing up the chapter of how she'd met Alex, partly because she'd told a little white lie and pretended to be ill so that she could stay at Beth's for a little longer. "I'm only human. That's in my past, but he was there and he started talking to me and Liam didn't like it."

"Does he have a name?" Ashleigh liked to know all the details.

Eloise's insides knotted. "What does it matter?" She didn't want to talk about her past. It was irrelevant. Alex was irrelevant. "He's not in my life now."

"But he was once, and you never said a thing," Ashleigh said.

"I don't want to talk about him. Alex. His name was Alex and I had some fun. Is that okay with you?" Eloise snarled.

Ginny looked nervous. "Calm down, it's okay. We don't have to talk about him. Leave it be," she said to Ashleigh. She reached for Eloise's hand. "We don't have to talk about any of this if you don't want to." Her voice was soft and manner comforting. Eloise felt a sense of relief. The subtle shift in Ginny was new. She was changing and maturing so quickly. Maybe being a mother had done this, or having, at last, a good, honest and trustworthy man in her life? Whatever it was, she was happy for Ginny.

"We can talk about it," she said, slowly. Ashleigh didn't know all the details, and it was only fair that Eloise told her everything. Besides, she'd been churning the whole sequence of events over in her head, trying to figure out what had gone wrong, and since Liam didn't seem interested in dealing with it, talking to her sisters was the salve she needed to heal her wounded heart. That was the thing about having sisters: they were always there, whether you wanted them or not. Whether they annoyed you or not. Friends came and went, but blood? Blood was binding. Blood was thick. Ashleigh and Ginny, while they might judge her, they would never walk away. They had gotten through the good times and the bad times together, and their sisterly bond had helped them through the decades. "Maybe he was jealous, but I don't understand why he would be. Alex was not important. He was fun for a short while. But he's in my past and he doesn't mean anything to me. It's Liam who I love."

Ashleigh scooped up some ice cream. "You had a fling."

"I told you it was a fling. I didn't cheat. Alex and I were only together for a few days and it's in the past. I'm not a cheater," Eloise retorted. She'd been cheated on in her marriage and had experienced the gut wrenching, heartbreaking effects of such a thing. She would never do that to anyone. "I don't understand what he got so worked up about. Then we went back to the hotel and he was grumpy, so I left it, and the next day he went for a run to clear his head." She rolled her eyes. "After a miserable lunch, we flew home."

"Something is clearly bothering him," her wise, older and judgemental sister remarked.

Ginny let out a sigh, her spoon digging into the ice cream tub and remaining there. "I understand him being jealous, even though he had no reason to be. Something happens to me when Vanessa appears. She'll suddenly show up in our lives, via a video call with Daisy, and then she somehow manages to reel Ryan into the conversation. I understand Liam's reaction."

"But it ruined our evening. We didn't even dance."

"Oh lordy. No dancing. Kill me now." Ashleigh plunged an imaginary knife to her chest. "Life is so hard for you."

Eloise narrowed her eyes. What did Ashleigh know? She couldn't even salvage her relationship with Ford who was the nicest, most down to earth guy. "I noticed you and that new customer's father getting on very well."

Ashleigh's face slowly turned pink. "Pass the bucket around. Stop hoarding it." She gesticulated with her hand, eyeing the ice-cream tub, and fully ignoring Eloises's comment.

Busted. Ashleigh ignoring her so casually proved that there was something. Having found her sister's Achilles heel, Eloise dug deeper. "What were you and Angelina McBride's father whispering about?"

"We weren't whispering!" Ashleigh replied.

"Was it pricing? Or something else, because he never left you alone for one moment."

"Who?" Ginny asked.

"No one." Ashleigh's jaw flexed and she dug her spoon into the now half empty tub with a vengeance.

Eloise was determined to not let this rest. "It wasn't *no one.* It was the father of the bride, a good looking, well maintained older man who seems to have the hots for our sister."

Ashleigh huffed. "It's not like that. He's just a well-mannered man."

"Maybe he's trying to be nice and angling for a discount or something," Ginny offered.

Eloise pushed back. "I heard him say that the price didn't matter. I saw the watch he wore. I noticed his clothes, and the way he carried himself. This man has serious money."

"And you wonder why Liam was jealous?" Ashleigh cried in a low blow that surprised Eloise.

"Stop this, now!" Ginny roared. An eerie hush descended on them.

"I'm sorry," said Ashleigh, after what seemed like minutes.

Eloise surveyed her sister. "I'm sorry, too." Now that she was going through a tough time with Liam, she felt sorry for Ashleigh. Her sister had been quiet and introverted ever since the time they'd seen Ford and Kayla at the beach when Daisy had gone missing.

"I forgot to tell you." Eloise slapped her hand to her forehead. "Beth is having twins!"

"Twins?" Her sisters cried, one after another, and clearly as shocked as she was when Beth first told her. She told them about the surrogacy, and all about Beth's lavish new nursery.

"Getting someone else to have her babies," Ginny mused, lines appearing on her forehead. "That's so weird. She won't ever know what it's like to carry them, and to give birth to them."

Eloise shrugged. "She must have her reasons, but I'm happy for her. I never expected Beth to have children. She never really wanted them. It must be something to do with Griff turning forty."

"Are you and Liam going to be well behaved at Ryan's on Saturday?" Ginny nibbled her lower lip anxiously.

"What's happening at Ryan's?" Eloise asked, her thoughts still on Liam.

"His housewarming. I told you! I've told both of you! He's having a small informal gathering at his new place, nothing like the full house shindig you had."

Eloise groaned loudly.

"Rude!" Ginny cried. "Everyone in Whisper Falls came to your housewarming, and we never behaved like it was a chore to go to it."

"She'll be there," said Ashleigh, scraping her spoon along the bottom of the tub. "If only to keep me company."

"Yes, I'll be there," Eloise replied, obviously wanting to be supportive even if her heart and mind were not in party mode.

"You and Liam," Ginny pointed her spoon at her, then at Ashleigh, "and you and Ford. You all need to be on your best behavior."

LIAM

"You didn't go through with it because of that?" Ford looked disappointed, and Liam felt even more of a failure. He'd messed up. He'd messed up bigtime.

"The guy was rich. He looked sharp." Liam had gone over that night many times. He now recounted the details of the disastrous weekend away with Eloise. The weekend where he should have proposed, and they should have come back bubbling with happiness.

"So, let me get this straight," said Ford, gesticulating with his hands as if he were solving a complex scientific problem. "The guy was an old boyfriend of Eloise's?"

"Yeah. You should have seen Beth's place, and met those people. Those people, that world, it's a completely different universe." Liam hated even thinking about it.

"So what? She picked *you*. She's with *you*."

Easy for Ford to say. It didn't feel so easy being at Beth's mansion, or talking to the birthday boy, Griffin, or meeting his friends. Liam felt like out of place. The pressure of proposing had made him look at everything with a critical eye. It made him look for reasons as to why they'd couldn't be together.

"Did you wear your tux?" Ford asked.

"I wore it."

"I'm pretty sure you looked sharp in it, too."

"That guy, Elle's ex, his tux looked ... designer." Liam couldn't bring himself to say the man's name. Ford swiped the back of his neck with is hand. "A tux is a tux. Were you checking this guy out like a woman would?" he asked.

"No." Liam scowled. "*Maybe*. Eloise and him, they had a thing a few summers ago."

"Listen to me, buddy. Again, this man is in her past. She's with you now."

"But I feel like she downgraded herself to be with me."

Ford gave a derisive snort. "What's gotten into you?" He stared up at the ceiling and shook his head. "Where's all this coming from?"

"This what?" Liam folded his arms, not liking Ford's tone. Getting told off. Being made aware that he had messed up. That this hadn't been Eloise's fault.

"This second guessing, and doubting. Do you want to marry this woman, or not?"

"I want to marry her. I just don't want her to have any regrets."

"Liam, buddy. You're putting too much weight on this. Do you love her?"

"Absolutely."

"Does she love you?"

He had to think about that. Having seen the world she escaped to at Beth's, and having met the Griffins and Alexs of the world, and taking into consideration that Eloise had once considered moving to Boston to be a part of that world, Liam was no longer sure.

He wasn't sure if Eloise was with him because she loved him, or because he'd been there, conveniently, while fixing up her house. She'd been lonely, and going through a tough time with Ashleigh away and Ginny pregnant and grieving.

For him, she'd been the cheerleader he'd always had his eye on.

For her? Who knew.

Maybe she had regrets.

CHAPTER 16

GINNY

"**I** knew you were hiding something!" One of the school moms cried.

Ginny didn't know what to say. "We weren't together then," Ryan replied, stiffly, putting a protective arm around her shoulder.

"What happened to *Mrs.* Jones?"

"We got divorced before I moved here."

"Leave the guy alone, Marion." The woman's husband looked pained, as if he'd stepped onto a six-inch nail. Ginny chewed her lip and tried to find a reason to make an exit. The woman was too nosy. Worse, she was plain rude and interfering. Ginny didn't like her. Some people needed a filter badly, and the way this woman was behaving, Ginny doubted she'd ever had a filter at all.

"Let me get you some more drinks," Ryan offered, deflecting the conversation sharply. Clearly, Ginny wasn't the only one who was suffering. She didn't want to spend a moment longer talking about her personal life with strangers, albeit they were parents of Daisy's friends. "Excuse me," she murmured and followed Ryan. She glanced over to see that Benjy was okay. Eloise was holding him, and she and Darcie were talking to Kayla. Liam was skulking in the corner talking to Ford, and Daisy and her friends were running around excitedly, playing games and having fun. Daisy was happy, and that was all that mattered. She'd given them all a scare when she'd gone missing that time, and they'd found her by herself at the beach, collecting seashells. The guilt of that episode had hit Ryan hard, and he felt for his daughter, especially with a mother like Vanessa who swanned in and out of the little girl's life. He blamed himself for Daisy's behavior, and feared that the little girl felt unwanted even though he did his best to shower her with love. He was as much a victim in this situation as Daisy, and Ginny's heart sometimes ached for this man when in down moments, he told her of how he felt a failure.

But things were changing for the better now. Moving into a new place they could call theirs, and with Daisy having a lovely room that she loved, one that overlooked the lake, they seemed more settled.

When he'd suggested holding a small housewarming, and asked Ginny to help, she'd accepted, feeling touched that Ryan wanted them to host this event as a couple. More than once he'd told her that it wasn't his housewarming, but 'theirs' and when she'd pushed back and pointed out that she didn't live here, that this wasn't her home, he'd told her it could be whenever she was ready.

The housewarming turned out to be a good idea, and as they began their preparations for it, cooking and getting the house ready, she got carried away in the spirit of things.

Daisy's excitement was at fever pitch levels. She was so

happy that her friends were coming to see 'her new home,' as she called it. Ryan seemed more at ease these days. More self-assured, more settled. He'd wanted to set down solid roots and now he had. This house was lovely and light and airy. It was modern, and everything was new and clean. Light tones, pastel colors.

"Where's Ashleigh?" she wondered out loud.

"I saw her go into the kitchen." Ryan laid his hand gently against her lower back. She liked it. Loved it. Loved that this man was in her life, and for the happiness and fullness he enabled her to have.

That was so typical of Ashleigh. "I should go and drag her out."

"I should go around offering more drinks."

"Good luck."

They exchanged loving looks before she walked over to the buffet table and picked up an empty platter. In the kitchen she found Ashleigh cutting a quiche into pieces. "What are you doing in here?" Ginny asked, refilling her platter with chips. She knew perfectly well what her sister was doing in here.

Hiding.

Ashleigh pointed at the quiche with her knife. "What does it look like?"

Ginny dusted her hands lightly. "Looks to me like you're hiding from Ford."

"Who?" Ashleigh returned to her quiche, and seemed to be taking a ridiculously long amount of time to cut it.

Ginny's mouth twisted. "You're behaving like a child."

"I don't know what you mean." Ashleigh set the knife down and picked up the platter of quiche.

"I suppose you've given Kayla the cold shoulder, too?" Ginny asked. She was in a difficult situation now because Kayla was nice to her these days, and Ginny didn't want any more drama in her close circle of friends and family. She didn't want there to be any friction between Kayla and her sister.

"Did I hear my name?" Kayla appeared out of the blue. A touch of lip gloss and mascara accentuated her features and turned her from a wall flower whom people barely noticed into someone who had been good at hiding her beauty.

"I was telling Ashleigh that you had Benjy." Ginny surprised herself with her fast reply, even if it was a lie.

"I wish I had Benjy," Kayla returned with an easy smile. "He's with Eloise and she won't let go of him. He's such a gorgeous little boy!" she cried, her face filling with love. "Everyone wants to hold him but your sister is being very possessive."

Ginny gave her a warm smile and held up the platter of chips. "Have some." Kayla took a handful, but she was eyeing up Ashleigh who had suddenly become mute.

"I'll have a word with Eloise," Ginny said, turning on her heel and heading towards the door. She wanted to give these women space to reach some sort of understanding. For her part, Ginny didn't believe that Ford and Kayla were an item. That wasn't the vibe she got from either of them.

"More quiche!" Ashleigh announced, overtaking Ginny and leaving the kitchen before she could.

Ginny frowned. Ashleigh was such a coward, and clearly avoiding Kayla who was now left alone in the kitchen.

CHAPTER 17

FORD

"You need to fix this, buddy, and fast. It's tragic watching the two of you, with Eloise in one corner, and you in another. That's not how it ought to be." Ford didn't like seeing Liam looking down, but that's all the guy had been lately.

"I hate it."

"You don't look happy," Ford agreed. The guy looked like a picture of misery.

"I'm not." Liam stared at the floor, as if the answer to his problems lay at his feet.

"Then why put yourself through this? It doesn't make sense." He felt like a hypocrite dishing out advice he hadn't taken himself. He was dealing with the same situation. Sort of. "Just go up to Eloise, talk to her and fix it."

"I will," his friend replied.

"Don't over think it. Just do it." Liam looked doubtful and Ford could sense the guy's dilemma. Money didn't faze Ford, but he was older, and in a different situation. This man was crazy about Eloise, as far as Ford could tell, but he couldn't for the life of him figure out what was plaguing Liam. Eloise had been married before. Maybe the guy was scared about living up to her expectations, and being able to make her happy. Maybe he was second guessing himself. Visiting Eloise's filthy rich friend would only have made the guy's doubts stronger.

The solution was simple, all Liam had to do was find Eloise and apologize. Like it was that simple. Ford shook his head. He had some making up to do himself. He glanced at Ashleigh again. He'd been keeping an eye on her the entire time he'd been here. She seemed to be in charge of the food, and was in and out of the kitchen, checking on the buffet table and refilling empty plates.

But he knew what she was really doing.

Avoiding him.

He wasn't going to let her do that any longer. He pointed a finger at Liam. "I've got people I want to talk to, but when I see you next, I want to hear that you've made up with Eloise."

"Okay. I will. I'll do it." Ford turned to leave, before Liam said, "Thanks for the advice. I appreciate it."

He nodded. "How about we go for some beers one evening next week?" he suggested, watching Kayla come out of the kitchen and make a beeline for Benjy who was stuck to Eloise's hip.

"That'd be cool."

He slapped Liam on the back, then made his move towards Ashleigh who was talking to someone. But as he headed towards her, Darcie grabbed him by the wrist. "Hi, stranger. How are you doing?"

"Hey yourself." He was slightly put out by the interruption

because his insides were in upheaval, the adrenaline pumping, ready to confront Ashleigh and to face the wrongs he'd inflicted on her. But now he had to stop and talk. Darcie was a good friend. He missed not seeing her as often. They talked for a while, exchanging details about what they'd been up to. He told her that Liam was working on his new office and he'd soon be opening the doors to his new accountancy practice.

"Good luck. Whisper Falls getting a hot shot accountant from Boston is a good thing. I know you'll do well."

"Coming back to Whisper Falls seems like I've come full circle." He wiped his hand over his face.

"You have second thoughts?" Darcie asked.

"No. This feels right. My mom not being here is what feels wrong."

She hugged him. "I know, hon. I know. Sorry for your loss. It can't be easy for you. I ought to check up on you more, especially now that we don't see much of you." Concern filled her eyes. He missed the gang. Ash, Eloise and Ginny and Darcie would also be at the house often. The Rose sisters' home was his comfortable place. He would routinely go over often, to see Ashleigh when they'd been together, and later, after they'd split up, to check in on Ginny when she was going through a tough time.

"You don't have to check up on me, Darc. I'm doing good. I'm keeping myself busy, and things will get even busier once the practice opens."

"I spent the weekend with Ashleigh," Darcie said, hurling that tidbit into the conversation as if it fit naturally. It didn't. "Did you know that she's had work done in her back yard and now she's transformed it into a beautiful rose garden?"

He recalled the time he'd last seen her. "I expected she'd do something like that."

"You've been over?" Darcie asked, as if this was shocking

news. The way Darcie asked hinted at something. He knew exactly what it was. It was no secret that he'd been avoiding Ashleigh. He felt bad about it, but at first he was hurt and then he'd had no choice when his mother fell ill. But now that had passed and he had his life back. Not wanting to waste any more time, he knew he needed to get his friend back.

"Not for a while," he answered slowly. "I saw her at the nursery when she was buying all those plants and roses."

"You used to be a regular at the Rose home." Darcie fixed him with a penetrating stare. As Ashleigh's wingwoman, he expected nothing less from her. "It's been a tough time."

Her face softened, and she placed a reassuring hand on his arm. "How's Maddie?"

"Enjoying college by all accounts, and Susan's making plans for her upcoming wedding."

"You okay with that?"

"Maddie going to college?"

Darcie rolled her eyes. "Susan getting married."

"I want her to be happy."

"And you?"

"What about me?" Rumors were flying around about him and Kayla, but as yet no one had said anything to his face. Kayla was sweet, and soft, at least in his experience, though Ashleigh and her sisters had remarked that they found her sharp and full of edges. Getting to know her was like peeling away the layers of an onion. Or the petals of a rose. He wasn't sure which one of those best described her. He appreciated the help she'd given to his mother, and he liked her, but it was nothing more than that.

"Are you happy, Ford?" There was a deeper question under that. Darcie was digging for information, but he had nothing to hide.

"I'm keeping busy, Darcie. Keeping busy. I put a lot of things by the wayside while taking care of Mom, and now I'm rushing to catch up and fix everything."

"I hear Liam's helping you."

"He's a good guy." He glanced at the guy and was disappointed to see that he still hadn't moved from where Ford had last left him. He was talking to some party guests Ford didn't know, and he was still avoiding Eloise. Ford shook his head.

"I noticed he and Eloise can't put enough distance between them," Darcie commented, with the hawkish insight of a woman.

His attention drifted to Ashleigh again. "Yeah. Seems like they need to sort things out." Just like he did. Just like he'd been about to when Darcie had accosted him.

"Ashleigh has an admirer," Darcie whispered, conspiratorially.

"A what?" He was sure he hadn't heard right.

"A customer, some rich, older guy. The father of a bride. He's taken quite a liking to her at the shop, from what I've heard."

The words were like a punch to his gut, leaving him temporarily winded.

An admirer?

Someone rich?

Making a move on Ash?

"Heard from who?" he asked, his curiosity growing exponentially.

"From Ashleigh."

He ground his teeth together, watching Ashleigh laughing with one of the guests. "That's nice," he said, slowly, feeling a pinch in his sides as he looked at her across the room. She was a beautiful woman who often turned heads, though she was oblivious to this. Didn't consider herself to be extraordinary. That rich mane of hair cascading down her back framed that gorgeous face of hers. But she had a golden personality, too, to go with those looks. The woman was as beautiful on the inside as she was on the outside, and she would do anything for anyone.

Just then Kayla came out of the kitchen and, after waiting for a few seconds, Ashleigh went back in.

She was avoiding Kayla, too, it seemed.

"It is nice," Darcie agreed, her eyes fixed on his.

"That's … that's great," he lied, trying to take in his stride the effects of the new bomb that Darcie had detonated. "I'll catch you later, Darc." He patted her shoulder before heading towards the kitchen. Hovering by the door, he was relieved to find Ashleigh alone. She was reaching for a jar of olives from a high shelf, but knocked the glass jar next to it accidentally. It crashed to the floor, shattering into little pieces.

"Fiddlesticks!" she hissed, as the fragments littered the floor.

He rushed to her side. "Hey, it's okay. I've got this."

She looked alarmed when she saw him; shock and surprise quickly followed by recomposure. Her gaze quickly swept around the kitchen before landing on his again. It was almost like she didn't know how to be around him.

"Sit down," he said, gently taking her arm and guiding her over to a chair. He half expected her to admonish him, to tell him that she was quite capable of doing this herself, but to his surprise, she was quiet.

Ginny rushed in. "What broke?" Her gaze fell to the shattered glass.

"I can take care of this, Ginny. You go back to being a

hostess," he told her, and she disappeared as quickly as she'd come. "Where's the broom?" He looked around for it, then Ashleigh pointed to the broom closet and started to get up again. "You don't have to do that. I can take care of it."

But he'd grabbed the broom and started sweeping the broken glass away along with the dried pasta shells into the broom stick holder. "I'm doing it, Ash. Just sit down and take a breath. I noticed you've put yourself in charge of the food and the kitchen."

"Ginny's busy being a hostess."

"And you?"

"I'm helping."

He wrapped the debris in paper and carefully disposed of it before putting the broom back. Leaning against the countertop, he hooked his thumbs into the belt loops of his jeans. "You okay?" he asked, knowing that he had a lot of ground to make up with her. Concentrating on his mom these last few months had made it easier for him to detach from Ashleigh. Now he needed to rectify things between them. He'd known this woman for so long that he couldn't imagine his life without her now. He could imagine his life without Susan because they had come to the end of their journey together. His ex-wife had moved on, but he and Ashleigh? They'd been given a second chance. Their journey had been thwarted before, and he was damned if he was going to let that happen again.

"What are you doing?" Ashleigh asked, getting ready to stand up again.

"Sit down, Ash. Just sit. Please."

She did as he asked.

He appraised her carefully. "You seem fidgety. Anything up?"

"No, nothing. I was reaching for a jar and –"

"I mean, *generally*."

Her brow creased in confusion, and he had an inkling why that might be. She'd tried to talk to him a couple of times but he'd pushed her away. At first it was because he'd been hurt. The idea gnawed away at him that perhaps she didn't feel for him what he felt for her, but then things got busy. Life had other demands. His mother's illness had been a big part of it, and it made it easier to put a distance between him and Ashleigh.

He'd been thinking about fixing it. He'd missed her and wanted her back and now he worried that someone else had beaten him to it. She'd been his first love, and he hers. They had history together, and dreams and plans, until tragedy weaved in and out of their timelines. Now that he'd returned to his hometown, to the woman he loved, he wasn't about to let a rich stranger snatch her away.

"I'm not fidgety, Ford. I'm trying to help Ginny. I want her to enjoy the party because this is a big deal for her. You know what sort of year she had before Ryan came along."

He pressed his lips together. He wanted to talk about them, but as ever, Ashleigh was focussed on her sisters. This was a deserved slap in the face for him. She'd tried so many times to reach him, to talk to him, but he'd ignored her. Now he was getting what he deserved.

She seemed restless and got up, looking ready to shoot out of the door again.

He wanted to talk. He'd snatched this moment with her just so he could do that. "You don't need to check the buffet table. You've refilled everything that could possibly be refilled. Can't you just stay a while?" he asked, anger rising inside him. The idea of another man making a pass at her made him see red.

His tone was sharper than he'd intended, and it halted her. "Someone's in a mood," she said, cocking her head.

I miss you and I want you back.

"I was hoping we'd get a chance to talk."

"You want to talk now, Ford? After all those times when I tried to get your attention, you think you can only talk when *you're* ready?"

She wasn't interested in him.

Like Susan, she'd moved on, too.

Because she had a new admirer.

Someone from out of town.

What was it Darcie had said? Someone with money? Someone older? Distinguished? Images popped in his head, filling in the blanks.

Ashleigh with this new man.

He only had himself to blame.

"There you are," said Kayla. Her face brightened when she saw him. He blinked once, twice. Still getting used to the new Kayla. Without glasses and looking ... *different*. Even though he'd already seen her here, it was still a subtle shock. She'd done something to her hair. "Hey," he said finally, having stared at her for longer than he should have.

Ashleigh stormed out.

"I'm sorry." Kayla spun around to see the dust trail Ashleigh left behind. "Did I say something?"

"No," he said, quietly. But he wished he'd gotten the chance to say more than he had to Ashleigh.

"Why are you hiding in here?" Kayla asked, a jovial tone in her voice. Her eyes sparkled. He swallowed. Getting to know her, he'd discovered that there was more to her than she let the world see. She could be harsh and cold and school teacherly on the outside, but the more acquainted they became, he realized that Kayla was racked by self-doubt. He didn't want to hurt this timid woman any more than he had to, but now he had to because it was becoming obvious that Kayla liked him in a way which he didn't like her back. "No, it's nothing you did. Shall we get back to the party?" He walked towards the door. The lightness in her eyes vanished, but she followed him out anyway.

CHAPTER 18

LIAM

"Hey." When he finally plucked up the courage to approach Eloise, his heart was racing. He wished the tension between them would disappear. He wished they could make up. "How've you been?"

"Hey, stranger." Elle's voice was somber.

He swiped a hand across the back of his neck, feeling odd around her. Feeling like the teenager in high school who'd admired the pretty cheerleader from afar. "I've been wanting to come over to talk to you. I saw you the moment you walked in."

"Why didn't you come over?"

Because he felt foolish, and this wasn't the place to approach her not knowing how she might react. "I wasn't sure how you'd be. I didn't want to upset you again."

"You need to examine your behavior, Liam."

He didn't appreciate the dig. *Already.* She was still in a

mood. "I didn't come over to start arguing again. I don't want to argue any more, Elle." He'd wanted to go up to her from the moment she arrived, but she hadn't even looked his way, even though she'd seen him. Their eyes had locked for the briefest of seconds, but she'd turned away and avoided him for the rest of the time.

He wasn't even sure he was going to come here today, but Ford pestered him into it, calling him a coward if he didn't. Also, Ryan might take it as a slight if he stayed away. He liked the guy, felt sorry for him and what he'd been through, all the hassle with his ex-wife. So he'd come, but he felt uncomfortable the entire time. If Ford hadn't been here, he would have left soon after arriving.

Ford's words replayed in his head again. He had to fix it. He had to make up. "Can we talk somewhere where there aren't so many people? Come outside?" He needed to explain why he'd behaved like a jerk and ruined what should have been a great vacation. Worse, he'd chickened out of doing 'the thing'.

"Outside?" She looked doubtful. She could be as stubborn as a mule when she wanted to be.

"Please." He needed to grab his chance to talk to her, while Ginny had taken Benjy. "I promise not to kiss you passionately."

He loved the way she fought that. The way she tried to keep her lips from curving into a smile, and reluctantly, she went outside.

They walked away from the house and towards a clump of trees. Elle leaned back against the trunk of one, her hands behind her back. Long legged and beautiful, she looked sexy no matter what she was wearing, but he loved her the most in her jeans and now found himself resisting the urge to put his arms around her and pull her into his chest. "I'm sorry. I hate this, Elle." Shoving his hands into the front pockets of his jeans, making his shoulders hunch, he waited for her to say the same, but she didn't. "I'm sorry I was so stupid at Beth's—"

"Why were you? Something was up with you before we even got there." Her eyes flashed with anger in an instant. It was if she'd been bottling it up inside her.

"Sometimes I wonder if I'm the one for you."

She looked shocked. He could kick himself. Where had that come from? He hadn't intended to say it like *that*. He wanted to tell her he loved her and that he felt inferior when he'd met the guys at Beth's husband's party. Those guys with their old money, and new money, their bags of money, and *that* world.

A world he didn't understand. A world he didn't fit into. A world he sensed Elle felt at home in. For crying out loud, she'd been thinking about moving away from Whisper Falls to Boston, and now her plans had changed, but what if in years to come, she blamed him for keeping her here?

The way she looked at him, the hard eyes and twisted lips, it was obvious he'd said the wrong thing. "You still don't know how I feel about you?" Her voice in that deathly quiet mode unnerved him. "How many times do I have to tell you that I love you? Beth, her friends and her family, her husband and those guys, that isn't a part of my life anymore. I used to go there to escape the drama here, and the small-town gossip and rumors. I used to feel so hemmed in. Chained, you could say."

He flinched at her words and the raw anger in them. "You hated it here. You hated being tied to the shop. You hated being stuck."

"And then I met you."

"But is it enough?"

"What do you mean?" she cried.

"Everything you hated about this place, it's still the same. It's still a small town with its gossip and rumors, you're still working at the shop, and—"

"But you're here, you're in my life, with me. Or, you *were*. I don't understand what's come over you, Liam. It's like a switch flicked in your head and turned you into someone I don't recognize."

It was coming out wrong. He raked a hand through his hair and looked away, trying to find the words that would make sense. "I just want to make sure, Elle. I want to be sure you won't have any regrets." He'd been saving up for months to buy her an engagement ring, but now, having seen the rock on Beth's finger, as well as noting the rings worn by most women at the party, his ring looked small in comparison, even though it sparkled and was the best he could afford.

It didn't seem enough.

He didn't *feel* enough.

He worried about not being able to give her the life she'd once longed for. He didn't want her to push that desire away just because she'd met him. He didn't want her to change her dreams for him. People only had one shot at life, and it shouldn't have to be a life of regret, if one could help it. His last girlfriend had suffered a terrible illness and had her life cut short. It was a tragedy that marked him.

Elle tossed her arms up in the air. "You're over thinking, and over analyzing, and over complicating things. I wish I hadn't taken you to Beth's. I didn't want to go myself—"

"Are you ashamed of me?"

"What?" Her mouth fell open. "No, I am not ashamed of you. Why would I be? How could you think such a thing? How many times do I have to tell you, no!" Her words landed like bullets. She stared at the ground, and pushed off the tree. "I came here to have a good time. I've been miserable ever since we got back and I've missed you, but if this is all we're going to do, argue about stupid things that don't make any sense, then maybe we shouldn't be tog—" She paused.

In the silence that followed his heart hammered in his chest.

She was going to break up with him. He'd been right. "We shouldn't what?"

"Maybe we need to take a break. Have some time apart."

She'd gone and said it.

He hadn't expected this. He wanted them to make up but Elle clearly had other ideas. "If that's what you really want." His heart splintered into tiny fragments.

Her angry eyes bore into him. "I can't see any way around it. We can't stop bickering. Maybe we need a cooling off period."

"If that's really what you want, then fine."

He walked away in search of Ford.

CHAPTER 19

RYAN

"That was a success!" Ginny declared, yawning as she put away the last of the food containers in the fridge. Ryan put his arms around her, wanting to keep her here because he could see she was exhausted and needed to rest. "Thanks, for everything," he said, dropping a kiss on her lips.

"You are welcome." She looked up at him with her soft brown eyes.

"I'm sorry for the gossipy questions." He hated that the school moms were so eager to poke their noses into other people's business.

Ginny tilted her chin up and eyed his lips. "There will be no more gossip after today. No more stupid questions. There will be no doubt that you and I are together," she told him.

"No doubt, whatsoever." He pressed his lips on hers and kissed her again. Her soft body sank against him. "You're exhausted," he said, hoping to start the conversation.

She yawned. "Nothing that a good night's sleep won't fix." Another yawn followed, then, "Eloise and Liam must have patched things up because they left early."

He'd noticed that, but not for the same reasons. "They left at different times, though."

"Probably to throw us off the scent," she said, happily, wanting to believe the happy ending.

"Are you sure they made up?" he asked. He didn't seem to think so.

"Yes! They ran off to have some good times."

"How can you be so sure?" he asked, before dropping another kiss on her lips. A fire started low in his belly. He groaned inwardly, trying to rein in the passion.

"Yes! I'm sure." Ginny was indignant. "Otherwise they would have stayed and helped us to tidy up, even if they weren't talking to one another. They've gone to have some good times." She giggled when his arms wrapped around her, then felt her slide hers around his waist. She looked up at him with a mischievous smile. His heart hollowed out. Did she have any idea how much he loved her? "Good times?" he asked, even though he understood what it meant.

"You know what I mean." Her lips curved into a tantalizing smile. He nodded. He did know what she meant. It was a bridge they hadn't crossed yet. Ginny yawned. Benjy was asleep in the bouncer and Daisy had gone to bed, exhausted. "I should go."

"Don't go. Not yet." He held onto her, not wanting her to leave but she yawned again, and her yawn so infectious, it made him yawn.

"I have to go, Ryan. Ugh," she groaned. "I'm going to hate putting Benjy in the car."

"Then don't." He readied himself for the inevitable disagreement.

"I have to." She buried her face into his chest.

"You don't have to. Not now, after such a long and busy day. Benjy's asleep." He kissed the top of her head; felt his insides turn light. Wished she would stay, not because he had any underlying intentions–though it was getting difficult to resist her all the time—but because he loved being with her. All the time in the world wouldn't be enough.

"Please, Ryan. Not this again."

"Okay, okay." He didn't want to end this day on an argument. "On one condition."

"What's that?"

"You have to have a short nap, here, before you drive off. Or, I will take you back myself—"

"But that doesn't make sense," she protested. "I'll have to come back tomorrow and get my car."

She fell into his trap. He shook his head firmly. If she was going to be stubborn, then so was he. "Either I drive you and Sleeping Benjy back, or you have a little nap first."

"Sleeping Benjy." She giggled.

"He is. He's always asleep by the time you leave. I wish you'd stay over."

"We will. We will."

"When?"

"One day. I promise. Don't be angry."

"I'm not angry with you, Gin." He hadn't wanted to push her into anything, and had been remarkably patient. What he was most concerned about was her safety. She wrapped her arms around his neck even more tightly, making it even harder for him to suppress the ardor he felt. He tried gently to prise himself away from her, but her hold was firm. "Why don't we go away soon and have an overnight weekend-vacation with the kids?" Her searching gaze made his heart beat fast.

"Overnight?" he asked, his gaze penetrating hers. "Wh-what exactly do you mean?" He needed to make sure.

"We could spend the night together ..." She surveyed his reaction, while he did his best to play it cool. It was impossible. "We could get a connecting room for Daisy and Benjy so that they'd be next door, but not quite," she continued, "but they'd be safe and we could keep an eye on them."

He was falling apart inside. Spend the night together? What exactly did she mean? "W-why would we do t-that?"

"So that we could have some privacy, and be alone. *Truly* alone." The heat in those irises was like molten lava. He forgot to breathe. She did mean *that*. She really did. "Are you sure?" He was incapable of thinking clearly right now, with her so close, pressed against him, gazing at him like that.

"I'm very, very, very sure." She lifted up on her toes and sealed her answer with a long, soft kiss.

With heroic self-control, he was able to pull himself away. "There's no rush, Gin. We can wait a while if you—"

"I don't want to wait any longer, Ryan. I'm ready." She stroked his lower lip. "Are you?"

"Hell, yeah!" He looked at her and blinked. He hadn't meant those words to come out so enthusiastically. She laughed at him. "Hell, yeah," she echoed, softly, and kissed him again.

"Okaaaay," he said, his breath shaky. "Let's do it."

"The weekend after the next?" she suggested. "I need to recover from this housewarming first."

"Whenever you want. I'm free."

"The weekend after the next."

He lowered his head and she pressed her forehead against his. "The date's in my diary." He made a mental note of it and would start to look for a something amazing. Something that would take her breath away. Something charming, cozy and with the right ambiance. "But now, for me, you have to have a nap, or I'll drive you and Benjy back home."

"Okay, okay." They kissed again and he had to drag his lips

away. Then, he scooped her up in his arms, making her squeal. "What are you doing?" she cried.

He slowly went up the stairs.

"Ryan!" She kicked her legs, confused, and excited, and unsure. "You're carrying me over the threshold!"

He looked down at her, as something inside his heart jolted. He would love nothing more than to carry her over the threshold. One day. "I'm only carrying you up the stairs, Ginny." He smiled, and she giggled some more. But he had plans to do that one day; carry Genevieve Rose over the threshold. For now it would have to do to set her down outside the spare room; the one he'd been working on. He flung the door wide open, and she gasped.

He'd decorated it. Put in a bed, a crib, and a dresser.

"When did you do this?" she cried, walking in and looking around in awe.

"You can have a nap here, and then when you wake up, you can go back home." He leaned against the wall, his arms folded, trying to look casual.

"Ryan!" She turned around, her eyes wide with wonder. "When did you do this?"

"In my spare time. It's yours, to recharge in, to get short naps before you drive home, and not for any other reason," he said, sounding like a diplomatic.

"Ryan."

"I'm not telling you to stay the night, Gin. I'm giving you a place to recharge. You've been on your feet all day, and I can't have you leave just now. Not with Benjy. If anything happened I'd never forgive myself."

"I didn't bring my things."

"You're just having a nap," he reminded her. But he'd asked Ashleigh to sneak over a few of her belongings which were in the closet, and which Ginny would see if she opened the doors.

She yawned again, then crawled onto the bed. "Okay then. I'll just have a …" Her words disappeared in another yawn. A few seconds later, she whispered, "Ah, this is so comfortable. Ryan, this is … oh so comfortable." Stubborn as a mule, she didn't get under the covers, but lay on top. "This is more comfortable than my own ... bed ..." Seconds passed and her eyes fluttered shut, then flew open again. "Benjy's downstairs—"

"I'll keep an eye on him. Just rest up and come down when you're ready."

"I will." Her eyes closed again and he was sure she'd soon fall asleep. She'd been up early today and she'd been on her feet all day. She'd been the perfect hostess, and he liked that people finally knew they were both together. All he wanted now was for her to get some rest.

He went downstairs to see Benjy rousing from his sleep. "Hey, buddy." The little boy smiled at him, and made some noises, as if he were talking to Ryan. Ryan jibber-jabbered back, and the two of them had an entertaining, if nonsensical conversation.

Then, Ryan lifted him up, and gave him some milk, changed his diaper and let him play under the baby gym for a while.

A few hours later, after they'd watched some baby TV, and Benjy fell asleep again, Ryan gently lowered him into the crib. Ginny had turned to her side and looked to be in a deep sleep. He fetched a blanket and put it over her.

With no intention of waking her up, he closed the door behind him, and went into his bedroom to sleep.

CHAPTER 20

ELOISE

hat had happened to them?

Eloise awoke and lay in bed, staring at the ceiling. She hated being alone. Now, especially. Now that she had tasted life with Liam, she didn't want to go back to being by herself again.

How quickly things between them had fallen apart.

She'd been the one to suggest they take a break, but she hadn't really meant it. She'd said it in the heat of the moment because Liam annoyed her by saying silly stuff. All he seemed to do was come up with reasons for them to not be together.

It wasn't like him. Suddenly tempted to call him, she reached for her cell phone on the bedside table, but her fingers hovered on the buttons. He was obviously thinking things over, having some sort of existential crisis and maybe he *did* need his own space for now. She stopped herself from sending him a message and as she glanced through the rest of her messages, she saw a few from Beth.

They were baby scan photos of her twins. *'Meant to share these with you but you left in a hurry. These were the twins at twelve weeks.'*

Eloise stared at the image and her heart stopped. Two outlines could clearly be seen in the grainy photos. Before she knew it, tears were running down her face and she had no idea why. Sadness and a feeling of loss swept over her like a tsunami. She was adrift in a sea of hopelessness and despair. She missed Liam, and didn't know if he was gone for good, didn't know if they could find their way back again. Didn't understand what the heck had happened?

She stared at the scan photo again. Not only was Beth happily married, but she was doing the one thing she said she'd never do; having children. Her friend who hadn't wanted anything to disrupt her glamorous life party-and-vacation lifestyle—which was so much like a Ralph Lauren advert— now wanted more. Eloise still couldn't believe that Beth was now going to be a mother of twins.

As for herself, Eloise Rose, she was destined forever to be a single, lonely woman who would grow old alone.

What was it that Liam didn't understand? Why couldn't he believe that she wanted to be with him and that staying in Whisper Falls was a decision she'd made, because having Liam in her life made it better.

Why couldn't he see that?

But what if it was something else entirely? She sat up, pulling the duvet closer to her chest for comfort. Maybe he was secretly worried that she was older? He wanted children, but she wasn't keen and had told him as much. The pictures of Beth's scans had touched something deep inside her. Having Benjy in her life, she'd seen flashes of a future she'd never thought about much. Until recently. She'd selfishly kept her baby nephew to herself for most of the party, and seeing herself as a mother was no longer as alien a thought as it had been in the past.

Wiping the tears from her face, she sent Beth a message filled with heart emojis, and told her that she couldn't wait to see the twins.

Then she lied and told her that she and Liam were fine, and happy, and in love.

CHAPTER 21

ASHLEIGH

"Good morning, Ashleigh." The rich, male voice reverberated through her, making her feel as if she'd been on a rollercoaster ride.

"Oh, hi there." She gripped the phone tightly. The effect that Patrick McBride had on her was astounding. She'd been thinking about him just then, and it was uncanny, him calling her just now. Angelina's wedding had taken place on the Saturday just gone. "How was the wedding?" she asked as thoughts swirled around in her head like bats in an attic. Patrick McBride had no real business calling her anymore, especially first thing on a Monday morning right after the wedding.

Didn't he have better things to do? Or did he feel a pull to her? Something akin to the way she felt about him.

"It was magnificent."

She smiled, feeling happy for them. "It makes me so happy to hear that. I was thinking of Angelina at the weekend and I hoped everything was going well." It was strange how her heart somersaulted inside her chest. She'd been thinking of him ever since she'd missed him last weekend, on her day off. Patrick and Angelina turned up unannounced to make some final alterations. Eloise had taken care of them, but Ashleigh felt she'd lucked out on an opportunity to see him again.

Maybe it was a good thing that she hadn't been here last week. The charmer had a persuasive way about him, and while she enjoyed their subtle flirtation, her interactions with that man left her feeling giddy, like a teenager with a crush.

"That's sweet of you. Just Angelina?" he asked.

"Pardon me?"

"You said you were thinking of Angelina."

She sensed he was smiling at the other end of the phone, and immediately her mind went to his dimples. The insides of her belly did a funny turn. He was so handsome. So distinguished. So different from the types of men she usually found attractive. "Of her ... her w-wedding ..." Did he really expect her to say that she was thinking of him, too? This had to stop. And now. She was too old to be flirting with men like McBride. Men who flitted in and out. For a season. For a reason. But not a lifetime.

"She's in Turks and Caicos on her honeymoon now, but she wanted me to call and thank you sincerely. You really did turn things around so fast, Ashleigh. All that time and effort wasted in Europe, and you were here, under my nose, all along."

Her heart fluttered as his words sank in. Oh, he was good. So very, very good with his charm. "I wasn't quite under your nose. Whisper Falls is far from you."

"You were on the same continent, and that's close enough. I wish we'd met from the start of Angelina's wedding dress shopping."

"She must have looked like a fairytale princess," she

managed to say, trying hard not to let his compliments go to her head.

"She did. You can see the pictures from the wedding. They're doing a spread about it in The Island."

She chuckled at the casual comment, a comment which she suddenly realized wasn't a joke. "Oh, really?"

The Island? She didn't read it, but it was a well-known upscale magazine for the filthy rich. The front covers had photos of sprawling and decadent mansions, or a luxury island that people like her could only dream about.

"I believe it will be in next month's copy."

"Oh." She wondered why he was telling her this. They were from different worlds. He was from Manhattan. She from a small town. She was sure he must have attracted a dozen women at the wedding. Heck, he probably attracted every woman he ever met. She'd gotten to know him better during the last few visits where she'd become accustomed to his humor, but each time he left she found herself looking forward to his next visit. They'd gotten to know one another, and she learned that he got divorced when Angelina had been just a teenager. He was a businessman, with interests as diverse as finance and gold and software.

"I have my fingers in a lot of pies," he'd told her, "so if three or four pies fail, the other ten or so still keep me afloat. Diversification is the key."

"I only have one finger in one pie," she'd replied, and wondered why he was giving her so much attention. He was a playboy, surely? An older playboy, no doubt, but his charm, wit and charisma were dangerous and she would do well to heed the warning bells going off in her head.

"The dress was a hit, and I wanted to forewarn you that you'll be getting lots of new clients. So many young ladies there were in awe of Angie's dress. If you'd given me more business cards, I would have thrown them around like confetti."

She laughed. "Thank you, for spreading the word."

"Thank you, Ashleigh. I mean it, sincerely." His voice turned serious, even over the phone she could detect a change in his tone. "When the last designer let Angie down, it broke my heart, so it means a lot to me that you were able to save the day. You didn't just save the day, you overdelivered and the dress you came up with blew all the others out of the water." His appreciation was evident in his tone.

"Thank you for your kind words, Patrick. I'm just glad we were able to help Angelina be the beautiful bride on her big day." Ashleigh was used to this reaction. The Bridal Shop had done well and lasted for over twenty years because of their stylish dresses, their attention to detail and the way they treated their customers.

"I'd like to thank you, Ashleigh."

"Oh, you just did. Telling me that Angelina's day went so well, and that she was so happy, is enough thanks."

"But seriously." He cleared his throat. "I'd like to take you out to dinner."

"Pardon me?"

"Dinner. It's an eating ritual that humans partake in somewhere around the evening time."

Her stomach churned, and she couldn't bring herself to even force a laugh at his attempt of light humor. "There's no need to do anything like that." Her voice sounded tinny, and high pitched, not like it belonged to her. She flapped a hand in front of her face, like a fan, trying to cool herself down.

"But, I want to. I would like to see you again. Dinner, just you and me. No assistants. No Angie, or her friends. No one, but you and me. I'd like to get to know you better, Ashleigh."

She swallowed, but said nothing.

"I have a feeling that you're thinking the same."

Bold, presumptuous and confident. That was Patrick McBride all over.

But he was right. There was something between them. Some invisible force. Her insides turned liquid. She suddenly wasn't sure about having dinner, just the two of them alone, at a table, staring at one another. Yet a part of her wondered what it might be like, being with someone like him. He'd been her secret infatuation recently and each time he came to the shop, for fittings and alterations as Angelina's wedding date approached, she made an effort to dress more smartly, to wear a touch more of makeup and to take extra care with her hair. She'd been using the flirtatiousness between her and Patrick as a way to help her get over Ford.

Meeting Ford at Ryan's housewarming had awoken all her old feelings about him all over again; feelings she'd been trying to suppress ever since Kayla had appeared on the scene. He'd been so nice to her when she'd broken that jar, and he'd surprised her by clearing up the mess and talking to her like the old Ford she'd fallen back in love with. But she hadn't heard from since, and nor had she sought him out.

What was the point? He was with Kayla now, and she wished them the best of luck. Ford was moving on with his life and it was about time she did the same.

"Ashleigh?"

She coughed lightly, aware that she hadn't given him a reply. "Ah, um …"

"It's a simple yes or no. I'd like to see you again. If I've read the signals wrong, please tell me. Tell me I'm being forward and that you never want to see me again."

She'd be lying if she said 'no.'

Flicking through the diary, she pulled out the business card he'd casually handed her during one of his visits. Tapping it on the desk, she contemplated his offer. "Okay, then. Yes … it would be nice … to go to … dinner." It felt odd, agreeing to a dinner date with a man she barely knew. Flirting with a new man. She'd known Ford since high school, and there was a closeness and comfort she felt around him.

With Patrick, everything was new.

He was a rich Manhattanite.

Someone so rich he came to Whisper Falls in a chauffeured car.

Someone whose daughter's wedding would be written about in a celebrity magazine.

She heard his soft chuckle. "I'm looking forward to it, Ashleigh. I'll call you in a few days to make arrangements."

"I … I look forward to hearing from you."

"Take care, Ashleigh."

She hung up having heart palpitations, then looked around for Eloise who should have been at work earlier, but who now breezed in, with what looked like a croissant in her hand. Ashleigh glanced at her watch. "This is the second time this week that you've been late."

"Only by twenty minutes," her sister countered, before disappearing into the office.

"I wish I could be twenty minutes late," Ashleigh hissed under her breath. "Or thirty, or forty." Her sister seemed to be in her own little world lately. Sensing her misery, Ashleigh tried to be gentle with her. They'd all read the situation wrong after Ryan's housewarming when Eloise and Liam both left early. She, like Ginny, had wrongly assumed that Eloise and Liam had made up. It turned out that they hadn't. Eloise, that smart, clever and sometimes silly sister of hers had suggested they take a break, and now she moped around, looking as miserable as Ginny had done back when she'd gone through her bad times. But thankfully Ginny was doing well; that brain fog of hers had cleared, and she was happy, and content.

The love of a good man had helped. Ginny surprised her with the way she was quickly taking on tasks. She was determined to learn the ropes of the business, and Ashleigh was happy to delegate more tasks to her.

Both her sisters had taken time off work when they needed it, while she had to soldier through and make sure it was still business as usual. It didn't matter whether her heart was bruised or if she was overcome with worry. She still had to keep going.

She slipped Patrick McBride's business card into her bag. Maybe it was a good thing that she was meeting Patrick for dinner soon.

A few days later, she was going through the diary, checking to see what appointments were coming up when Rachel presented her with an enormous bouquet of flowers.

Not just any bouquet, either. Roses. Lots of them. Red, white and pink. Rich, velvety, petals and dark green leaves.

Expensive looking flowers.

"For me?" Confusion and hope circled around her like a desert storm and she blinked, as if she had sand in her eyes.

"It's got your name on the envelope." Rachel beamed at her. Ashleigh stood there, holding the bouquet, inhaling the sweet, honeyed scent of the roses. It took her back to her younger days; to the precious memories of her father presenting roses to her mother. She closed her eyes and relived the past for a few precious seconds, her body shuddering with the recollection that seemed so real.

"Open it," Rachel insisted.

She laid the flowers down and opened the small white
envelope. It bore her name. Ashleigh Rose.

Slightly formal.

Someone who didn't know her too well.

She opened it, and inside, in printed writing saw the words:

'For you'

She frowned.

No name.

Nothing else.

For you.

"Who are they from?" Rachel asked.

"I have no idea." Ashleigh handed the card to her assistant who
turned it over in her hands. "An admirer! You have a *secret*
admirer," Rachel announced with a grin.

"I doubt anyone—"

"It was the McBride wedding last weekend, wasn't it?"
Rachel asked. Then nodded to herself, realizing that it was.

Heat crept along Ashleigh's cheeks. She gave a vehement
shake of her head. "No. *No.* Why would Patrick McBride send
me flowers?"

"Now, now, Ashleigh. Don't be so modest. I saw the two of
you flirting whenever he was here." Rachel winked at her.

"Flirting?" Ashleigh cried with all the indignance she could
muster. Thank goodness Rachel hadn't been around when he'd
called earlier. But maybe she'd overheard the conversation, at
the final dress fitting where he'd expressed sadness that they
would not meet again. When he'd jokingly told her that if she
was ever in New York, to look him up.

"They're from Angelina's father, as a 'Thank you,' I bet." Her assistant seemed rather sure of it. "I'd stick them in a vase quickly if I were you. They look expensive."

Ashleigh smelled the roses. Sweet, floral, with a hint of spice. She smiled to herself. They were from Patrick. She wished he'd written more of a message. He told her he'd be in touch with arrangements for the dinner but she hadn't heard from him since then.

And then he'd sent these.

She closed her eyes and inhaled a long, deep breath. She'd thank him when she next saw him.

CHAPTER 22

GINNY

"Me and Benjy get to sleep in our own room?" Daisy cried.

"He'll be in the travel crib and you'll have your own bed," Ginny explained.

"In the same room?"

"Yes. In the same room."

"Where will you be?" Daisy asked, looking fearful.

Ginny looked at the five-year-old carefully spooning out blobs of cookie dough onto the baking tray and pondered telling her that she and Ryan would be in the room connected to theirs. "Right next to you," she said, keeping it vague. She was making cookies with Daisy, while Benjy watched from his baby bouncer. Ryan was in the study, working.

"Yay!"

She'd started staying at Ryan's place from Friday through the weekend. She loved being here with him and with Daisy.

Benjy loved it too, and he had company. It had started from the night of the party when she'd fallen asleep and woken the next morning to find Benjy sleeping peacefully in the crib beside her. It had been Ryan's doing. He'd set up the spare room in secret because he wanted her to be safe. But she'd been wary of Daisy's reaction the following morning. The little girl had rushed into the room and squealed at seeing both Ginny and the baby. She'd rushed straight to Benjy and started jibber jabbering away with him. She hadn't batted an eye at Ginny lying in bed.

Ryan was so thoughtful, such a gentleman. All her dreams about finding the perfect man and being happy one day, had come true. She'd never been happier. Her life had been so bleak, and now she had everything. This coming weekend they were going on their short break. Ryan told her he'd found the perfect place to stay and it was a two-hour drive away. She was so excited. She'd been shopping with Talia and bought new clothes and sexy lingerie, feeling confident having lost a little of her baby weight.

"Are you nervous?" Talia had asked.

"A little."

Because this was new, her first time with Ryan, and she was conscious of her body after a baby. There was so much to think about, and yet she had an instinctive feeling that he would be good, and gentle, and that everything would work out fine.

"Read the instructions and tell me how long these go in the oven for," Ginny said, coming back to the present as she slid the baking tray into the oven.

Daisy peered at the recipe book. "It says twenty minutes."

"Good. Now set the timer, please."

Daisy did just that.

"Okay, good. Now, let's clear up."

"Can I lick the bowl first?"

Ginny grinned. "Sure, lick it so clean that we won't have to wash it up."

"Ew." Daisy made a face and got started on the bowl as if she'd been handed a plate of sweets. Ginny had no doubt that she would lick that bowl completely clean. She crouched down and kissed Benjy. "Hey, baby." He bounced in his bouncer, getting excited.

"Would you like a piece of banana, baby?" She made eating noises which perked Benjy up even more. Cutting a small stick of cucumber, she gave it to Benjy. His teething troubles had subsided, and he'd been happier lately. "I think that's enough, sweetie," she said to Daisy who was still licking the bowl. "Anymore and you'll be ingesting glass." Ginny held her hand out for the bowl. "I'll chop up a banana for you seeing that you're so hungry."

Daisy recoiled.

"Benjy's eating a piece of cucumber. A nice and healthy snack. How about an apple if you don't want a banana?"

"Okay." Daisy reached into the fruit bowl for an apple when Ryan appeared, looking pale. "I smell cookies," he said, but his tone had a brittle edge to it. So unlike him. Ginny surveyed his face carefully. She'd seen that look before.

"We made sixteen," Daisy informed him, cheerily oblivious to the tension.

"Huh." Ryan seemed faraway, worry swimming in his eyes.

"Sweetie, watch the timer and let me know when it goes off." Ginny walked out, reaching for Ryan's hand and leading him away. "What?" She sensed that the news wasn't good.

Hands on hips he stared at the floor as if a weight pressed down on his shoulders. "Vanessa ..."

It was enough for a tiny knot to fist in her gut. She should have known it would be something to do with her. Ryan's ex-wife was the only one capable of turning Ryan's mood somber.

Ryan scratched his brow. "She ... uh... she's throwing a birthday party at the weekend and she wants us to come. Me and Daisy."

"I know it's you and Daisy," Ginny replied, anger festering under her skin. He moved towards her and put his arms around her. "I didn't mean it like that."

She looked up at him, her mood softening. "I know. I'm sorry."

"You're sorry? For what?" He put his hand to her face. "I'm sorry. I'm sorry that Vanessa does this. Her birthday is two weeks away and she's chosen this weekend to throw a party. It's deliberate. Daisy told her we were going away. Maybe we should have kept our weekend under wraps."

"It's okay." Vanessa did this all the time. Not more than two weeks went by without Ginny getting a glimpse of Vanessa's big, round and possibly Botox'd face. She would suddenly appear, via a phone call to Daisy, and break up whatever Ginny and Ryan were doing. Kissing, or watching TV, or cooking or just sitting down together and talking. Vanessa had punctured their cosy little bubble on many occasions. The woman was going to be a thorn in their sides for a long time. Possibly forever. "We can go the following weekend, or the weekend after that. How many obstacles can she throw in our way?" Ginny was determined not to let her think she'd won.

Ryan's face was hard as steel. "I dread to think, knowing Vanessa. I've half a mind to tell her we've planned a weekend away and we can't come."

"You must go, Ryan. Daisy will want to. Let Vanessa play games, but you must always do the right thing, and the right thing is to take Daisy to her mother's birthday party. It's okay. We'll postpone our break to another weekend."

He framed her face with both his hands. "It's not okay. You

must think I always push you to the back, that you're second place, but you're not."

"Ryan." She pressed her forehead against his neck and took a breath, inhaling his scent. He tightened his hold around her. No matter the situation, no matter what was going wrong, being in Ryan's arms was a salve to the curveballs in her life. She looked up at him, her eyes falling to his lips. "I understand. Daisy comes first, and Vanessa is her mother, and I don't think I'm second best. You always make me feel special."

"You, Daisy and Benjy are first in my world, but Vanessa …"

"Pulls the strings. So, let her. Go to the party and make sure Daisy has fun. We have time."

He pressed his lips against hers and she melted into a soft kiss. The timer went off in the kitchen, and she heard Daisy's running footsteps. Then a giggle from the little girl. This hadn't been the first time Daisy had caught the two of them making out. Ginny gently pulled away from Ryan. "Good luck in breaking the news to Daisy."

CHAPTER 23

ELOISE

She wouldn't ordinarily avoid Beth's phone calls, but lately they had been coming thick and fast. Faster than usual.

Prior to her and Liam's recent visit to see her friend, Eloise had only heard from Beth a few times. It seemed as if they'd both drifted and started to go their separate ways. Yet ever since Griffin's birthday, Beth seemed determined to make an effort.

Either that or she was bored. Eloise felt bad because whenever her friend called her, she flinched. She hated being this way. Their friendship which had been waning, seemed now to be healing after that rift. Beth called more; whether it was because she was eager to talk about her soon-to-be born twins, or because she had nothing better to do, Eloise wasn't exactly sure. Maybe her friend was just curious to find out why Eloise and Liam had left the party so suddenly, and why they'd missed the post-party brunch. Eloise didn't know, but, as she lay in bed with the phone in one hand, listening to Beth going on about her unborn babies, her heart sank. Her friend twittered on about how proud Griffin was and how they were doing up the nursery. She kept talking and talking and talking.

Jealousy sliced through Eloise. She longed for that familiarity, for the security. To have someone and to be loved and to have a future they both looked forward to. It was something she'd had with Liam once, but now her hopes and dreams evaporated into thin air.

When Beth asked where Liam was, Eloise kept the topic on the twins. She'd already had to deflect more than once when Beth asked her how she and Liam were doing. Then she'd casually noted that Liam was never around. Her comments put Eloise on the defensive, and she was forced to lie and make things up. But she didn't lie well. It was something she couldn't do. She was too forthright. Instead, Eloise had asked her friend to send photos of the nursery they were doing up for the twins, both girls.

Beth obliged and the photos came through in the next few seconds, followed by a video recording done by the proud mom-to-be of the nursery. She gave a panoramic and up close view of everything. Eloise's heart sank as she stared at the pink and white walls with the white furniture and light pink dusky blinds. Two identical white cribs with soft white and pink canopies above, from which draped what looked like silk curtains. A dresser, changer unit with drawers, crib mobiles, night lights—one shaped like a moon one, the other like a star —caught her eye. She imagined a scene with the lights turned on, and two beautiful little babies gurgling in their cribs. Her eyes turned moist and she turned away, not understanding her reaction. She forced herself to look at the huddle of blankets in palest pink and white shades folded up and placed on a dresser. Her throat felt dry. Beth had even gone and bought some clothes and hung them up on the small wooden clothes rail suspended from the wall. Tiny tulle dresses and baby onesies were displayed in cute little hangers.

"Won't they get dusty?" she whispered.

Beth waved her hand dismissively. "We'll buy some more."

"Or you could just get them cleaned," Eloise suggested.

"Or that."

How had this happened, and so fast? Beth's wedding had taken place just over a year ago, and here she was, happily married and now expecting twins.

Life wasn't fair.

They were college friends, and both shared so many parallels in their lives. Beth had got married late for the second time. She was in her late thirties, like Eloise, but Beth had got married for the first time at the age of nineteen to the son of a hotel magnate. It lasted all of two months, and after that, Beth turned into a party-loving animal, refusing to settle down or commit. She had lots of romances, and breakups, lots of happiness and tears, and heartache and joy. Eloise remembered the numerous times her friend only had to call and Eloise would be there, much to Ashleigh's consternation. She and Beth were similar in their attitudes about men and romance. They both had lots of breakups. Eloise had been married also, but it hadn't worked out either.

So it surprised Eloise when Beth announced that the guy she'd met while snorkeling in Bermuda was the guy she was going to marry. And now they were having twins. Beth had done a complete one hundred and eighty degrees shift in her life plan. Settling down and having kids? It was the type of future Beth said she never wanted. She'd been footloose and fancy free ever since her divorce.

"Everything has happened so fast to you, Beth," Eloise said, her thoughts taking voice.

"What do you mean?"

"You got married just over a year ago and now you're having twins."

"It's coming up to fifteen months since we got married" Beth announced smugly.

"Exactly, and now soon you're going to be a mother."

Beth chuckled. "It happens like that when you find the right guy. I found the right guy and so have you."

A pause filled the air.

"You have, haven't you?" There she was again, digging, digging, digging.

"Yeah. Liam's busy right now." Eloise coughed lightly, tried to prepare herself for the fabricated version of the truth. "He's always working on fixer uppers. Ford's got him working on the accountancy practice."

"Still?"

"Yeah. Liam's got a small team of people he can use but mostly he likes to—"

"To do the jobs himself unless it's a big one," Beth finished the sentence for her.

"He's just been really busy."

"I'm sure he is."

CHAPTER 24

FORD

Ford blinked when the door opened, and Kayla stepped inside holding what looked like a plastic container.

His mouth hung open in shock because she was the last person he expected to see. She, no doubt seeing the shock on his face, suddenly looked very anxious and took a step backwards. "I went to your house," she said, in a voice that was so breathless, it didn't even sound like her, "but nobody was there."

He assumed she'd called him first, and pulled out his cell phone to check, but there were no recent calls from her. "You should have called," he said, sliding the phone back into his pocket, and wondering what had possessed her to come straight to his office.

"It wasn't anything urgent." Her voice was so quiet, he almost had to strain his ears to hear her. The sound of the drill starting up didn't help. They stared at one another. He was dumbfounded, not knowing why she was here. "Something wrong?" he asked, when the drilling noise stopped.

"Who's here?" She seemed surprised that there was someone else around. He waved a hand over his shoulder. "Liam. He's fixing a couple of things for me. Something wrong?" he asked again because this was most peculiar.

He'd helped her to get her confidence back with her driving and she'd been very helpful regarding his mom. As Kayla now seemed to be driving perfectly fine, he had no idea what would bring her here, to his practice, over the summer holidays.

But a niggling feeling gnawed away at him. It was that same uneasiness he'd had when he saw Kayla at Ryan's housewarming. "Everything okay?" He sensed her nervousness. She was still frozen to the spot and hadn't taken a step towards him. "I made you these." She held out the plastic container, causing him to walk towards her. "They're cookies. I got the recipe from Ginny. It's their mom's recipe and Daisy loves them."

"Daisy, huh?" He managed a smile. "Thank you. That's very kind of you," he said, graciously. But Daisy was a child, and he a grown man.

Cookies?

"Ginny said you liked these. I mean, *everybody* likes them. Who doesn't like cookies?" She was rambling and digging herself deeper and deeper into a hole of embarrassment. He gave her a reassuring smile when her face tinged a shade of pink. He'd never seen her so frazzled. It was most unlike her. He liked Kayla, but he sensed that she liked him a bit more. He'd tried to ignore it in the past, even at Ryan's party, and was glad that they no longer needed one another's help, but now that she was here in his accountancy practice, having deliberately sought him out, he felt uncomfortable sensing what was coming. "I don't think I can eat all the cookies by myself—"

"I made a batch because Daisy likes them and I went over to drop them off and Ginny said you might be here, so … here I am." She smiled nervously.

The insides of his stomach prickled. This was so awkward. He was aware that in the past people might have assumed he and Kayla were together. It suited him, at the time. They'd done nothing more than talk, and help one another. Back then he'd been happy for the rumors to spread around Whisper Falls like a flashfire. But now the situation was starting to get out of hand.

"She told you to come here?" he asked, wondering what Ginny and Liam believed. No one had outright asked him yet if he and Kayla were together. Liam had asked once, but in a roundabout way, back when Ashleigh was trying to make up with him. He'd pushed them both away, because he didn't have the headspace to deal with either of them. Not when his mother was slowly dying. He'd let Liam think something was going on. He hadn't lied, he'd just been economical with the truth. He'd wanted word to get back to Ashleigh because he didn't want her around him, trying to mess with his head, trying to win him back, trying to apologize and help.

"She said if you're not at home, you'd likely be here, because Liam was working on your office."

"Did I hear my name?" Liam came out, shirtless and wet with sweat. Beads of perspiration ran down his face as he wiped his hands on a towel.

"Kayla's here," Ford told him. Kayla's face turned tomato red as her eyes ran down the length of Liam's chest. She looked away, staring up at the shelves on the wall, or admiring the plasterwork. Ford couldn't tell which it was. She looked incredibly, painfully embarrassed.

"Oh, cool," Liam remarked.

Ford cleared his throat. "She made cookies."

"For me?" Liam asked her, jokingly, not before glancing at Ford, his eyes popping wide open with a she's-got-the-hots-for-you expression.

"Why don't you take them, buddy, and put them somewhere?" Ford passed the container to him.

Liam grabbed a cookie and popped the entire thing into his mouth. After a couple of seconds, "Thanks," he said to Kayla. "They're good."

"It's Ginny's mom's recipe," Kayla declared.

"Yes, it is. I can tell. " Liam made an exaggerated noise of enjoying another cookie.

"Don't you have work to do?" Ford snapped, wishing the man would disappear and get back to his work. He didn't need this visit of Kayla's to be reported back to the Rose sisters. Liam would talk to Elle—maybe not right now—but eventually when the guy plucked up enough daring to fix that situation. Ford didn't want Ashleigh to hear that Kayla had come to see him with cookies she'd baked especially for him.

Now was the perfect time to fix the situation between him and Ashleigh, but there was already a wrench in the works. Ashleigh had someone else on the scene. Someone slightly older, distinguished, rich. The news landed like a bomb when Darcie told him, and even now, weeks later, it still didn't sit well with him. He'd been hoping to make it up with Ashleigh, but now he'd been forced to stay on the sidelines to watch what developed.

He scratched the back of his neck as the room turned silent. Kayla wrung her hands together. "It's been a while since I saw you," she said, slowly.

"At Ryan's place," he answered, just as slowly, thinking that it wasn't so long ago. But at the same time thinking, *here it comes.*

"We haven't met since then?"

He was sure they hadn't. "Nope. Just at the housewarming. It's been about a month."

"Such a long time," Kayla answered, breathlessly.

"Huh." Ford scratched the itch that suddenly appeared along his jaw. Sounded to him like Kayla was working herself up to something. "How are you?" he asked because he couldn't think of anything else to say.

"These are delicious!" Liam reappeared with the container of cookies. Thankfully, fully clothed now, having thrown a tee over his chest. He handed the cookie container to Ford. "Take this, before I devour all of them."

Ford, while grateful for Liam's interruption, took the container and wished his friend would disappear again.

"That was nice of you, Kayla." Liam nodded at her, and she blushed even more. Before she could answer, Ford growled at his friend. "Thanks, buddy. You can go now." The guy had the audacity to wink at him. Ford let out a sigh and turned to Kayla again. He smiled, waiting to see what she might say next, because clearly, she'd come here for a reason and didn't look as if she'd be leaving anytime soon.

"I was wondering …" she said slowly, her cheeks turning as red again as when she'd seen Liam shirtless. "Did you want to … I don't know… maybe go watch a movie or something?" She shifted uncomfortably from one foot to the other.

Go watch a movie?

Those were usually his lines. The sort of thing he might say when trying to win Ashleigh over. It didn't quite feel right coming from a woman like Kayla; a woman who had once been shy and reserved and who now looked so different. She seemed a little more daring. But he had a feeling it was something more. She liked him. Problem was, he didn't like her back. Not in the way she liked him. He liked her *enough*. As a friend. But that was it.

"A movie?" he asked, his mind going into overdrive, trying to find a way of letting her down gently.

Her mouth twisted, and something like disappointment shadowed her face. To his horror, he realized this wasn't the answer she'd been expecting. Not that he'd given her an answer. He was wavering. She was a lovely woman, a good friend, and he hated to break her hopes, but to give in, to pretend to go along would be wrong. "Just you and me?" he asked, then immediately wished he hadn't when her face turned beetroot red.

"We could take Daisy," she suggested, quickly.

He stared at the floor, considered the best way to do this, and decided to go with being truthful. "I'm sure Daisy would love to go to the movies, but, with you and me? I'm not so sure. You're a lovely person, Kayla, but I … I just don't think it would be something that would work out."

Her body slumped. It was a miniscule movement, but enough for him to notice. He hated himself for doing that to her. Kayla backed away towards the door. "It was … it was …" She couldn't even look him in the eye. "It was just a suggestion." She smiled at the door. "I don't even know why I asked."

He stepped forward, his hands flailing by his sides as he tried to figure out what to say to put things right. He was determined not to let her leave thinking there was anything wrong with her. There wasn't. But he had no romantic feelings about her and he didn't want to lead her on. "Don't leave like that. Look at me, Kayla." Her head was still turned away. "Kayla," he urged, his voice gentler now. "*Please.*"

She was biting her lower lip when she finally faced him.

Her face was so red that he was alarmed. "It's not you. It's me," he told her, placing a hand on her arm.

"It's okay. I shouldn't have asked."

"No, it's—"

"It's okay, Ford." She released her arm and turned to go. "It's okay. Please let's not ever talk about this again."

Not three seconds had passed since she left than Liam reappeared. "She likes you."

"You think?" Ford growled, his voice thick with sarcasm.

"She *really* likes you."

"I heard you the first time, pal."

"She's got the hots for you big time."

"Dude, get back to fixing my walls."

He didn't feel the same way about her, and he never would.

CHAPTER 25

GINNY

She had to do something to keep busy.

Ryan and Daisy were in Seattle this weekend for Vanessa's alleged birthday party. Ryan looked guilty as he said his goodbye to her, but Daisy was excited to see her mom. With the innocence of a child, she'd asked Ginny why she and Benjy weren't coming. Ginny and Ryan had exchanged hopeless glances, then Ginny had made up an excuse about needing to see her friend.

She was happy for the little girl, but it niggled her that this was the weekend they'd all planned to go away. She wasn't too upset by having to postpone their little getaway. What upset her more was the idea of Ryan going to see his ex-wife. It made her wonder if their relationship—hers and Ryan's—would forever revolve around Vanessa in some way.

She felt certain that Vanessa would always be concocting a new and cunning plan to reel Ryan back into her life. The woman had a penchant for interfering even from all the way in Seattle. Would Ryan feel obligated to go to Vanessa whenever she snapped her fingers? Ryan would go not because he wanted to, but because he felt obliged to, and because Daisy would want to visit her mom. The child was too young to see her mother's conniving machinations.

After they left, Ginny was by herself for the first time in a long time and had the whole weekend free, and nothing much to do. She usually went straight to Ryan's place on Friday evenings and stayed for the weekend. She loved going there, and as time went on, it felt more like home than her than her own home did. She was still touched by how he'd done up the spare room for her and Benjy. Ryan's little acts of kindness made Ginny feel that she belonged. He'd even brought over some of her clothes and a few of Benjy's things to store in the closets. This man went over and above and always did what was right for her. He was proving in so many little ways that he wanted her in his life.

But this morning she felt on edge. It was the same pervading sense of unease that rendered her sleepless last night. She didn't want to sit at home all day just her and Benjy, because then all she'd do was think about Ryan and his ex-wife.

It wasn't that she didn't trust Ryan; more like it was that she didn't trust Vanessa.

Feeling paranoid led her to doing something she'd been putting off for a while. Making a visit to Ben's parents at their house. She hadn't met up with them since they'd met at the mall. They'd called a few times and invited Ginny to come over with Benjy, but she'd always made an excuse. But now, prompted by Ryan and Daisy visiting Vanessa, she felt the urge to let Benjy at last visit his grandparents at home. It was the right thing to do. The poor boy didn't have any grandparents on her side at all and no matter what had happened between her and Ben, his parents were related by blood to their grandchild. It was a relationship she could not ignore, but she couldn't face them alone; she wasn't ready to go to their house alone with Benjy. So she enlisted the help of her friend, Talia, to come with her, to give her the confidence and strength she lacked.

She had already called Ben's parents and spoken to them on the phone. Cindy was so happy to hear from Ginny that she invited her to come for lunch or dinner, whatever suited her. Ginny didn't relish the idea of that. She wouldn't be able to eat. No. This was going to be a short visit. Maybe under an hour. She would go to their house, so that they could hold Benji and spend time with him. She felt nervous about the visit and her insides were doing cartwheels.

What would they talk about?

Hal, Ben's father, was more the quiet and introverted type. The couple were such opposites, and Ginny realized she didn't know them more than at surface level. That would have to change because she wanted Benjy's grandparents to be in his life, even if it wasn't an easy thing for her to deal with.

She drove to Talia's house and texted to let her know she was outside. "Ready, baby?" Ginny asked, glancing over her shoulder at Benjy as she waited for her friend. Her little boy's face lit up the moment she made eye contact and his smile widened each time she spoke. He was happily babbling gibberish back to her by the time Talia got into the car.

"Thanks for picking me up." Her friend leaned in and kissed her on the cheek, before twisting her body and bending to chat to Benjy. The boy giggled and squealed louder.

"I'm tickling his legs," Talia explained as Ginny drove off. "You're looking very handsome today, aren't you, Benjy?" Talia cooed.

Ginny smiled. "He has to look smart. It's his first visit to his grandparent's place. Thanks for coming with me."

"Glad to help."

"I'm nervous."

"This is a big deal, Gin. You having the determination and grit to visit Ben's parents, when it can't be easy for you."

Ginny kept her eyes on the road. "It has to be done. Visiting them at the mall was easy, compared to this."

"How are you feeling?"

"Like throwing up."

"Not pregnant are you?"

Ginny glanced and her and scoffed. "That would be a miracle, given that *this* weekend was supposed to be our getaway so that we could …"

"Oh, yeah, I forgot." Talia blew out a whistle. "Sorry, honey."

"Don't be. We'll go in a few weeks' time." Ginny didn't dwell on that too much. Ever since she'd gotten in the car her insides were doing cartwheels and now her mouth was parched. She couldn't swallow if she tried.

Talia stuck her arm behind her, presumably to play with Benjy's feet or legs, because her little man laughed uncontrollably, shrieking in hysterics. He was such a joy to be around, such good baby, especially when he wasn't having problems with his teeth. These days he was sitting up unaided and starting to crawl. He'd grown from the tiny, lifeless, scrawny little thing that had come into her world and now transformed into this lovely, chubby, bouncy, beautiful baby boy.

"How long do we have to stay there for?" Talia asked.

"I told them we couldn't stay for too long. Hopefully less than an hour."

"Okay, okay. I can do that." Talia seemed anxious herself. "I can stay for as long as you need me to. We have the whole weekend now that you're all alone."

"Stop reminding me," Ginny groaned.

"Have you heard from Ryan? What's the low down on Vanessa?"

Ginny let out a sigh and wished Talia wouldn't keep going on about it. "I haven't heard from him since he got there. I'm not going to bother him. It's fine. I'll get all the details when they come back."

"You know, one of the managers at work almost had a breakdown when her husband left her for—" Talia abruptly stopped talking.

"Left her for what?"

"Don't worry. It's not important."

But Talia's comment fueled the burning paranoia that was already simmering in Ginny's head. "He left her for what?"

"It doesn't matter, Gin. This is nothing like your situation. Forget I said anything." Talia made a sound in the base of her throat as if she were annoyed at herself.

"Do they have kids?" Ginny asked softly.

"They do, but they're in their teens. Let's not talk about that. I shouldn't have said anything."

"What happened?" Ginny asked, her curiosity sticking to her like a leech as she tried to put together the pieces of this invisible jigsaw puzzle that Talia had hinted at.

"They figured things out. He realized he'd made a mistake, and the kids were suffering, and his wife, too, so he must have regretted it at some point because he went back to his family."

"She took him back?"

"Uh-huh. I don't know why." Talia tried to make light of it.

"For the sake of the family. That's why." The roles were reversed in her situation. Ryan's wife had left him for another man, and while Ryan had told her that he would never go back to Vanessa, Ginny wasn't so sure. He loved Daisy more than his own life, and Daisy loved her mom. There could be a situation one day when Ryan saw just how happy Daisy was around her mother. Once Vanessa dug her nails into him enough, she would wear him down and reel him back. This was what Ginny feared the most. Ryan was such a good man. Maybe he would eventually, over time, give in and succumb.

"Look, honey." Talia grimaced. "I'm sorry. I shouldn't have said anything."

"It's okay." A scenario like this was her worst nightmare; she always considered the worst case scenario because she was Benjy's only parent and her son always came first.

"After we meet Ben's parents, why don't we take Benjy out?" Talia suggested. "We'll go to the park or somewhere, some soft play center, and we can go for pizza after."

"That sounds good. Let's make a day of it," Ginny agreed. But her mind was elsewhere. On Ryan and Vanessa in Seattle. An image of a smiling Daisy suddenly popped into her head.

A happy family.

The image stayed with her even when she knocked on the door of Ben's parents' house. Cindy's hand flew to her face as she looked at Benjy, before bursting into tears. Once they were inside, Ginny handed Benjy over to his grandmother, while Ben's dad, with tears in his eyes, thanked her. He hugged her gingerly at first, then properly, as he, too, sobbed.

Ginny and Talia looked at one another. It was only now, that she was witnessing their raw emotion, their brokenness, that she wished she'd done this sooner, and not prolonged this pain for them.

They sipped iced tea and watched Benjy's parents fuss and dote over their grandson. Looking around the room, Ginny saw that one side of it was filled with toys so new, she saw the boxes in a corner. These people had been waiting for family to return; their bloodline, their one link to their only child who had died. .

Whether it was for the tragedy they all shared, the life that had left them, or gratitude that she had returned with their grandson, Ginny would never know, but this, being here, didn't feel too bad. In fact, it was quite the opposite. It was comforting to be with Ben's parents, in the house he grew up in.

The thought shocked her. This was family.

It was what Ryan had in Seattle.

She needed to focus on her future with Benjy because romance was fickle. Eloise and Liam were living proof of that. Ryan was the most amazing man, but things could change in an instant.

She didn't put it past Vanessa to get her tentacles into Ryan and pull him in. It could happen. Just because Ryan told her he would never go back to Vanessa, didn't mean he wouldn't change his mind.

Men could be fickle when it came to love.

CHAPTER 26

ASHLEIGH

It had been a while since she'd heard from Patrick.

Maybe she never would again. After all, who was she to think that Patrick McBride might be interested in her? She had no doubt that man charmed every woman he came into contact with, and that he made them feel special, just like he'd made her feel special.

She smoothed down the sleeves of the dress hanging on the mannequin; it was similar to his daughter Angelina's dress. Ashleigh shook her head, as if it might shake Patrick out of her thoughts. In a small way, she'd been waiting for him. He'd given her something new to think about, and had stopped her feeling regretful about Ford.

It had helped, having that slight if cursory flirtation with Mr. MacBride, because try as she did, she hadn't managed to successfully move on from Ford. He still slipped into her thoughts every now and then, and she often found herself wondering what he was up to because she hadn't seen him for a while.

She turned away, to find May, her assistant walking towards her with a large bouquet of multi-colored flowers in her hand. They were rainbow colored roses with splashes of glitter on the petals. A riot of colors, so eye catching and beautiful that they held her attention. She stood riveted, unable to take her eyes off them. Roses weren't meant to be blue or green or purple, and yet these were eye-catchingly spectacular. She stared at May in confusion, as if to say 'Why are you pointing those at me?'

"They're for you." May raised an eyebrow.

Rachel sidled up to her at that very moment. "From Mr. McBride?" she asked, before gasping in admiration. "They're beautiful, Ashleigh! And they look very expensive."

Ashleigh's insides quivered with excitement. "I don't know who they're from."

"Look and see!" Rachel and May cried in unison. Her assistants seemed more excited about them than Ashleigh did. She was excited, but also a little wary. Two large and expensive bouquets of roses.

She took the bouquet and examined it, before opening the envelope. This one said,

'Been thinking about you'

Ashleigh smiled. He still wanted to keep in touch. A phone call would have sufficed. He didn't have to keep plying her with flowers.

Funny how she'd only been thinking of him this morning. Maybe this was a sign. He hadn't called her but he'd sent her something meaningful—her favorite flowers, and this proved that he was thinking of her. He was a businessman and his daughter had just gotten married. He had people to see and things to do. It might take a few weeks or months for their dinner date to happen—and she wasn't holding her breath about it—but still, it was nice to be courted like this.

"Are you sure these are from Patrick McBride?" Rachel asked.

Ashleigh shrugged. "I'm assuming so. He never signs the card with his name. It's always some sort of cryptic message."

May pressed a hand to her chest. "How romantic." She sniffed the roses again. "They're beautiful! And they're your favorite."

"They are indeed."

Rachel chortled. "He's such a romantic man. We saw the way he used to corner you and talk to only you the whole time."

Ashleigh huffed, and was about to roll her eyes but didn't want to come across as being too theatrical. She feigned nonchalance instead. "He was waiting for his daughter to try on different wedding dresses. You ladies need to get back to work. These dresses won't fix themselves."

She caught sight of Ginny heading towards her with a diary in her hands, and hoped that Benjy was okay in the office alone. He was a lot better now, a lot quieter now that he was over his teething episode. Also, he had gotten used to being here. Ginny had set up her corner of the room which now looked more like a kindergarten than a working environment.

"Are those from your secret admirer again?" Ginny asked, lowering her head to inhale the scent of the flowers.

"It's not a secret admirer if I know who he is," Ashleigh retorted.

"When is he taking you to dinner?"

"Whenever he has time."

"It's been a while."

"He's busy," Ashleigh cried, and wished everyone would get off her back.

"These are beautiful." Ginny ran her fingers over the roses carefully. "What awesome colors! Blue?" She gaped at Ashleigh.

"They're different. I like them."

"They're stunning." Ginny took another inhale. "He knows the way to your heart." She stroked the petals of a rose.

"Where's Eloise?" Ashleigh asked. "She's supposed to be at work today. Is she still moping around at home?"

"Oh, don't worry. I'll stay for longer today," Ginny volunteered, without answering her questions.

Ashleigh was grateful that her younger sister, who'd never showed much interest in the family business, now seemed so invested in it. It helped, especially now that Eloise was lacking. That girl seemed lost and distant lately, and Ashleigh knew exactly where her mind was. She was sick of holding the fort just because her sisters were going through tough times. She had experienced tough times herself but had to solider on, no matter what happened.

"That's all well and good," Ashleigh retorted, "But Eloise can't just decide not to come in, and not tell anyone. Not tell *me*."

"She's coming in later," said Ginny, being defensive. "She's tired."

"There are times when I'm tired, too," Ashleigh snapped.

"Be gentle with her, she's nursing a bruised heart."

"She knows how to mend that bruised heart. There's nothing I can do to help her. She needs to woman up and get to work."

Ginny sighed. "She's going through what I was last year."

"Your situation was far worse." She stared at Ginny, remembering that awful time when Ginny hadn't even wanted to get out of bed. When she'd lost the will to get up and do anything. When she'd given up. "What's Benjy doing?"

"He's fast asleep."

"I'll feed him lunch when he wakes up," Ashleigh offered. Whatever happened in her day, her adorable little nephew always made everything okay again.

"Thanks."

"But first I need to find a vase to put these in."

She found a vase, filled it with water and rearranged the flowers in it, before placing it on the countertop. Lowering her head, she smelled the flowers again. Her insides felt light, and if fairy dust were a thing, she imagined herself basking in it.

Patrick McBride had brightened up her day. She pulled out his business card and called him. He answered immediately, not even letting it ring twice.

"Thank you for the flowers, Patrick. That's very sweet of you."

"Uh … You're welcome." His delayed response told her that she'd caught him off guard.

"You sound busy, I don't want to take up any more of your time."

"No, no it's fine. Stay. I'm so glad you phoned. I love hearing your voice."

"I just wanted to thank you for the flowers, Patrick. They're beautiful."

"You like them?"

"I love them. But Patrick, it's too much."

"Too much? Nothing is too much when it comes to you, Ashleigh."

"There you go again, paying me way too many compliments, being so charming."

"That's because you are a lovely woman. You should be showered with compliments."

She laughed.

"About our dinner date. Are you free next week?"

Her social diary was completely empty.

"Good. I'll arrange dinner. Somewhere in Whisper Falls."

"You'd come all this way again, just for dinner?"

"It's not *just* dinner, Ashleigh. I'm coming to see you. And I'm looking forward to it.".

Not as much as she looked forward to seeing him.

CHAPTER 27

ELOISE

She felt like death, and when she opened her door to find Ashleigh standing there and looking at her with a face like thunder, Eloise wished she'd picked herself up and made the effort to crawl into work today.

Staying at home and facing her older sister's wrath now wasn't worth it. Her stomach twisted. It had been playing up all day and she didn't feel too good. Maybe she shouldn't have eaten that two-day old pizza.

"I came to check on you," Ashleigh announced, walking in and giving her a once over. Eloise put a hand to her mouth. It was that time of the month again and she felt sick and bloated, though she'd never felt this bad before. She blamed her current malaise on Liam. She blamed everything on him, even though this situation was her fault. She was the one who'd decided they needed a break and now she was stuck in some sort of standoff, but her pig-headed pride wouldn't permit her to go crawling back to the man she loved and admit she'd made a big mistake.

"What's wrong with you, apart from the broken heart?" Ashleigh sat on the couch and made herself comfortable. Eloise wished her sister's expression would soften because she looked scary. She wrapped her arms around herself. Liam's oversized sweatshirt was big on her, but she liked wearing it. Not because she was cold, especially not in the middle of summer, but because it carried his scent and she wanted to wrap herself in it. "I told Ginny I wasn't well."

"She said you were coming in later in the afternoon."

Trust Ginny to only deliver half a message. "I didn't say I'd be in *later*, I said I would *try*."

"And you never came," Ashleigh protested. "Did you ever consider the groundbreaking idea of picking up the phone and calling me to tell me?"

"Sorry. I should have." She wished she had now. She'd been scared of what Ashleigh might say, but that wouldn't have been as bad as dealing with her face to face now. She swallowed, feeling guilty. Ashleigh looked so worked up. "It won't happen again." Whatever happened, she'd have to go in tomorrow, no matter how bad a state she was in.

"We run a family business. *Family* business," Ashleigh said sternly. "Which means that us three, the sisters, who are part of one family, need to be responsible for the running of it *equally*. This isn't *Ashleigh's* business. It doesn't belong just to *me*. It belongs to the three of us. This is Mom and Dad's legacy. This is something they created and we decided this was what we would do. This was how we would continue their legacy."

"Okay, okay, calm down," she cried, trying not to raise her voice because it would only antagonize Ashleigh further. "You don't have to talk to me like I'm a teenager. I already feel bad enough." She wished Ashleigh would disappear.

"Do you?"

Ashleigh's retort caught her off guard. "Yes, of course I do. Why are you so worked up? It can't only be because I didn't come to work today. You're not there by yourself, Ash. Ginny's there now and she told me she was going to work some extra hours." They eye-balled one another. "I heard you got some more flowers," she said, wanting to deflect the conversation to something else.

"Who told you? Ginny?" There was a harshness to Ashleigh's words, as if she felt left out of her sisters' conversations.

"We weren't talking behind your back," Eloise countered.

"She called to tell you about the flowers?"

"I called her to ask how you'd taken the news of me not coming in," Eloise replied.

"I didn't think you *weren't* coming in. I was expecting you to come in *later*."

Ooops.

Ashleigh continued. "Maybe next time call me and tell me instead of, you know, you and Ginny talking among yourselves. The pair of you obviously seem to talk more with each other than you do with me." Ashleigh sounded angry.

"That's because you've been pretty miserable lately, Ash." It needed to be said. These days Ashleigh was mostly in a bad mood. Thank goodness for Patrick and the bouquets he'd sent her because they partially relieved her temper.

"I'm miserable? And you're not?" Ashleigh glared at her.

"You don't look so miserable today, just mad." Eloise tried to smile. "I heard the roses this time were spectacular; blue and green and purple. Is that right?" she asked, trying to appeal to Ashleigh's good nature.

"They've been dipped in dye and they had glitter along the edges."

"Wow."

"I liked the first bunch more," Ashleigh declared. "I prefer natural colors; the pinks, whites and reds. They're the color roses ought to be."

"How awesome that you have a secret admirer!"

"He's not so secret if I know who he is." Ashleigh rolled her eyes. She seemed to have loosened up somewhat and Eloise was eager to keep her in a good mood. "It must be exciting, having a man like Patrick send you flowers, and not one bunch but two!"

"Is it?" Ashleigh didn't seem that enthused.

"Isn't it? He's so good looking for a man of his age."

"He's not *that* old," Ashleigh pushed back.

"He looks older than Ford. How old is he?"

Ashleigh visibly flinched at the mention of Ford's name. "I don't know. I've never asked him."

"When's he taking you out on that date he promised?"

"He didn't promise. It's not a date, and whenever he can, I assume. He's busy. His daughter recently got married and I imagine they still have lots to do. They know lots of people."

"You're making excuses for him."

"This is what he told me. I spoke to him. I called him and thanked him for the flowers."

"You have his number?"

"We exchanged business cards," Ashleigh replied, defensively.

"So, this is a date?"

"We'll see."

"You're going to move to Manhattan," Eloise told her.

"And leave you and Ginny to run the business?"

"You've considered that idea?" This news came as a surprise.

Ashleigh shook her head. "We haven't met for dinner yet

and you have me living in Manhattan. Of course I haven't considered the idea, because it's not happening. It's just dinner, and it will probably never happen."

"But he lives in Manhattan, doesn't he? Have you considered how this might work?"

"How will what work?" Ashleigh blew out a breath and dismissed the notion with her hand. "Nothing's going to happen. This is purely dinner, or will be when he gets around to arranging it. It's a bit of fun for me, and fun is what I need after dealing with you and Ginny."

"What does that mean?" Eloise cried, offended.

"Like when Ginny has issues with Benjy, when he's teething, and like last year when she was languishing in misery, pretty much like you are now. You and I ran the shop. Now you're going through your little miserable chapter, so Ginny and I have to run the shop, and she's not even full time. And she has a baby."

Eloise wasn't sure what point Ashleigh was trying to make but clearly something was bothering her. "She wants to be full time," Eloise pointed out. "She's excited. She's motivated."

"She's a single mom and she has another more important duty and responsibility."

"She's not going to be a single mom for long. Have you seen the way Ryan looks at her?"

A smile softened Ashleigh's demeanor. "Ryan is the best thing to happen to her."

"Yes he is," Eloise agreed, feeling a twinge of bittersweet regret.

"I dread to think where she'd be if she was still wallowing in misery, lying in her bed and not wanting to get up and face the world. Look at her now. We just need you and Liam to make up." Ashleigh sat back and clasped her hands before resting them on her lap. "Then you'll also be running around like a happy little bunny rabbit."

"Bunny rabbit?" Eloise wasn't sure she liked the reference, but she'd take it, if it meant that her sister was now in a better mood.

"What's going on with you and Liam now?" Ashleigh asked.

"Nothing. It's still the same status quo."

"You have to snap out of this, Eloise. You have to get back into the land of the living."

"I am. And I've been coming into work, haven't I?"

"True, but even when you're at work, you don't look like you want to be there. Why don't you go to him and talk things out?"

"I told him to cool it, I was the one who said we needed to have a break."

Ashleigh gave her a disapproving look. "Seeing you this way, I wonder if it was the right thing to say."

"You should have seen how he was, Ash. I'm scared that he might be different to the man I've fallen in love with. That he's changed, like Matt changed." Her ex-husband's infidelity had broken her. When they married she never imagined he would do that to her, and now she was scared having seen a side to Liam she'd not seen before.

"But Liam's different," Ashleigh pointed out. Eloise appreciated that her sister was trying to reassure her, but she didn't feel any better. "He's just different. Don't you feel safe with him, and secure, and as if you belong? Don't you feel it in your gut? Doesn't he make you feel comfortable and solid, as if what you have is unbreakable? *Unshakeable.*" Ashleigh's voice dropped an octave and she had a faraway look in her eyes.

"Who're you talking about? Ford or Liam?"

Ashleigh seemed to snap out of it with a jolt. "I'm talking

about Liam." But she looked away as if she'd been caught in a lie. "What does Liam make you feel?"

That was easy. Having listened to Ashleigh and the things she'd said, it was *all* those things and so much more. "He makes me feel all the things you said."

"Then don't waste any more time feeling miserable." Ashleigh picked up the TV remote and turned the TV on. "What shall it be? A thriller or courtroom drama?"

CHAPTER 28

FORD

*H*e had ulterior motives for tonight, because he was curious to know what Liam and Ryan knew about Ashleigh's new suitor.

He'd planned to have a few beers with Liam and, at the last minute, had also decided to ask Ryan to join them. Ginny's new man was a good guy and good company, as Ford had discovered at Ryan's housewarming. He'd been surprised to learn that he'd even been invited to that event. Now he deemed it was about time that he returned the favor and invited him out. It was also time that they all got to know one another better, especially if they were all going to end up with the Rose sisters.

Something like that wasn't impossible. It could happen. It was just a matter of waiting it out to see what happened with Ashleigh and the new guy who seemed to be smitten with her. Ford hadn't been able to get that news out of his head ever since Darcie had told him.

"Thanks for this," Ryan raised his beer bottle and clinked bottles with Ford and Liam.

"Yeah, thanks." Liam's voice was gruff, just like his appearance. Ford had been alarmed to see him walk into the bar. He wouldn't have recognized him were it not for the ball cap he wore backwards. The guy looked rough as hell. Even Ryan seemed a little shocked by Liam's appearance but he was being polite and not calling him out on it.

"No problem, buddy. How're you doing?" Ford asked.

"Yeah, good. It's all done, shelves are up. The plastering is done, the painting is almost finished. I'll be done in two more days and then your place is ready to go."

"Hey, congrats. This is your new accountancy practice, right?" Ryan asked. "When do the doors open?"

Ford sighed. It had taken longer than he'd anticipated to reach this stage. Life's curveballs and all that. "It is my new practice, and it should have opened a few months ago, but better late than never. It will open as soon as Liam's finished doing whatever he's doing."

"Are you throwing a party?" Ryan asked. "A grand opening, maybe?"

Ford wrinkled his nose. He didn't like the idea of that. "I don't have any clients from Boston that I can bring here, so I'm starting over again. I don't foresee anyone turning up even if I had a grand opening, which I don't plan on doing, not for an accountancy practice."

"But you're from this town and so many people know you," Ryan pointed out. "They'll get the Boston expertise at small town prices. You most definitely should have a little soiree, or *something*."

Ford marveled at Ryan's enthusiasm. The guy was in love, and everything was likely going well for him, judging by the how he'd seen Ryan and Ginny at the housewarming. He side-eyed Liam who looked as miserable as Ford had felt on hearing about the new guy hitting on Ashleigh. He and Liam were two losers when it came to love. He frowned. "It's an accountancy practice. We're boring people. Who'd come?"

Ryan looked askance at Liam as if waiting for him to contribute to the conversation, but Liam's gaze was on his bottle of beer. He was a man deep in thought. A silent man.

"Ashleigh, Eloise and Ginny will come, for sure. And then there's Darcie and her husband and son. Besides, you know so many people. You grew up here," Ryan remarked.

Ford shook his head. He didn't want to throw a party. All he wanted was to get Ashleigh Rose back in his life, and he sure as hell was going to try, but first he needed to know where things stood between her and the new guy. Needing more information, he was about to slip Ashleigh's name into the conversation when he remembered something about Ryan. "How was your weekend? You went to see your ex, didn't you?"

"Ouch. Don't even go there. That's a touchy subject," Liam muttered. Ryan looked at Ford in confusion, as if he didn't understand the comment. Ford waved a hand dismissively in Liam's direction. "Don't mind him. He's had a hard day at work." He didn't know what Liam was talking about, either, or how the guy would know anything, given that he and Eloise weren't talking much.

"It's okay. I don't mind," Ryan said, good naturedly. "It is a touchy subject but Ginny's not here and I could do with both your opinions on it."

"On what?" Ford was intrigued.

"Ginny's angry with me. I wasn't going to meet you guys tonight because I was going to see her. I haven't seen her since we got back, but she told me she was too busy; that she had other plans."

Ford chuckled. "Sorry for the short notice about tonight." Monday evening didn't seem like the right time to have a boys' night out, but he was desperate for news and he didn't have the patience to wait until the end of the week.

"It's not the short notice. It's just that I was hoping to see Ginny and Benjy tonight," Ryan answered.

Ford nodded in understanding.

"We're second in line then?" Liam mumbled.

Ryan shrugged. "She's giving me the cold shoulder, so I'm glad I came out."

"Cold shoulder, eh?" Ford pondered the news carefully and was a little surprised by Ryan's confession. He'd assumed all was well when it came to Ryan and Ginny.

"Get used to it, especially if you're dating one of the Rose sisters." Liam seemed especially bitter.

"Are all three of us in the doghouse?" Ford wondered out aloud.

Ryan gave him a searching look and when no one replied, said, "I guess we are."

"Why is Ginny annoyed with you?" Ford asked. "Is it because you spent the weekend with your ex-wife?"

Ryan set down his bottle. "I take issue with the way you're phrasing it."

"Sorry, but that's literally the only way I know to say it. You did, did you not, spend the weekend with your ex-wife?" He grinned mischievously.

"Only because she decided to throw an early birthday party for herself. Her birthday is still two weeks out."

"She wanted to mess up your weekend with Ginny. She must have known about it, right?" Liam asked, perking up.

"This is news to me., about you and Ginny going away." Ford hadn't heard about this. There was a time when he would have known what the sisters were up to. Not that he was nosy, just that he'd once belonged to the inner group, and felt like family. It had helped a lot when his divorce had come through and he'd moved back to Whisper Falls. With Susan no longer in his life and Maddie at college, and his mother old and frail, and not altogether there, being with Ashleigh was like coming home. It was easy going, and natural. There was no place he'd rather be than home. No one he'd rather be with than her.

Ryan scratched his jaw. "We … uh … we were going to go away for a few days. Ginny, me and the kids."

Liam leaned across the table, looking ready to join the conversation. "You think that's why your ex threw the party early? To mess up your weekend?"

"That's kind of how Vanessa rolls."

"And Ginny's angry with you because?" For the life of him Ford couldn't figure it out.

"Who knows?" Liam got up. "Women are a species unto themselves. I'll be darned if I ever understand them. I'm getting another round of beers."

The two men exchanged glances when Liam disappeared. "He looks rough," Ryan remarked. "I didn't want to say anything before, but is he okay?"

"I've seen him in better days. He just needs some time, though I don't know what Eloise is playing at," Ford answered, then decided to broach the subject now, and kill two birds with one stone while Liam was away. "I hear there's someone new on the horizon, someone interested in Ashleigh. You heard anything about that?"

"Was Kayla a cover?" Ryan asked, shocking Ford with his directness.

"Pardon me?"

"My sister. Was she a someone you used?" There was a hint of menace in his tone.

Oh, boy. Ford didn't want to end up having an altercation with Ryan. That wasn't why he'd invited the guy out tonight. "Kayla and I helped each other. You know that, don't you? She lost her confidence with driving, and I was struggling with my mother who was sick. It was Kayla who suggested the arrangement, not me."

Ryan's shoulders slouched. He sat back, as if digesting the news. "I thought it might be something like that. My sister … she's not … she's not one to get romantically involved."

Ford raised an eyebrow at the news which came as a surprise to him, but he wasn't going to comment on that. "She's a great friend. She's been such a great help and I appreciate all she did for my mother, but I promise you, buddy, there was never anything more on my part than friendship."

Ryan gave him a knowing look. "I figured she was sweet on you."

The guy knew. "I tried to let her down gently. I'm sorry. I didn't want to hurt her. I didn't realize at the time how she felt, but there's only one woman for me."

"Yeah? If that's the case, then why's the only woman for you getting flowers from some random stranger?" Liam asked, handing out the beer bottles.

"He's not a random stranger, he's the father of one of the brides. Ginny said he's 'dashing.' Don't do that," Ryan cried, when they made throwing up noises. "That's how she described him."

Ford flinched as if he'd been pricked by a six-inch needle. Desperate to change the topic he started on Liam. "What about you, dude?"

"What about me?" Staring at him now, it was clear that he hadn't shaved in days or slept much. "Are you and Eloise still not talking?"

"She told me we needed to cool down. We needed a break. So I'm giving her a break."

Ford shook his head. "That break isn't doing you any wonders, buddy. Have you looked in the mirror lately?"

"No point. No need to," Liam muttered to himself.

"We've talked about this before," said Ford, not wanting to divulge their private conversation to Ryan. "You're crazy about that woman, so you need to go and get her."

"How? Why? And especially when she told me to—"

"It doesn't matter what she told you," Ford interjected firmly. "It doesn't matter what they say. The way you're feeling, you think she doesn't feel the same way? She's always said she loved you. What's the issue? You feeling inadequate because her ex's tux was expensive?"

"What?" Ryan asked, new to the story. Ford was about to explain when he thought better of it. "Can I tell him, about the party and what happened?" he asked Liam. "Or would you rather we don't talk about it?"

"Sure. Go on."

He briefed Ryan on the matter. Ryan sat back, his finger sliding over his chin. "You just have to be who you are, Liam. Don't change yourself, because Eloise loves you for who you are, not for someone you think she might want you to be."

Liam looked up at him, his brows pinching together. "It's not as simple as that," he growled, before lifting the bottle to his lips.

Ford felt sorry for the guy. It was easy enough to see that Liam was too angry to be thinking straight. Too angry because he was so hung up on Eloise. It was a crying shame those two were both as stubborn as mules. "If I can give you guys one piece of advice, it would be to hold onto someone if you have even an inkling that she's the one. Sure, you'll have fights and disagreements, but never ever forget the good times, and why you once thought she was 'the one.' 'Cause when you let them go, you might not ever get them back."

He would know, because he was in danger of losing Ashleigh forever.

<h1 style="text-align:center">CHAPTER 29</h1>

ASHLEIGH

"Too much cleavage." Darcie shook her head.

Ashleigh stared down and had to agree. She felt a little naked. A little exposed.

"Try this one. I like this on you." Eloise threw her one of the many dresses Ashleigh had set down on the bed as possible outfits for her date with Patrick. Climbing out of her current dress she slipped into the one Eloise was holding.

"That's better." Darcie's face was a picture of approval.

"That dress says elegant, sexy and confident," Eloise agreed. Ashleigh patted down the dark green dress which didn't hug her curves too tightly, yet still showed off her hourglass figure. It didn't dip too low, either, which meant she would feel comfortable instead of looking down every few minutes to make sure she didn't reveal too much. It was stylish and classy, and the color contrasted beautifully with her dirty blonde hair.

Patting a hand over her smooth stomach, she admired her reflection in the mirror. "That's the look I want." She was nervous about meeting Patrick. It was one thing to see him when he was at the shop, and his daughter was hovering around and trying on dresses, but it was a completely different thing for it to just be the two of them. To be sitting across the table from him in a restaurant, sharing a meal. There would be no Eloise or Ginny, no Rachel or May, or other customers to make her feel at ease.

"What about your hair?" Eloise peered at it.

"What about it?" Ashleigh snapped. She hadn't asked her sister to come over, but Eloise had turned up anyway. "It's just dinner."

Darcie and Eloise snickered amongst themselves.

"It's dinner, just dinner, and *nothing else,*" Ashleigh retorted.

"I told her if she's not careful, she's going to end up moving to Manhattan." Eloise winked at Darcie.

Someone wolf-whistled. In the mirror Ashleigh saw Ginny and Benjy reflected back. Her little nephew was wrapped up in a towel, looking fresh and clean after a bath. "Wow!" Ginny wolf-whistled again.

"Where did you learn to do that?" Eloise sounded impressed.

"You look gorgeous, Ash. Go knock him dead." Ginny carried a slightly wet Benjy on her hip, with Darcie and Eloise now fawning over the baby .

"It's just dinner," said Ashleigh, spraying perfume over herself. "This is going nowhere." Nothing would come of tonight. It was purely dinner with a man who she'd enjoyed flirting with.

Something fun.

Something different.

A nice evening out with an attractive man; someone she would not ordinarily have met. As a successful businessman, Patrick traveled around the world and probably mingled with high society. He had no doubt met plenty of beautiful women recently at his daughter's wedding and he probably had their phone numbers in his address book.

But, for some reason she still couldn't fathom, he was coming all this way to take her out to dinner.

Why?

It didn't make sense.

But, even she couldn't deny that there had been an attraction. They'd flirted with one another and talked, and she had enjoyed their conversations at the shop. But she was fully aware that this man was out of her league. They mixed in different circles. It was preposterous, this idea of her and him being together. He was a rich man who could do what he wanted, and him coming all this way to take her to dinner seemed odd.

"Don't downplay his interest in you." Darcie seemed to have read her mind. "You are an attractive, beautiful woman, Ash. You have a lot to offer. You're a business owner, a wonderful friend, you have a big heart and a great personality and you're in great shape. You look amazing for your age."

Ouch. Ashleigh sighed. "For my age. I don't like those three words."

"Hon, we're all getting older," said her friend.

"That may be, but I don't like to be reminded about that." It was another reason why she was forcing herself to shuffle out of her comfort zone and go on a date with a man she barely knew. She wouldn't be in this position if she and Ford were still together.

But that ship had long sailed, and coming to terms with it

had been difficult. It could have been perfect. Her first love returning to her after all these years. Returning to his hometown and wanting to settle here. There could have been a beautiful future for them. One made up of sunsets and sunrises. A good life filled with love, joy, and happiness. She didn't need new and exciting. Ford was her north star. He was solid and dependable, like a rock. With him she could be who she was, and remain true to herself. If only she could take back time and change that conversation. If only she'd let him come to Europe when he'd wanted to surprise her. He hadn't even wanted to join her on her travels. His main purpose for that trip was to break the news of Ginny's pregnancy to her in person, so that he could be there to help her absorb the shock.

It wasn't her fault. She'd gone round and round in circles trying to explain it to him. But they were now in this situation because he was acting like a big baby and not giving her a chance. Maybe that's what men became in their middle years, though that wasn't Liam's excuse. The man was slightly younger the Eloise, and still in his early thirties. Though it was obvious to her that Eloise could drive a man crazy. As much as Ashleigh loved her pig-headed, fun-loving sister, Eloise wasn't always easy to be around.

"Put this on." Eloise held out a bracelet.

"That's perfect." Darcy's face lit up. "And earrings, too. You need something for your face."

"I don't want to wear earrings if I'm wearing the bracelet." Ashleigh admired the rose-gold bracelet adorned with an intricate pattern. It shimmered under the light.

"Put on some earrings," Eloise insisted.

"No." Ashleigh pushed back. She wasn't a Christmas tree, waiting to be adorned with glittery, shiny things. "I don't want Patrick to think I've spent a long time getting ready."

"But you have!" Eloise and Darcie cried in unison.

"He doesn't need to know that." She slipped the bracelet over her wrist and admired it. It was lovely, and it was just right. A nice simple bracelet. She gave her audience of two a little twirl. Ginny had left, presumably to settle Benjy for the night. "This will have to do."

"You don't just 'do,'" Ash. You look breathtakingly stunning." There was approval in Eloise's eyes. Darcie gave her a chef's kiss before clasping her hands to her chest. "He won't be able to resist you."

Ashleigh rolled her eyes. "We're just having dinner, and after that he's dropping me back home."

"Hmm." Darcie smiled at her with amusement. Eloise gave a wickedly evil cackle. "Somehow, I don't see why he would drive all this way just to eat. Dinner could lead to other things," her sister said mysteriously.

Ashleigh glanced at her watch, desperate to leave. It was two minutes to seven. Her phone rang at that very moment. It was Patrick.

She answered immediately, her insides quivering like jelly. "Hi," she said, her voice shaky.

"Hey, Ashleigh. I'm outside." His voice vibrated inside her. The words, the meaning, the intent. Patrick McBride was outside her house, waiting for her.

"I'm coming." She cut the call short when she heard Eloise and Darcie squealing in the background. They hugged her as she tried to make her way to the door, grabbing her clutch bag, and sliding her heels on. She considered wearing her soft, comfy pumps, but knew her fashion critics wouldn't let her leave the house in them. "'Bye!" She rushed out, feeling the pinch of the shoes along her heels and the squeeze along her toes. Thank goodness she didn't have to walk much.

To her dismay, Eloise and Darcie were standing in the

doorway, refusing to shut it and they watched as she made her way to the car; as if they were her parents and she was going to prom. Patrick waved at them with a smile. He'd stepped outside and was standing by the sleek, black and shiny car.

She walked towards him slowly, praying she wouldn't trip because she wasn't used to these heels. Gripping her clutch bag tightly she tried to feel confident, tried not to totter as Patrick strode towards her, a look of admiration on his face, his lips curved up slightly at the corners. When they were face to face, he put his hands on her shoulders, leaned in and kissed her on both cheeks. "Ashleigh, you look divine. You take my breath away." Something sparkled in his eyes. Heat crept along her skin. He noticed her bracelet, and then his gaze settled on her neckline, before moving higher, to her lips, then her eyes. It was so knowing, the way he surveyed her; as if his time, his attention, his appreciation was reserved only for her. This was his charm. His master-of-the-universe special power that made her feel so cherished.

She had no idea how he did it, but she basked in the glow of his admiration.

"What?" he asked, puzzled. She must have made a face or something, because he looked at her expectantly.

How do you do it?

How do you make me feel so special just by the way you're looking at me? "Nothing," she said, keeping her thoughts to herself. "I can't believe we're finally going to dinner."

"I'm sorry I delayed it for so long."

"Don't be sorry. I understand. You're a busy man, Patrick."

"And you're a very busy woman. Shall we?" He opened the door for her, and waited her to climb in. It wasn't easy, trying to slide in smoothly in heels and a dress.

It was a sleek black car. It looked so clean she was scared to make a mess. Once inside she suddenly felt nervous. It smelled of leather and luxury. The car handles and the dashboard shiny and clean. Not a speck of dirt on the seats or the floor. It didn't even feel as if she was in a car.

She glanced at Patrick as he got in. He looked so handsome in his navy-blue shirt and blazer with dark trousers. It wasn't a business suit, or an informal suit, but a coordinated and casual looking outfit that looked expensive, and made her do a triple take. Butterflies rushed around in her stomach. He looked like something out of those expensive watch advertisements. Someone from a world filled with old-style elegance, vintage cars, and steam trains.

She tried to swallow, and not make it obvious, but she was in trouble. How would she ever get through a meal, and not worry about table manners, or having food stuck between her teeth? This man had asked her out to dinner. He was interested in her. He wanted to spend time with her. The thought sent her insides into another tailspin. What was he doing with her?

Don't underestimate his interest in you. Darcie's words replayed in her head.

She took in a slow breath and tried to keep her friend's advice in mind. This was probably how Liam must have felt at Beth's; out of his depth, as if he didn't belong to that world. She needed to explain this feeling to Eloise, to let her know that what Liam felt was genuine. He wasn't being a big man crybaby. The poor guy felt inferior. *Less.* Inadequate. She understood it perfectly. "I've never been in a chauffeur driven car before."

"You haven't?" Patrick sounded surprised. It made her think that as much as this was an adjustment for her to make, going out with someone so wealthy. He was likely dealing with the same thing. Getting used to someone 'normal'.

Where she had been so relaxed, she now experienced her first twinge of anxiety as she saw the chauffeur in the front. A sheet of glass separated them from him, but she needed to know. "Can he hear us?"

"No."

"What if you need to talk to him?"

"Like this?" Patrick flicked a button on a panel on the door. "Say hello to Ray, Ashleigh."

"Hi, Ray," she said, feeling self-conscious.

"Good evening, Miss Rose."

She turned to Patrick with wide eyes. "He knows my name!"

Patrick laughed. "I would hope so." He stopped pressing the button.

"Tell me about Angelina's wedding. How is she?" Ashleigh asked, settling against the soft yet firm car seat.

And he was off, talking about the wedding and about Angelina, and telling her of the many emotions he experienced at seeing his only daughter getting married. He didn't say much about the guests or the venue, or any of the other things Darcie had been itching to know about, and had wanted her to ask him, but instead focused on his daughter, and the friends and family, and what the day had meant to him, and how sad he was when she left.

The car came to a stop outside the new restaurant which had recently opened in town. *Allendium.* It was an expensive place. She'd heard about the French inspired restaurant, but as yet hadn't been. Nor would she have. "Have you eaten here before?" she asked, curious why he'd come here.

"No, but it's been highly recommended."

"Recommended by whom?"

"My friends."

"They've eaten here?" In her narrow view of his life, she wondered who from Patrick's circle had trekked all the way to Whisper Falls to eat at this establishment.

"No, but the chef has two Michelin stars."

"Oh." The remark was so typically Patrick.

From the moment they walked in, from the moment the head waiter—she assumed it was the head waiter judging from his smart black suit—saw Patrick, they were treated like royalty. Patrick talked easily as if he and the man were the best of friends. She marveled at his ability to make everyone he met feel at ease.

Not just her.

"Do you know him?" she asked, when the man left them alone.

"Who? The maître d'?"

She blinked. "Yes, him. It looked as though you were both long lost friends."

"Never met him before."

She blinked again. "You were talking to him as if you knew him."

"I was congratulating him on the new restaurant."

"I know, Patrick. I understood." She felt a little wound up, as if he was being patronizing. "You just have a way with people."

"You're annoyed with me," he stated, his handsome face staring at hers, his voice low and soft, as if he was concerned. She wasn't annoyed. But what was it? She couldn't put her finger on it.

"You're good with people," she said, finally.

"It's the secret to being successful, Ashleigh. You know that because you're very good with people." He was doing it again, being charming. Pleasant. Showering her with compliments. "You are. You can't run a business like yours, where people come to you from far and wide, through word of mouth and recommendation, unless you're good with people and you have an amazing product with phenomenal service. You have all those things, Ashleigh, whether you believe it or not." He moved closer, his hands on the table. "I suspect you don't believe it, and you're also not comfortable with me praising you."

Oh my word.

This man could read her mind. Sweat formed around her the back of her neck and she so badly wanted to fan her face, fearing another hot flush coming on. Instead she reached for her glass, then realized it was empty.

"Let's order. Drinks?"

"Cold water, please." She kept her hands clasped tightly together on her lap.

"Some wine, too?" he asked.

"That would be nice."

They perused the menu and ordered, and then after some recommendations from the sommelier they decided on a bottle of red wine to go with it. She liked that Patrick didn't order for her which she'd feared he might. That would have riled her for sure. Sitting across the table from this handsome man, her right leg started to shake. She placed a hand on her thigh to steady it. This typically only happened when she was nervous, and though she felt a calmness being around Patrick, something clearly was off. Something deep in her core that didn't sit right. She couldn't work out what it was or why she felt like this.

But their conversation flowed easily. Patrick told her some more about Angelina's wedding, and mentioned the article in The Island that was now out. Ashleigh made up her mind to buy a copy. He told her that his daughter was on a whirlwind honeymoon traveling around Europe. The mention of this spiked Ashleigh's interest.

"Tell me about the high points of your European vacation?" Patrick asked. So, she did.

Their first course came and went, and she was still talking about her trip to Europe, while Patrick would add in his little observations and anecdotes. He'd been to every place she mentioned. And even the places she hadn't been to, but which she'd planned to visit in the future.

By the time the main course arrived, her leg had stopped shaking, and she no longer felt nervous. Patrick had this uncanny ability to make her feel at ease, as if they were together, like a real couple, not just on their first date. He listened attentively to each word, and asked her questions as if he were genuinely interested instead of asking out of politeness.

His background and wealth were soon forgotten. She settled back in her chair, feeling comfortable and was shocked to learn that the hours had flown.

"I'd like to see you again," Patrick said, as they were drinking coffee.

"You would?" she replied, feeling unsure. She'd had a great time, but something was missing. That fire in her belly wasn't there. Even though she thought she was at ease, deep down she wasn't. Maybe it was his wealth, his background, the world he lived in. Telling herself that his wealth didn't matter was a lie.

How would this work? Patrick lived in Manhattan. It was a car journey that took a few hours.

"Don't think about the obstacles," Patrick told her, making her nervous now because it seemed as if he'd read her mind.

"Why?" she asked, the words jumping out of her mouth before she could stop herself.

"Because you're a beautiful woman, Ashleigh. Forgive me for saying this but I meet many women, and they tend not to hide their hunger, or their desire. Maybe it's the money that attracts them." He sounded resigned, almost sad, downcast "But you didn't even know who I was at first."

"I sort of did soon enough. When you said you had an unlimited budget, it gave me an idea of the type of man you were."

"But you didn't seem to care. You didn't have dollar signs in your eyes. You're grounded, and nice and genuine, Ashleigh."

Grounded and nice and genuine. It was hardly a compliment. Were they plastic, and difficult—the women he was used to? She wondered what they were like and if Patrick was deliberately going against the grain, maybe he'd been burned lately, and had a broken heart so was trying a different tack. Something different, *someone* different.

"And beautiful," he continued, when she stayed silent. "You've got a heart of gold. I'm fifty-five years old and I've seen enough in my lifetime so far to know when people are genuine and when they're not."

Fifty-five?

Not bad.

He looked like he was in his mid-forties.

There were twelve years between them. Not that it mattered at this age. He looked so good; so well maintained, so groomed. This man took good care of himself.

"I've met a lot of fickle women and in comparison you're different. Honest and earthy."

She laughed. It might have been that the wine was going to her head, but honest and earthy? He might as well have described a wine. She giggled.

"You're laughing," he noted, his eyes twinkling with amusement.

"I'm still looking for the compliment in your 'honest and earthy'."

"It is a compliment!" he insisted, with a devilish grin.

They talked more, about life, and travels and the places she wanted to go back and visit, and he talked about his businesses, and his life back in Manhattan. He sounded lonely, as if after working so hard, something was still lacking in his personal life. Seeing his only child get married and start a life of her own with her new husband must have been some sort of milestone for him. He casually mentioned that he and his ex-wife were amicable, after the divorce. "Because I gave her everything she wanted. Desiree is well looked after."

"Desiree? She sounds exotic," Ashleigh remarked, but what she'd been thinking was that she sounded *young*, which was a ridiculous thought for her to even have because of course there was no way of being able to tell that from a name.

"She's French."

"Ah ... how ... very ... glamorous." A montage of glamorous women flashed through her mind and she instantly felt inferior.

He grinned. "She is."

She smoothed a hand over her unruly hair, feeling even more inferior in comparison. "But glamor is no substitute for a great personality, or for being interesting, and having a certain ... a certain flair. Something deep, and mysterious. I'm talking about you now, Ashleigh. You are all those things."

She blinked, then picked up her glass of wine and sipped it.

"She had Angelina when she was only eighteen," he said, moving the conversation forward smoothly, as if sensing that she didn't like being showered with compliments.

Ashleigh did the calculation in her head, having remembered that Angelina was twenty-one. Which meant that Desiree was only thirty-nine. *Not even forty yet.*

Once again she was reminded of the difference between them. And as she laughed with Patrick and looked into his twinkling eyes, crinkled at the corners by fine lines. As much as she admired his chiseled and well-maintained face, as much as her heated by the idea of him wanting to see her again, she didn't quite feel the same way.

She wanted to, but it wasn't there. Her mind kept drifting to Ford, As much as she tried to deny it, she still hankered for that man, even now when she told herself that he was with Kayla and that he'd moved on. She needed to move on, too.

It wasn't normal, or fair to Patrick, for her to be sitting across the table from him and to be thinking about another man.

"What's wrong?" he asked.

"Nothing. Nothing." She swallowed, feeling guilty.

"I don't know what's going to happen, Ashleigh, but I like you. I really like you and I can't stop thinking about you."

She smiled.

Say it back.

But she couldn't. She couldn't because Ford was in her head.

"You don't feel the same way." His voice lowered. The light went out of his eyes.

"I like you too, Patrick—"

"I feel that there's a 'but' coming."

She rushed to deny it, but the truth couldn't be held in check for too long. "I reconnected with someone recently."

"*Reconnected?* Ah. There's a lot of power in that word." He nodded, but his expression turned somber. He looked down at the table. She had a feeling women didn't often turn this man down.

He said nothing more and she didn't know whether to continue or wait for him to say something. In the end, the empty silence irritated her enough for her to confess. "Someone I was in love with twenty years ago."

"As long as that?" He nodded to himself, his eyes falling to the table instead of meeting hers. "I can't compete with that."

She hated that the conversation had veered down this path, because the evening had been so pleasant up until now. "Oh," she said suddenly remembering. "Thank you so much for the flowers. They were gorgeous. So beautiful. I've never seen roses that color before."

"No?" He looked suddenly unsure.

"Where did you get them?" she asked.

"Just ... some florist online."

Something about his demeanor, shifted. Something subtle yet noticeable. "Why don't you ever sign your name?"

He cocked his head, but didn't answer.

"On the card. Why not sign it?"

"It's just how I am," he said, finally. Which didn't seem like him.

"You sent them, didn't you?" she asked, because his change in demeanor was a red flag. "Patrick?"

He sat back against his chair. "Not quite." His Adam's apple bobbed.

She felt as if her spine had snapped in two, the way her body sagged under the weight of his reply. "Not quite? What do you mean 'not quite?'"

"I assumed my PA had sent them."

She was aghast. "You ... you ... you didn't even pick them?"

His chin tilted upwards. "No."

"You didn't write the messages?"

"No."

"You asked your PA to send me flowers that you never picked with notes you never wrote."

"Notes?" He scratched his chin.

"Notes." She stared at his face. A few moments ago it had

been the epitome of quiet, understated old money, and now. Now she saw this man as someone who hadn't been entirely truthful. Someone who'd tricked her. Someone who'd made her believe something that wasn't so. "Did you even see the flowers she sent? How many bouquets did you—your PA—send me, Patrick? Do you even know?"

His lips twisted as if he wasn't sure what to say.

"Did you not know that there were two bouquets?"

He looked to be in pain. As if someone had just trodden on his chest. "I know it sounds bad, but I can explain. I've been busy with business deals ever since the wedding, but Lena, my PA, she'd obviously heard all about you because Angelina wouldn't stop talking about the dress, and then at the wedding, everyone was in awe and wanted to know where we got it. I told Lena all about you and she must have decided to send you flowers and that's why ..." He rambled on, which was something this man never did.

Ashleigh felt aghast by the new revelations. "Did your PA make the reservation for this restaurant?" she asked quietly.

Patrick's lengthy silence gave her the answer.

She shook her head, feeling betrayed and humiliated. She wasn't important enough for him to take time out of his day to send her something himself. Dazed, she thought of all the nights she'd lain in bed, thinking about a man like Patrick thinking about her.

"She made the reservation, but I told her where to make it. I called you, because it's you I wanted to get to know better. Sending flowers and making reservations aren't things I have time for. I make time for the important things, and you're important to me, Ashleigh."

"But you weren't honest with me." That's what hurt. There had been no reason to lie. He could have come clean. The fact that he hadn't, until pushed to confess the truth, made her wary.

"Don't hold it against me, Ashleigh. I'm a very busy man. I have people who do things for me."

"Yes, you do, Patrick."

And there it was.

He wasn't who she thought he was. He was a phony. He meant well, but he was not the man for her.

CHAPTER 30

GINNY

She'd been avoiding Ryan.

She would normally go over to his place on Fridays and stay there for the weekend but ever since he'd returned from his weekend with Vanessa, she'd felt conflicted. Hadn't wanted to see him, and hated herself for feeling that way.

But it was Friday night, and round about now they'd all be having dinner together and watching a movie afterwards. Daisy would be excited and playing with Benji would no doubt be gazing at her in adoration.

It would have been so good.

Instead she now sat on the couch with Benjy on her lap who was playing with a fabric baby book. Ginny had already read it to him a few times, but each time she came to the end, he clapped his hands together excitedly, wanting her to start all over again.

She was home alone because Ashleigh had gone out on her date with Patrick.

It was silly, sitting here alone, being miserable and thinking of what might have been when all she could think about was Ryan and Daisy. But she was trying to make a point. She couldn't become dependent on Ryan. She couldn't go to his house every weekend. The man had just come back from seeing his ex-wife. She needed to heed the warning signs. Even Talia's story confirmed Ginny's own fears about that situation.

Too bad it didn't help her. She missed him and would catch herself thinking about Ryan and Daisy despite vowing not to.

He, on the other hand, seemed eager to see her. He'd called her every day since his return. She hadn't called him. He wanted to see her on Monday night but she'd made up an excuse and he'd met up with Ford and Liam instead. Sensing her aloofness, he'd held off coming to see her and then earlier today, when he called to ask if she was coming over, she told him that she was still busy and no, she wouldn't be coming. The conversation had been short, and Ryan surprised her by telling her that it was fine, and then he hung up.

That hurt.

She'd expected more pushback from him. Maybe it was for the best. Maybe he was torn from the weekend with Vanessa and maybe, just maybe, he needed time alone to gather his thoughts.

No wonder he didn't seem too upset about her not coming over tonight.

Fickle.

That's what men were, and relationships, too.

Dipping her hand into the bowl of popcorn, she pulled one out, took a little nibble and gave the remainder to Benjy. He instantly shoved it into his mouth and clapped his hands together; Benjy-speak for 'more.'

"You want another one, huh, sweetie?"

Benjy clapped his hands again.

"Okay then, just another half."

She bit a piece off another popcorn and gave it to him. He chewed, and smiled, and a trickle of drool slid down the side of his mouth. She wiped it away with her fingers. "How about some milk now, baby?"

He understood the word and bounced up and down on her lap, vibrating with pure joy.

"Then bed, I think. You and me both."

She glanced at the TV screen and had no idea what she'd been watching. She'd put on a romcom an hour ago when Benjy had been sitting on the floor playing with his toy laptop. He liked to mimic her. She'd started bringing paperwork home and would do some work in the evenings, eager to prove to Ashleigh that she could juggle both roles; as a mother and a shop owner.

But it wasn't easy. At work she was more concerned about keeping Benjy busy and entertained and quiet, and unless he was asleep, she didn't get much work done. Yet she was so desperate to show her sisters that she was capable of it. There was nothing else she wanted to do. She didn't want to get a job. It would be harder to commit to a nine-to-five shift, and to answer to a boss, plus she'd have to get childcare.

What she had at the shop worked—for her and for Benjy. She was grateful for the family business that the parents she barely remembered had started.

She sensed her sisters were getting bored with it, and maybe even felt chained, but she felt a new sense of hope. She wanted The Bridal Shop to continue and prosper. She wanted her parent's legacy to live on, and in the back of her mind, if Eloise and Ashleigh no longer wanted it, she was preparing herself to take it over should the opportunity ever present itself. Because she needed something solid and reliable to secure Benjy's future.

She didn't know if Ryan would be around forever, but their family business would be, for as long as they invested it in. She was determined to make it work. Turning the TV off, she was about to head upstairs with Benjy when the doorbell rang. She was surprised that Ashleigh had come back home so quickly from her date and was wondering why her sister didn't let herself in with her keys. Preparing to interrogate her, she opened the door only to find Ryan and Daisy standing there, grinning at her. "We've come to get you, Ginny," Daisy said.

"Get me?" Ginny's gaze flew to Ryan in confusion.

"It's Friday. You always come over on Friday." Ryan raised an eyebrow, the slight hint of a smile on his lips. It annoyed her that he looked so happy. And that he had the audacity to turn up on her doorstep as if he hadn't been to see his ex-wife last weekend.

"Daddy said you're angry with him, Ginny. Are you angry with him?"

Ginny tried to soften the great-thanks-for-landing-me-in-it glare she gave Ryan.

"Are you, Ginny?" Daisy persisted.

"Huh? Uh ... no, sweetie—" She lied.

"Then why didn't you come over like you always do on Fridays?" She was always there for the weekend, and now she dreaded to think how empty the house must have been for Daisy without her and Benjy there.

"Can we come in?" Ryan asked, sounding wary. He looked sad and somber, and despite her initial irritation, she was nonetheless happy to see him. He looked so good in his business suit.

"Sorry, come in."

Daisy ran in, calling out Benjy's name, and his excited

shrieks at seeing his favorite little person pierced the air. All Ginny could hear now as the two children were reunited were cries of pure joy from them.

"Benjy's missing out," said Ryan. "And I miss you both. *We* miss you both. " He stepped towards her then wrapped his hands around her waist, caging her to him. It didn't feel bad at all.

Her defenses crumbled, and her determination to stay steely and firm melted at his touch.

"What's wrong?" Ryan thumbed her lower lip, teasing her. It was so good to see him, to be in his arms, to have him here. She tried to stand tall, and rigid. Tried to strengthen the body armor that protected her fragile heart. But she was failing miserably, especially when Ryan's eyes filled with concern. "You've been avoiding me all week."

They stayed in the hallway, as the sounds of the children laughing and enjoying one another's company filled the air. They were so thrilled to have finally found each other again.

Nothing like her and Ryan who faced one another like strangers.

"Did you kiss her?" she asked, giving in to the worst of her fears which were over exaggerated and bordered on crazy.

"Who?" His response should have allayed her fears, that his ex-wife was so far from his thoughts he hadn't even realized she was talking about her. But her fears stuck to her like superglue to paper. "Your ex-wife."

His gaze swept over her face, as if he was looking for clues as to what he'd done wrong. She had an inkling that he was not to blame. That, maybe, she was being paranoid.

Being with Ben had done that to her. But she wasn't dealing with Ben now. This was Ryan. And maybe she was the one who looked and sounded like a crazy woman.

"You saw Daisy's mother," she reminded him.

He cocked his head. "You told me to go."

"How was it?"

"Great, for Daisy. Boring for me."

"And how was she?" She couldn't bring herself to say the woman's name. Ryan's eyes narrowed in suspicion. Or maybe because she sounded like a lunatic asking insane questions.

"Did she do her usual and make a play for you?" Ginny couldn't stop herself. The week's insecurities meshed with jealousy.

"It was a party for twenty or so people. We were the only family. The rest were her new work friends."

"And, did she seek you out?" Ginny demanded.

"Her boss was there. They're dating."

It was as Ginny feared. "She's a flirt and I wouldn't put it past her to do something like that to make you jealous."

"You think she's dating someone to make me jealous?" Ryan asked, not sounding convinced.

"I wouldn't put it past her."

"I barely spoke to her, Ginny."

"But *she* spoke to *you*."

"Yes," he said, carefully, his eyes locking on to hers. "But she was the hostess. Did you want me to ignore her? What's really going on, Ginny. What's all this about?" He lowered his head and pressed his forehead against hers. With him being so close, it was impossible not to inhale his scent. Her insides turned skittery. The thrill of excitement put her body on high alert. Her heart rate rocketed, her pulse raced. A myriad of reactions that left her reeling and confused. Good reactions, to a good man.

This wouldn't have happened with Ben. He would have walked out by now if she'd interrogated him the way she had Ryan. She was always tip-toeing around Ben, but now that she had a man who would move heaven and earth for her, she was pushing him away.

Messing things up.

She was scared. That's what this was about.

Scared of being left behind. Scared of being cheated on.

Ryan would never cheat on you.

"What are you scared of Ginny? It's only you. You're the only one in my thoughts. You're the only woman I want, and if this upsets you, me going to see Vanessa, then I won't go."

She couldn't do that, either. She rested her hand on her cheek, knowing that she sounded like a jealous woman, a paranoid woman. A woman she didn't want to be. She couldn't stop this man from meeting the mother of his child. It would be unfair to Daisy. "Daisy needs to see her mother."

"Then tell me, what should I do? I love you. You know I love you and I don't know what more I can say or do to prove it to you."

She felt silly now, with his arms even tighter around her and his warm, sweet breath against her skin. His face an inch or so from hers. She was ready to sink against him. To melt into a toe-curling kiss and get swept away again. "I'm sorry for being this way," she whispered.

"I don't know how I can fix this. Ginny. You feel insecure and I understand why. I know it's because of everything that's happened to you and I don't want you to ever doubt my feelings for you. I can see you're unsure, and you're suspicious but—"

"I'm scared."

His penetrating gaze flitted from one eye to another. "Of what?"

"That you'll go back to her. You say you won't, but you might for Daisy's sake. Vanessa can be so persuasive, and I'm scared that one day she'd reel you in to her life again."

"Never. That's never going to happen. I'll never go back to

her again. I swear to you, and I've told you as much before, but you clearly don't believe me. I'll do whatever it takes to prove it to you."

Her heart melted.

"I've booked our getaway for next weekend," he said, throwing a surprise at her.

"What?"

"I checked with Ashleigh to make sure you weren't working."

"I don't work weekends."

"I checked anyway. I thought it best to, given the sibling rivalry regarding the roster."

Ginny's heart fluttered. Wasn't she the luckiest woman alive? To have such a thoughtful man?

This.

This was why this man was unlike any she had met before.

The complete antithesis of Ben.

Ryan was always so thoughtful and caring and kind.

And he was hers, if she'd let him be. She tried to wrap her head around his words. "We're going away?"

"Come hell or high water or Vanessa, we're going away." And then he kissed her again.

CHAPTER 31

ELOISE

She couldn't shake it, this bloatedness that still plagued her.

Despite not feeling so great, she'd still gone into work. She had no choice, it was her name on the roster to work this weekend and she didn't dare risk Ashleigh's wrath by calling in sick. But at the same time she wondered if this was what being heartbroken felt like? She felt lethargic and didn't want to do anything; just like Ginny had been, and this worried her even more.

She'd been putting it off, but now, slouching on the couch and hugging a cushion, she found herself in a dilemma. She wished she hadn't answered Ashleigh's phone call just now. Tonight of all nights, she would have preferred to be alone. Taking that test was a big deal, and she'd know the answer soon enough.

Her time of the month hadn't happened despite all the usual

symptoms and she'd felt weighted down by a heavy feeling. She had no option but to consider the other possibility; the one that could change her life forever.

She was falling apart. Feeling scared and sorry for herself, she burst out crying.

After a short while, and conscious that time was marching on, she glanced at her watch. Ashleigh had told her that she wouldn't be over for another hour yet which meant there was time for Eloise to find the answer; according to the instructions she'd read. She got up and decided that it was best to get this over with.

But her insides hollowed out as she took the small box out of her bag, before going into the washroom. There, she opened the home pregnancy test kit and followed the instructions. After, she rested the plastic stick on the closed lid of the toilet, and walked away, setting a timer on her phone.

Nervous and restless, she turned her face towards the door, her back to the test and waited with bated breath as her heart thumped wildly in her chest.

Her life was on the line, and she would know in a few minutes.

Either she turned around and her world didn't change.

Or ...

She had to keep a steady head. She and Liam were no longer together, and her future was more uncertain than ever. But there was still a small possibility—and she prayed it was this—that the recent split from Liam and the stress of it, had messed up her body clock. It was possible that the trauma of their breakup had affected her more than she'd thought.

Take a deep breath.

In the next few seconds, the trajectory of her life could be changed.

She leaned against the door and tried to resist the urge to go over and check before her timer had gone off.

This was painful, the long, torturous wait. Maybe the timer on her phone wasn't working. Maybe—but it went off suddenly, making her jump.

The results were in.

Turning around slowly, her heart in her throat, the noise of blood pounding in her ears, she stared at the pregnancy test. Then, with every ounce of courage she could muster, she forced herself to walk over.

One look was all it took.

Two lines.

She burst out crying.

Not tears of relief, but something else; fear, uncertainty, her life changing.

She was pregnant.

Sliding slowly to the floor, misery filling every cell in her body, she sat with her back to the bathtub. Folding her knees, she rested her elbows and lowered her head. There, in the dark space of her collapsed body, she sobbed. They were loud, racking sobs that filled the air as it all came pouring out. She was consumed by fear and hopelessness, but most of all she was scared about her uncertain future. She didn't know what to do.

She was pregnant with Liam's child, and they weren't even talking to one another.

She was going to be a mother.

The shock of those words stilled her into silence.

She was going to become a mother.

A child hadn't figured in her future. This accident was because of one careless time. Or two.

This time next year she would have a baby in her life.

A little person, like Benjy.

It wasn't what she'd envisaged.

She'd be an older mother, soon to be thirty-eight.

Two years from forty.

Forty.

Oh, dear God.

The revelation sent her into another tailspin of fear and she burst out crying again.

Liam wouldn't want her.

She was older, and having a baby would age her quicker. He could have his pick of young women. The floodgates well and truly opened. She cried and cried, until she could cry no more, and then she heard the knock on her door.

She lifted her head in shock.

Ashleigh was here earlier than expected.

A loud, long groan escaped her mouth and she considered, briefly, the idea of pretending that she wasn't at home. But of course it wouldn't work. Ashleigh had told her she was coming over, and she'd probably heard her bawling.

Wiping her tears away, Eloise got up hastily, smoothed down another one of Liam's old sweatshirts she'd put on, and glanced in the mirror.

The door knocker rapped again, this harder, and the doorbell sounded a few times. Ashleigh was angry and impatient. The worst combination. "Eloise!" Ashleigh shouted.

Eloise quickly smoothed down her hair and wiped her eyes with the back of her hand before rushing to open the door.

"What took you so—" Ashleigh stopped mid-sentence. "You were crying. That was *you* I just heard." She rolled her eyes before storming into the house, a bottle of wine and a big bag of chips in her hands. "Why are you *still* crying?"

Eloise followed her sister into the kitchen. She forced a smile and said, in an equally forced happy voice. "I get like that sometimes. I told you, it's my time of the month."

Ashleigh pulled out two glasses of wine, a bowl into which she emptied the chips, handed the bottle and the bowl to Eloise and strode into the living room.

She was clearly comfortable here. They sat down, and when Ashleigh started to pour a glass for her, Eloise stopped her. "I'm not hungry, thanks."

"I'm not feeding you. It's *wine*." Ashleigh gave her a peculiar look. This was how they'd always caught up with one another. "Why are you crying so much, even now?

"It's not that. I ... I'm just feeling tearful for no reason. It's that time of the—"

"It's been your time of the month for the past few weeks. You've never had it that bad before. I think you're depressed. Why can't you just go and make it up with Liam if it makes you so miserable being apart?"

"I will. I want to." The voice that said those words sounded weak and tinny. It didn't sound as if it belonged to her. "Tell me about your date with Patrick," she asked, hoping to move the conversation away from her. Luckily Ashleigh didn't need much encouragement and started talking as if she'd been bottling up the news inside her. As her sister recounted the event, Eloise pretended to listen but her mind was on her own shocking news.

She had to toughen up. She had to be strong now. This secret was bigger than her, and she couldn't risk it coming out, not until she told Liam.

Her heart sank. When would she tell him? How would she tell him? What would she say?

How would he take it? Could he cope with the news? Or would he see it as a burden? Given that the man already seemed to have doubts about them as a couple, she didn't want him to get back with her just for the sake of their unborn child.

She'd have to keep it a secret, until ... until ...

"Are you listening to me?" Ashleigh suddenly cried, her voice louder than usual and jolting Eloise from her thoughts. She hadn't heard a word her sister had said. "Yes." But her shaky voice indicated otherwise.

"You weren't paying any attention," Ashleigh huffed, before lifting her wine glass to her lips and taking a big gulp. She sat back, her glass on her lap. "You and Ginny, you're both the same. You never listen to anything I have to say, yet you expect me to be around, to be all ears, to be there for you, to drop everything when you have something to tell *me*. You both expect me to cover for you at work if there are things going on in your lives. I'm expected to be the robot who keeps on going despite any issues in my own life."

"I went to work today!" Eloise cried indignantly. She wasn't going to take this lying down. She hadn't felt well and still she'd gone in. Who was Ashleigh to say otherwise or to even accuse her of being lazy?

"You weren't listening to a word I said about Patrick."

"I was."

"Then, what should I do?"

Eloise blinked. She had no idea what her sister had said.

"If you were listening, tell me what I should do about Patrick," Ashleigh demanded. Eloise bit the inside of her cheek while she struggled to recall what, if anything, she could remember. The date, with Patrick, last night. She examined Ashleigh's face. Her sister's cheeks were slightly red. Like when she was frazzled, or angry. Or excited.

Ash wanted to talk about it and dissect the date. Clearly, it had gone well. "You should see him again," Eloise blurted out.

"What?" Ashleigh hissed.

"If you like him so much, if he's such a gentleman, you should definitely go on another—"

Ashleigh stood up, downed the contents of her wine glass. Picked up the bottle of wine, and stormed out.

Eloise rushed out after her. "What did I do wrong?"

"You haven't heard a word I said." Ashleigh slammed the door after her, prompting Eloise to burst into tears again.

CHAPTER 32

ASHLEIGH

*Y*oga was the only thing that would help her to release the anger that simmered inside her.

The summer sun shining down made Ashleigh feel grateful. She was lucky, she tried to remind herself. She had family, and friends, good health, as well as a roof over her head and food on the table.

It didn't matter that her date with Patrick hadn't gone well. It didn't matter that the man she thought had bought her the roses she so loved, hadn't really bought them at all.

She was lucky.

But even as she repeated the mantra over and over, while doing her sun salutation, she didn't *feel* lucky. She felt let down.

So much for all her daydreams and romantic notions about Patrick. To make matters worse, Eloise had also let her down. Her sister had too much drama in her own life and when

Ashleigh needed her to be there, to listen to her and to show interest in her news for a change, Eloise had tuned out.

It was always the same.

The sisterly support was mostly one-sided. As they'd grown older, as more drama slipped into their lives, Ashleigh bore the brunt of being the only calm and guiding force. She'd become a matriarchal figure without meaning to. She was always there to support them, and to take the reins when chaos ran rampant.

Eloise's non-interest in her date with Patrick hurt. At a time when Ashleigh needed empathy, support and sympathy, a listening ear, too, she'd received nothing.

Doing yoga in her backyard, against the beautiful backdrop of her rose garden was her only reward. Yoga brought her peace. For once, she was prioritizing making time for herself, and was determined that no one or nothing could take this away from her.

But something chewed away at her while she was in her downward dog pose, admiring the pink roses upside down. Was this all her life was going to be? Sunday mornings spent on her yoga mat in the backyard?

At least the view was nicer these days.

She inhaled a deep breath as she held the pose, felt the blood rushing to her head. She was still angry with Eloise. Her sister was a much happier and nicer person to be around when she was with Liam, but, of course, she was too pigheaded and stubborn to make up with the man, and now they all had to suffer the consequences. Away from him, Eloise was falling apart. That was the problem with her. She seemed to invite drama.

Ashleigh stood up, then bent forward and placed her hands flat on the ground, under her feet. She was flexible and nimble for her age, and proud of it. Having stretched out, she got on all fours then, holding her core, she lifted her right hand in front of her, while at the same time moving her left leg in a straight line behind her. Then she alternated the movements with her other arm and leg. After a few repetitions, she sat in the lotus pose and closed her eyes.

This was peaceful.

This was nice.

This was time to herself, nourishing her soul and being kind to herself.

She took a deep breath and savored the moment.

Maybe later, she would call Darcie and ask if she was free to meet for lunch.

That would be a pleasant way to pass the afternoon.

The doorbell rang, catching her by surprise as it punctured the silence. Groaning, she opened her eyes and stood up slowly, wondering who it could be. She was forever cursed by constant interruptions and prayed it wasn't Eloise. Her sister had probably come to apologize. Ashleigh grumbled to herself, not wanting to suffer an apology. Why couldn't everyone leave her alone? All she wanted was a Sunday morning to herself. Marching to the door she pulled it wide open, but her breath released on a gasp when she saw who it was.

Ford.

"You." It was a complete sentence. What in the world was he doing here? What possible reason could he have for turning up here, and now?

Ford seemed taken aback by her reaction. "Good morning." His eyes quickly raked over her, making her feel self-conscious of her shoddy appearance. She was in a baggy t shirt and yoga pants, and her hair was pulled up into a wild pineapple atop her head.

"Did I wake you up?" he asked.

"I didn't get out of bed," she snapped, hating the

interruption, but more annoyed that Ford was seeing her in this state. "I was in the backyard doing yoga."

"Can I come in?"

"Do you have to?"

He raised a brow at the acid tone of her voice. "Someone's not in a good mood," he said, rather casually given that she was giving him the death stare. "I was passing by and I thought I'd come in to see Benjy."

"Benjy? Benjy's not here. Ginny's gone to Ryan's place." She glared at him. "There's no one here."

"You're here."

"Ginny spends her weekends with Ryan. I thought you already knew that."

"Why would I know that?" he asked.

She knew him well. Knew that his reply sounded suspect. He knew Ginny wasn't here. "Because you're suddenly very friendly with the boys," she replied.

"The boys?"

Once more, his question didn't ring true. She examined his mouth, trying to gauge if he was being sarcastic. Looked for telltale signs of lying. "Liam and Ryan. Your new drinking buddies." She'd heard all about it from Ginny. How Ryan had been inducted into the little group along with Ford and Liam.

"Are you going to let me in, or do we have to conduct this conversation in the doorway?" he asked. She walked away, leaving the door open. She didn't buy his reason for passing by, but now that he'd interrupted her yoga session, he might as well come in so that she could find out what he was after.

She wandered back into the yard. Ford followed but once outside she took one glance at the yoga mat on the floor and decided that there was no way she was going to get into a downward dog position, not with him standing there, watching her. She couldn't relax, didn't feel like she could continue.

There was something in those electric blue eyes of his that still held her captive even after all the drama between them. This man was so handsome, he took her breath away. And he didn't need to drive up in a chauffeur driven car or take her to a fancy restaurant to do it. He just had to turn up on her doorstep unannounced.

She looked at him expectedly. "What do you want?"

"Why are you always so angry, Ash?"

The way he said her name irritated her. *Ash.* She wasn't Ash to him anymore. She wasn't *his* Ash. "I was busy."

"You're home alone!"

"I'm busy taking time out for myself," she clarified.

"You want me to go?" he threatened. She didn't, not now that he was here, now that he'd interrupted her and messed up her morning routine, and her head. After Patrick, seeing Ford unexpectedly, in her house, with it being just the two of them, the way it used to be before, brought back fond memories. But she wasn't going to tell him to stay. "You interrupted me. Ginny's not here, so if you want to see Benjy you'll have to go to Ryan's place."

"Let's not be strangers, Ash. I don't want to be at war with you. I don't know why you're so mad at me all the time."

"You don't know why I'm mad at you?" she snapped, wondering where to start. He hadn't given her the time of day until recently. He hadn't really spoken to her much during all those times she'd tried to get through to him. All those wasted months when he didn't have time for her. He'd been nice to her at Ryan's housewarming, when he'd cleared up the mess of broken glass, but otherwise he'd done his best to avoid her. Now that Kayla was on the scene and his life was happy and he had someone, he suddenly wanted to be friends again.

Now that it suited him.

He wanted to make up. He wanted things to be good again between them, even though they were no longer together.

For what?

"I need you to tell me," he answered, the intensity of those eyes piercing through her, unnerving her.

Dear God. Now he had her.

"Can we be friends, Ash?"

His question stalled her. It was the way he said it, the softness in his voice, the subtle pleading. The way he looked at her, no longer with his guard up, but speaking to her like the old Ford. Softer and nicer. And yet his words disappointed her.

He just wanted to be friends.

She had to be tough.

Act like it didn't matter.

As if she didn't care.

"Well, yeah," she said, with a shrug. "I've been trying to be friends with you, but I don't think you've noticed. You've pushed me away at every opportunity, but I understand now that you were *busy*."

"Things happened."

Yes, she thought. Things happened. Kayla happened.

"How have you been?" he asked. She pulled out a patio chair and sat down. He did the same.

"I've been fine," she answered, if a little woodenly.

"This is pretty, what you've done with this place." He gestured around the garden.

"Isn't it? I love this place now."

"It's beautiful," he agreed, nodding his head. "You've done wonders with it, Ash. I could sit here for hours."

"Please don't."

His gaze went from admiring the rosebushes and settled on her. He raised an eyebrow at her desperate plea. She hadn't intended for it to come out like that. Whiny, and desperate. But any more time spent with him, staring at that gorgeous face and his broad shoulders and strong hands, would make her feel even more jittery and funny inside. She was struggling with his presence as it was. It would be better for both of them if he just left.

"Anything interesting happening?" he asked, as she opened her mouth to tell him to leave.

"Where?" she asked, confused by the vagueness of his question.

"How's the business? How's the shop?"

"Great. Ginny's back at work now and we have a little play area for Benjy in the office."

"I heard you had a high-profile client recently."

She looked at him. "What are you talking about?"

"Liam, or maybe it was Ginny, or Eloise mentioned something about a wedding, a big wedding that was covered in some society magazine or something."

His mention of specific details, then being equally as vague, made her suspicious. "We did have a client like that ..." she said slowly, the cogs in her brain starting to whir.

"You got some flowers, and you had a date?" he asked, casually, but she knew Ford. Knew the difference between him being genuinely casual and pretending to be so.

"What are you now? Big Brother?"

"Pardon me?" His lips slanted into a smile.

"Are you watching my every move?" Was he pretending to be concerned? Interested? What a shame that they'd been reduced to this, to talking about each other's lives casually and non-committedly as if it didn't matter that they had once been together and in love.

I can't do casual with you.

She couldn't, and sitting across from him when he looked so delectably delicious, and she still had feelings for him, was difficult. Being around him made it so plainly obvious to her; this was the fire that had been missing on her date. Patrick didn't compare to Ford. Not one bit. Patrick with all his money, his charm, his distinguished good looks and personality, just did not compare.

Ford was rough and rugged and down to earth, and for a few seconds she forgot what she was doing out here in her backyard.

But now he wasn't hers. She was at a loss with what to do or say, or how to be when footsteps in the hallway startled her. For a second she wondered why Ginny had returned early. She didn't usually come back from Ryan's place until late in the evening.

But it was Eloise's face that she saw. Eloise's worried, haggard face. The girl looked as if she'd hadn't slept for two days.

Ashleigh's insides sank like a heavy weight. Eloise was the one person she didn't want to deal with right now, not on top of trying to deal with Ford. It was unbelievable. Her home was like the opening night on Broadway. All she wanted was peace and quiet and she now had these two people—problematic people as far as she was concerned—demanding her time and attention. Life was so unfair sometimes.

"Hey." Eloise hovered in the doorway, sounding as sorry and as weak as she looked. "Hey, Ford."

"What happened to you?" Ford didn't hold back.

"I didn't sleep well."

"I can see. Everything okay?" He looked so concerned, as if he was going to stand up and go to her.

Eloise glanced at Ashleigh.

"What?" Ashleigh hissed. "What now?" From the periphery of her vision, she could sense Ford being shocked by her sharp words. "What?" she cried, addressing him. "I just wanted some time to myself, to do my own thing. Why can't people leave me alone?"

Ford flinched, as if she'd slapped him.

"She's in a mood because of me," Eloise explained to him apologetically.

"I'm here. I can hear you," Ashleigh snapped. She hated being talked about in the third person.

"I'm sorry, okay?" Eloise's eyes filled with something that looked like fear. It startled Ashleigh. Something was going on with Eloise. Something she needed to get to the bottom of. "I'm sorry," Eloise continued, her eyes never leaving Ashleigh's face. "You just caught me at a bad time last night. I'm here now, and I want to hear all about Patrick and your date." She pulled a chair out and sat down beside her.

Ashleigh groaned quietly to herself; it was more of a growl. If there was one thing worse than Eloise showing up now, it was Eloise showing up and talking about Patrick in front of Ford.

"Patrick?" Ford asked, sounding eager to hear the story.

"She had a date," Eloise explained.

"Can you not talk about me as if I'm not here!" Ashleigh cried. "Ford doesn't need to know about my date."

"On the contrary ..." Ford's eyes widened as they locked gazes.

"On the contrary *what*?" Ashleigh hollered. He was interested in finding out what was going on with her, was he? Wanted the low down? The gossip?

There was no way he was getting anything.

She glared at him, causing him to sit back like a wounded dog. She turned to her sister. "Save the dramatics, Eloise. It's fine. It's okay. You don't look so well yourself. I'll come over later and we can talk, but you look like you're falling apart and if you miss Liam that much you should go and see him and make up with him."

"This isn't about me," Eloise protested. "I'm sorry I wasn't there for you yesterday but you can tell me everything now—"

"It doesn't matter. You never are. Nobody is ever there for me," Ashleigh snarled. She wanted these two people gone. She wanted to be left alone. What she didn't want was Eloise sitting here listening to her while Ford took in all her news. She would not play to this audience of two.

"You're in such a bad mood, Ash. What's going on?" Ford asked.

"Oh, really? You think so?" Ashleigh snapped back. This morning had gone from an interruption by Ford to a full-blown drama with Eloise's arrival. Ashleigh resented the intrusion and wanted an end to it all.

She wanted them gone. Inhaling a few long, deep breaths she stared at her rosebushes. She needed to calm down. Most times, she had a reservoir of patience, but lately, it had run dry. She couldn't break down now, she couldn't show Ford that she, like Eloise, was slowly unraveling. That her future seemed bleak, once more, and that she longed to escape again, to return to Europe to visit the places she'd missed out on last time.

But that dream was slowly slipping out of her hands again. She wouldn't be able to go away. She couldn't leave the business in Ginny's hands, not with Eloise being the way she was. Irritation pinched her thoughts. Once again, it all fell to her; the responsibility and the fixing of everything.

She was sick of it.

"It's not you," she heard Eloise whisper to Ford, "She's angry with me."

"I think Ash needs some time to herself," she heard Ford say. "I just wanted to see how you were," he said, standing up and placing a hand on her shoulder. She forced herself to not stare up at him.

Eloise got up, too. "I'll leave with you."

Ashleigh still didn't turn to acknowledge them.

They disappeared quickly, obviously having taken the hint, and she was left alone, just how she wanted it to be, only, now that they were gone, she didn't want to be by herself anymore.

CHAPTER 33

GINNY

"We're staying here?" Daisy covered her mouth with her hand, her wide-open eyes were filled with delight.

"Ryan, really?" Ginny gasped as the car pulled up outside the log cabin. "You booked *this*?" She stared in awe at the log cabin that would be their home for the next few days. The quaint home was nestled in lush greenery, with no neighbors and no other buildings in sight.

Ryan had kept it all a secret, and hadn't told her what he'd booked and where they were going. She'd assumed it was a hotel room, a big family room, but as they drove up and he parked the car outside, she was speechless. She looked around, surveying their surroundings; there were tall trees everywhere. It took her breath away.

A large porch graced the front of the house, with a couple of rocking chairs and a large swing seat. The wooden railing around the porch area was adorned with hanging flower baskets. She imagined having her morning coffee out here, very early in the morning before the children woke up. Just her and Ryan talking about their plans for the day. For their lives, even.

It was beautiful. "Ryan, this is … I'm at a loss for words. It's too much. Where did you find this?" She gawked at him in awe. She didn't want to think about the cost. This wasn't a room. It was a whole house.

He reached for her hand. "It's not too much. I wanted to make it up to you. I wanted it to be something for us to remember when we look back."

"Look back?" She suddenly felt fearful. Was he fed up? Going back to Vanessa? Was this goodbye? Deep down she knew it wasn't. This was her knee jerk reaction to anything good that happened in her life. So much goodness, so many lovely things. She wasn't used to it after the year she'd had. It would take some getting used to, being able to accept, without doubt, the good things that came in her life.

"When we're old and remembering our youth, and how we met, and what we did." He squeezed her hand.

"Daddy! I love this," Daisy cried excitedly from the back.

"I'm glad you do, Dee. Come on, let's get out and explore our new home!"

"I wanna go inside!" Daisy cried.

Ginny smiled at her. "Let's go inside."

They got out of the car. Ryan picked up a sleeping Benjy and carried him in his arms. It was a miracle her baby boy hadn't woken up given the screeching levels of Daisy's excitement. "I'll grab the luggage later," he said. "I want to show you the house."

They followed Ryan inside, and it took her breath away again. She walked around, examining the wide-open living space. It had a stone fireplace that promised warm, cozy nights, though they wouldn't need it in the middle of summer. The décor was a mix of modern comfort and rustic charm. It was light and airy, with lots of floor to ceiling windows. Soft plush couches looked inviting, and the hand-woven rugs added warmth and character to the surroundings which were further embellished by antique furnishings. This was so much better than a hotel. So much more. So beautiful and amazing. She was running out of superlatives. Daisy ran around, super excited.

"Ryan, this is beautiful!" Ginny gushed, the thought of them living here for a few days was too much to take in. This was her dream home. And time with Ryan and the children. Had life really worked out so well for her? So quickly and easily, it felt like.

This was more than she had ever imagined. Her body relaxed and she felt lighter in herself. She was so glad to be away from the house and from her sisters who had been so weird around one another at work. They weren't talking, and Ash seemed off with Eloise who looked even more tired and ill these days. Ginny made a note to check in on her when they returned. She needed to have a one-to-one girlie talk with Eloise because Ashleigh could be hard and unsympathetic when it came to these things.

Poor Eloise.

Ginny pushed the thoughts away, determined to enjoy an amazing few days here. It didn't even matter if they never left this cozy log cabin and stayed inside the entire time. Still holding Benjy in his arms, Ryan slipped an arm around her waist. "Like it?"

"I love it." She put her arm around his waist and tilted her head against his shoulder.

This man.

This man was precious, and good, and hers. He was a keeper, and she was the luckiest woman on the planet. In her darkest times, fate had brought them together. With Ryan she'd found light in her tunnel of despair, and she had finally moved to a better place, with a better person, and a future that blossomed before her.

Ryan had thought of everything. The house was on one level. No safety gates required, no need to worry about Benjy trying to make his way up the steps. "How did you find this?" she asked again in wonderment. "Where? How?"

In answer, he placed a kiss on her lips. "Come and see our room," he whispered, still carrying Benjy in his arms.

"You'll need to put him down," she said, wanting Benjy to get a good sleep, seeing that his schedule had been messed up ever since they'd been on the road.

"First let me show you the kids' room. We can put Benjy down in there."

"Yay! Our room!" Daisy's excited shriek woke up Benjy. His eyes flickered open, and then his lips wobbled, and he started to cry.

"Oh, baby, baby." Ginny took him from Ryan.

"Dee, you've woken Benjy up." Ryan sounded annoyed.

"It's okay. It was about time for him to get up." She lifted Benjy into her arms and he immediately turned quiet, then looked around, as if realizing that he was in a new place.

"Benjy, come!" Daisy, still deliriously excited, grabbed his foot, the only part of him she could reach when he was in Ginny's arms. He let out a happy shriek at seeing his favorite person, and Ginny's heart filled like a balloon, overflowing with so much joy she thought it would burst. These children loved one another so much. For Benjy, Daisy was his world. He needed Ginny for the basic things such as food and comfort, but it was Daisy who made him roar with laughter. Around her, he would shake his arms and legs with excitement, wanting to go to her. Daisy was the big sister to her son.

"Give us a tour of the place, Dee. Just walk around and show us all the rooms one by one," Ryan suggested. Daisy happily obliged, opening doors to the different rooms, the washrooms, and study, and reading room, and then the various bedrooms.

"That's your room," Ryan told her, as she stopped by one of the doors. Daisy opened the door and ran inside. "Bunk beds!" She squealed as she looked around the spacious room which had two bunk beds and a crib. "I wanna sleep on the top. Can Benjy sleep on the bottom?" She stared up at them with huge pleading puppy dog eyes, then pointed to the bottom bunk and without waiting for an answer, told Benjy, "Benjy, that's your bed. You're gonna sleep there." Benjy babbled back right on cue. Daisy could have said the sky was falling and her son would have laughed with her.

"Not now, sweetie," Ginny replied. "Benjy's too little to sleep on a bed. He'll be in the crib, over there." She pointed to the nice, big crib near the window. "Won't that be exciting?"

Ryan patted his daughter's head. "Later on, when Benjy's older, you can share bunk beds then."

Ginny smiled to herself, feeling ridiculously happy.

Later on.

The future no longer filled her with dread. She welcomed it. She was ready. Like she would be tonight. Their first time.

Ryan placed his hand on the small of her back. "Do you like it?" She blushed, hoping he hadn't read her mind. She turned to him. "I love this place. This is so much more than I imagined, and I've been imagining this weekend in my head for a long time."

"Yeah?" His mischievous smile made her blush even more.

"Not about … *that*," she whispered quickly, letting Ryan take Benjy from her. "About … about … uh … just being away from my sisters, and being in a new place, just the four of us."

He didn't stop grinning, and with Benjy who was rocking excitedly in his arms, he pressed a kiss on her head. "Let me show you our room."

Our room.

She was probably beetroot red by now. He took her hand and led her to a room across the hallway, then he opened the door. Inside was a huge bed, and fireplace, a couple of lamps, a bookshelf and a dresser. Huge windows looked onto acres of greenery. This would be a memorable place for a first night.

"What do you think?" Ryan asked, obviously proud of himself.

"This is awesome!" Daisy ran around the room in excitement. Ginny stared at the large bed. "I'll get lost in that," she whispered, feeling Ryan's heated gaze on her. Seconds passed as they stared at one another. Longing wrapped itself around her heart like vines, crushing the thorns that had sprung up to keep trespassers out. Ryan had changed her world, and for the better. He set Benjy down on the floor, before whispering, "You'll never be lost. You'll always have me." He left a kiss in that highly sensitive space between her ear and her neck, and she arched her back instinctively. "No picking him up, Dee," he told Daisy over Ginny's shoulder. The man had eyes everywhere. Ginny spun around as Daisy crouched to the floor beside Benjy. "You're too small yet, sweetie." Ginny picked Benjy up. "He'll be walking and running soon." She stroked the girl's face, wanting to make her feel better. "Come and help me to unpack, sweetie."

"Good idea," agreed Ryan. "We should unpack, eat something, then go out. We can go on a short hike and there are some children's play areas nearby. What do you say, Dee?"

Daisy exploded in excitement, and Benjy followed suit.

~

They settled in quickly. Ginny unpacked while Ryan fed Benjy. They finished off the rest of the food that Ginny had packed for the trip, before leaving for a hike through the woods. Ryan wore a baby carrier, and strapped Benjy in.

The hike was scenic and short. Nothing too taxing, which also meant they could stop and admire their surroundings. Nearby was a children's play area, where Daisy had a lot of fun. Benjy was too little to go on many things, and could only go on the baby swings, but he seemed happy enough to be in Daisy's orbit. Every ride she went on, she involved Benjy, sometimes if only to yell out at him and tell him to watch her.

And he would. Happily.

"I'm so happy," Ginny gushed, watching Ryan pushing Benjy on the swings.

"You've forgiven me?"

She bit her lower lip, feeling silly for the way she'd been with him after he'd visited Vanessa.

"You know I did before we even came here." They'd spoken and cleared things up. It was so good being able to talk out their problems, clear up miscommunication and resolve disagreements.

It hadn't always been like this for her. Ben had upset her so many times, but Ryan, perhaps because he was older, or just because he was Ryan, was different.

This was different. She felt it in her bones, the love she had for this man, what she felt for him and his daughter, and how she secretly imagined spending a life with them.

They had a great day, and when they came back it was bathtime for the children, then dinner. Daisy fell asleep on the sofa and Benjy in his rocker. Ryan picked Daisy up and put her to bed, while Ginny laid Benjy in the crib.

Without the children around they were free now and had time to themselves. Ginny suddenly felt nervous. Ryan walked towards her as she hovered in the hallway, leaving the door to the children's room ajar.

"Hey." He enveloped her in his arms and pressed a kiss against her forehead.

"Hey." She was nervous, and excited at the same time. Ryan stroked his finger along her face.

"I started the fire."

"You did?" It wasn't cold, but she felt goosebumps all over her skin.

"It's romantic," he whispered in her ear. She shivered, as he cupped her face. "I wanted it to be romantic for you, something you'd never forget."

She looked up, and let him kiss her, and knew that for as long as she lived, she would never forget any of this.

ELOISE

Ginny sounded so happy. Eloise couldn't believe the exuberance in her voice.

Her little sister had called to tell her they were leaving their log cabin—Ginny had been sending them numerous photos over the weekend—and she wanted Eloise to be at the house when they all returned.

Eloise had tried to get out of it, but Ginny insisted, saying 'Benjy missed her and needed to see his aunt.' Ginny could be silly like that, but Eloise had no intention of letting her sister down. Not the one sister who was nice to her and cared. She didn't relish the thought of going back to Ashleigh's place. Not after that time last week when Ford had been there and Ashleigh had been in a spiteful mood.

Besides, there were other weightier matters on Eloise's mind. She'd called Liam, knowing that she had to tell him her news. It was the right thing to do, but the call had gone to his voicemail. Left feeling disheartened, unsure if he'd done that intentionally, she decided not to call him again for a few days.

The man had a right to know, but now he was at the back of her list of people to tell. She was desperate to tell someone. She couldn't keep it to herself, this deep secret—the same secret Ginny had hidden from Eloise once upon a time. Remembering how things had been for Ginny, she couldn't believe she was in the same predicament now. Same, but different.

How life unraveled. It was mysterious and mystical. Timings and cycles.

Things hadn't been right between her and Ashleigh, and the strain of it at work was too much for her to bear. It was too much on top of the nausea she was experiencing. Now, standing at the door of the main house, she rested her hand over her belly and took a deep breath as she rang the doorbell. She still had a key to the house, but it didn't seem right to turn up unannounced.

Ashleigh opened the door. She had a questioning look on her face; almost as if she were wondering what the heck Eloise was doing here so late in the evening. Eloise braved a smile. "Ginny told me to come over. Is she not back yet?" she asked, even though she knew her sister might be an hour yet.

"I expect she'll be here soon enough. They left a few hours ago," Ashleigh responded, if a little stiffly. Eloise followed her sister inside, and they made small talk, the kind of small talk they didn't make in front of the assistants and the customers back at the shop.

"What did Ford want?" Eloise asked, curious to discover the reason behind his visit. It spoke volumes that she hadn't found out sooner. She and Ashleigh had purposely stayed out of one another's way at work.

"He said he wanted to see Benjy."

"Doesn't he know Ginny always goes to see Ryan at the weekend?"

"You'd think so." Ashleigh sat back down on the couch and flicked the TV remote. Eloise sat down tentatively on a different couch. She watched her sister, hoping to see some softness instead of the frown that had taken up permanent residence there.

"What?" Ashleigh asked, catching Eloise staring at her. Her tone startled Eloise. "Why are you still angry with me?" she asked. "I'm dealing with a few things."

"It's been weeks, Eloise. The answer to your problems is sitting in his own place being miserable as well, I expect."

"I called him."

Ashleigh blinked a few times. "And?"

"He didn't pick up."

At this something that looked like pity crossed Ashleigh's features. "He didn't?"

"He didn't."

"Maybe he was busy," Ashleigh suggested. "He's been working on Ford's new office and he probably has a lot of work at the moment."

"Or he didn't want to take my call." The idea of that hit Eloise like a baseball bat. Placing a hand across her stomach, she willed herself not to break down and cry, as she'd done ever since she'd found out she was pregnant. "There's something else," she said, getting ready to jump off that cliff and tell Ashleigh. Unlike Ginny, she couldn't keep this secret all to herself.

"What?" Ashleigh frowned, expecting bad news.

"It's ... uh ... it's just that ... uh." She couldn't bring herself to say it; the words that had changed her life—and no doubt would indirectly change Ashleigh's—had difficulty leaving her mouth. Before she could string a coherent sentence together, she heard a cacophony of noise; Benjy's shrieks and Daisy's laughter. Then the sound of someone trying to hush them.

"They're back!" Ashleigh cried, standing up and walking towards the door.

At that very moment Ginny, Ryan and the kids tumbled in, their beaming, happy faces staring back at her and Ashleigh.

"You all look very happy—" Ashleigh started to say.

"Eloise!" Ginny's face lit up even more. "You're here."

"You told me to come." Eloise folded her arms over her stomach protectively and wondered why Ginny was staring at them both in wonderment. This was most unusual.

"I'm engaged!" Ginny cried. "I couldn't wait to tell you both. Ryan proposed and I said yes!"

The words were like a thunderbolt striking Eloise's body. Ginny engaged? How could that be? Feeling as if she'd been punched, she placed her hands over her stomach protectively. She'd have faltered back a few steps if the wall hadn't been in the way.

"Engaged?!" Ashleigh cried, flying to Ginny's side she threw her arms around her. "You proposed?" she asked Ryan, who nodded, a huge grin on his face. Daisy jumped up and down in excitement, and Benjy watched her, howling with laughter, finding her achingly funny.

"*Again?* Isn't it too soon?" The words flew out of Eloise's mouth before she could stop herself. The air suddenly fell silent.

"It's the best news!" Ashleigh cried, hugging Ginny all over again.

"Yes," Eloise forced herself to sound more jubilant. Ginny was engaged, and Ryan was a good man. He was perfect for her. Deep down inside she was happy for her sister, she really was, but the news made her want to curl into a ball and cry, and she hated herself for it.

CHAPTER 35

ASHLEIGH

Ginny was engaged.

Ashleigh jumped up from her chair and rushed over to Ginny's side. "Engaged?" She threw her arms around her as tears welled up in her eyes. "You proposed?" she asked Ryan, trying to hold herself together. This was such a happy occasion, a monumental moment, something to celebrate, and she was overwhelmed, yet sad and happy and all over the place.

Ryan beamed at her, his smile reaching from ear to ear.

"I'm so happy for you, Gin!" She hugged her tightly, holding the memory of her parents in her mind's eye. She was overcome by an overwhelming sense of joy. Her sister was with a good man, and would be looked after.

"Ash." Ginny gently prised herself apart and looked into her eyes. "Why are you crying?"

"I'm not." She wiped her eyes, sounding sniffly.

"Ashleigh." Ryan touched her arm. "This was supposed to make you happy."

"I *am* happy," she insisted, breaking out into a laugh-cry. She moved her hands, gesticulating between Ginny and her new fiancé. "This is the best news. It really is. I couldn't be happier."

"Again? Isn't it too soon?" Eloise asked, her words splintering the bubble of happiness. Determined not to let her sister's sour reaction ruin the moment, Ashleigh ignored Eloise and threw her arms around Ginny again, to reassure her sister. "It's great news! The best."

"Yes." That came from Eloise, but she didn't look as if she meant it. Ashleigh wished she would just leave and take her negativity with her. With her lips pursed together, she held Ginny's hand. "I'm so happy. Another wedding!" she cried, hoping her excitement would drown out Eloise's lack of enthusiasm.

They turned to look at Eloise who stood quietly watching from where she sat. Ashleigh's anger spiked. What was wrong with the woman? Was Eloise still so wrapped up in her misery that she couldn't even find the decency to congratulate Ginny and Ryan? "Don't mind her," Ashleigh whispered close to Ginny's ear so that no one else heard.

This was the best news and it was about time their small family had some good things happening. Apart from Benjy's birth, it felt like the Roses had been dealing with nothing but obstacles and curveballs. "Ryan." Ashleigh moved towards her soon-to-be brother-in-law. "Congratulations, and thank you for taking Ginny off our hands. At last!" She looked upwards and placed her hands together as if in prayer, before glancing at Ginny to make sure her sister wasn't offended and had taken this in jest, as she intended.

Ginny didn't look the slightest bit offended. If anything, she was busy admiring her ring.

The ring.

"You already bought her a ring?" Up until that moment, it hadn't occurred to Ashleigh that this had been planned.

"You planned this?" Eloise asked. Ashleigh was aghast that her sister still hadn't expressed any happiness at the news. She was about to say something when Ryan told them that he'd been planning to propose to Ginny ever since he'd visited Vanessa. Being with his ex-wife had shown him so clearly the contrast between what he once had and no longer wanted, and what he now had and could no longer live without. He felt blessed for Ginny and Benjy and the new lease of life they had given him and Daisy. Thankful to have found them, he didn't want to let them go. "But it was something Ford said, that really cemented my decision for me."

"Ford?" The mere mention of that man made Ashleigh's breath hitch. "What did he say?" She struggled to keep her voice level.

"Oh, yes. That was sweet of Ford." Ginny snuggled up to him, her head resting just under his neck. They looked like they were joined at the hip. So cute. So in love. So blissfully happy.

"Was Liam there?" Eloise asked.

"Where? On vacation with us?" Ryan asked, confused.

"No, when Ford said whatever you're about to tell us."

Ryan frowned, then nodded. "Yes. He was."

"What did Ford say?" Ashleigh asked again, irritated by Eloises's interruption.

"Something about how once you find 'the one', to never let them go because you might lose them and never get them back."

"Awww," whispered Ginny, breathlessly. She looked up at

Ryan, her expression radiating joy, and her eyes so shiny, Ashleigh thought she might cry.

"That's sweet …" Ashleigh placed a hand on her chest. Ryan was all sorts of wonderful and she was thankful that this caring and amazing man was going to be a part of their family. Ginny couldn't have asked for a better husband, or a better father for Benjy. She put an arm around Ginny and Ryan and they group-hugged. Casting a quick glance in Eloise's direction, her heart sank. Eloise looked miserable.

Can't you be happy for them? Ashleigh was tempted to wrench her sister out of the room and give her a stern telling off, but this wasn't the time or the place for that. "I'm floating on air hearing all this good news from you two. I thought it was just a short break away and nothing more than that," she said, determined to keep the conversation flowing.

"It *was* just a short break away. That's what I thought, too." Ginny laid her palm against Ryan's face. "I never thought I'd come back engaged. He surprised me completely."

Ryan looked at her as if she were the only woman on the planet. The only one for him. Ashleigh sighed with happiness, then glanced at Eloise again, and her heart plummeted. Her younger sister was standing there, wringing her hands and saying nothing. She might as well have been a part of the furniture. Ashleigh sensed that even Ginny didn't know what to make of Eloise's lackluster reaction.

"How did he do it? The proposal?" Ashleigh was itching to know.

"He just … one morning we were having coffee outside on the porch. It was *very* early, about five in the morning, and the kids were sleeping. The sky was a vanilla pink in color. It looked beautiful. It was quiet, so peaceful out there. We were sitting in the middle of a forest. All I heard was birdsong."

Ashleigh sighed. They'd painted the picture perfectly. "And?" The proposal, she wanted to hear about the proposal.

"And I asked Ryan if he wanted another cup of coffee." Ginny had tears in her eyes as she recounted the story.

"And I said, I want something else." There was a huge grin on Ryan's face. "I said, I want ... and I got down on my knee and pulled out my ring."

A tear rolled down Ginny's cheek. Ashleigh sighed, tears forming in her eyes. Ginny continued the story. "And he said, 'I want to marry you, Genevieve. There's nothing more I want than for you to be my wife. Will you—'"

"And before I could finish, she jumped up and screamed 'Yes!'" said Ryan. They looked at one another, saying nothing, sharing secret memories they probably wanted to keep to themselves.

"That's so *beautiful*." Ashleigh felt so ridiculous happy, she thought she would burst out in tears herself.

"Are you feeling okay, Eloise?" Ginny asked. "You don't look so well."

Eloise smiled weakly, making Ashleigh wonder if something else was going on. It wasn't like Eloise to mope around for too long and not get up and do things. "I'm ... yeah ... I don't feel so good." She walked over and hugged Ginny, then Ryan, finally congratulating them. She'd taken her sweet time to do it. Then she suddenly announced that she was leaving.

Ashleigh didn't want to keep Ryan and Daisy too long, but Daisy was watching TV, and Benjy was asleep, and she wanted to know all about the proposal, all the little details, because listening to the happy stories from other people's lives sure beat having to deal with Eloise.

∼

She and Darcie were having lunch at the diner again. Eloise hadn't come to work, *again*, and Ashleigh's patience was wearing thin.

She kept quiet about Eloise being moody and miserable, and was most eager to share what little good news they had in the family. She told Darcie about Ginny's engagement.

"So fast?" Darcie asked, not one to keep her thoughts to herself.

Ashleigh had wondered this, at first, for a fleeting moment, but she no longer had any reservations. "It's not even been a year since they met but it feels like Ryan has been a part of our family forever. More than that though, it feels like he and Ginny have been together for the longest time. He's strong, a rock, a great person and a fantastic father, but what's even more endearing to watch is how he is with Ginny. How she lights up around him, how the smile sets on his face from the moment he sees her, and it doesn't dim. "

"And the age gap?" Darcie asked. "That doesn't bother you?"

"What age gap?" Ashleigh threw back. "The eight years? Barely notice it. Ginny seems wiser around him." She shrugged. "Ben was as young as Ginny, and he was so immature. He had a whole lot of growing up to do until ... sadly ..." She couldn't finish the sentence. "Ryan is everything Ginny needs, and she completes him. I don't believe in miracles, Darcie, but these two were meant to be together."

Darcie beamed a smile at her. "That's great news, Ash. Truly it is. He seems like a nice guy, though you can never tell until you start living together for a while and discover all their flaws and mannerisms."

"There's that," Ashleigh agreed. She'd never had that experience, and now she found that the older she became, she liked her own company. She was getting particular and could be cranky at times, and she wasn't sure, after all these years of living only with her sisters, how she might find it to live with someone. How cranky and irritable she'd get if she had a partner, a lover, a soulmate. "But Ryan and Ginny fit together like a glove and I couldn't be happier for them."

"I'm glad they have your blessing," Darcie remarked, drily. "Are you over Patrick yet?"

Ashleigh had already told her friend about her disaster date the day after. "I was over him before we left the restaurant."

She'd been so disappointed in Patrick. She could see now that everything about him seemed phony. Well, maybe not *everything*, but enough things. And maybe phony was too strong a word. He wasn't phony in that he'd tried to scam her. He just hadn't been authentic. Of all the qualities Ashleigh most liked in a partner, honesty and truth were high on the list.

Pretending to buy flowers for her had soured her impression of Patrick. Darcie was appalled when Ashleigh told her. She had a sneaky feeling that her friend was keeping an eye on her. Today's lunch was further confirmation of that.

CHAPTER 36

GINNY

"**W**ant me to have a word with Liam?" Ryan asked. He had arranged to meet with Ford and Liam later that evening, to tell them of their good news.

"I would rather you didn't. I don't want to spread news to him about Eloise, not until I've spoken to her first."

She finished running a soft baby brush through Benjy's hair. They'd been discussing Eloise's strange reaction to their engagement news and both agreed that Eloise not only didn't look too well, but didn't seem like her usual self.

"That's a good idea. I guess you need to speak to her first." Ryan glanced at his watch. "Are you ready, Dee?" he shouted.

"Coming, daddy!" Her shout floated back. Daisy was off to a summer day camp this week. The summer break was flying by fast. Ginny marveled at how their lives had changed over the last few months, at the events which bookended those lovely summer days. Ryan had moved into his new place around the time school ended, and here she was, engaged, a few weeks' before Daisy returned to school.

"I wonder what their reaction will be," said Ryan, picking Benjy up from his highchair and kissing his head.

Ginny giggled. "I wish I could be a fly on the wall."

"Why don't you come along?" he suggested. "We can tell them together."

She didn't feel that this was a great idea, not now, while Eloise was not her usual self. "And bring Ashleigh and Eloise along, so that we're one big happy group of six?" She sighed. She couldn't see that working out, not with the other two couples still not on great talking terms with one another. "It's good that you're going out with the guys tonight. It's nice for you to get to know them without us girls being in tow. Besides, I need to check up on Eloise. I'll try to persuade her to come to the diner with me and hopefully she'll open up more if it's just me and her."

"Are you okay with me telling them we're engaged?"

She laughed. "Ryan, you don't need my permission about these things. Of course you can tell them. It's great news. Share it!"

"Okay." He bent down and kissed her on the lips. "It's a shame we can't all hang out together," he said, turning pensive.

"Hopefully we will be able to, one day." She didn't know when that would be. Months or years in the making. It was a shame because they were all so good together.

He bobbed Benjy up and down and the little boy giggled. She was filled with immense gratitude. Ryan was a wonderful father, not only to Daisy, but to her little boy. "I love that you're making friends and doing things on your own." Ryan seemed to have settled in nicely in Whisper Falls and life was working out for them both.

"They're good guys. I like their company."

"I also need to tell Talia." She wanted to meet her face to face rather than to break the news to her over the phone. "And Beth." They looked at one another. Happy times. The breaking of good news to friends and family. If only Eloise had been as elated. The fact that she wasn't had given Ginny a sleepless night. Something was up with her sister and she was going to find out what it was.

"Benjy where are you?" Daisy shouted, her voice was nearer now and Ginny guessed that she was probably looking for Benjy in his room. Her son wriggled happily in Ryan's arms at the sound of Daisy's voice, wanting to be let loose on the floor, so that he could try to crawl to his favorite person. He'd learned to crawl at the log cabin, just as they were about to leave to come home. His first crawl was another memory to add to the priceless moments on that unforgettable trip. Ryan set him down carefully on the floor and they watched as he tried to push off with one leg and move forward.

"Go on, son. You can do it," Ryan said softly, crouching down. "Yeah you can. Come on, Benjy." Benjy wrinkled his face at Ryan, then giggled. Ginny watched them, her heart overflowing with love. Then Daisy came flying in and immediately stopped as she saw Benjy on the floor. She got down on all fours, mimicking Benjy, and making funny faces and doing silly things, anything to make him laugh. Ginny held out her hand and stared at her ring happily. It glistened in the sunlight pouring through the windows. The life she was now living was like a miracle.

A dream come true.

A manifestation of her deepest desires. To belong, and to have a family. "You love that ring, don't you?" Ryan asked, sidling up to her.

"I'm never taking it off." She pressed her hand to her chest. Ryan looked like he wanted to swoop down and claim her mouth again, and truthfully, she was thinking the same but Daisy rushed up to her and immediately put her arms around Ginny's waist, burying her face in Ginny's stomach. "What's that for?" Ginny asked, surprised.

"Because you're my new mommy!"

Over the little girl's head, Ginny looked at Ryan wondering how best to deal with this situation. Ryan didn't come to her rescue. "I won't be your mommy, sweetie. I'll be more like your … *stepmom*."

Daisy's eyes, usually so wide and mischievous, were now flat. Like the light had dimmed. "I don't want a stepmom. Stepmoms are nasty."

Ginny chortled. "It's not like how it is in Cinderella, sweetie."

Ryan finally stepped in. "It's not like that at all, Dee. Your mommy will still be your mommy, always."

Ginny crouched down so that her face was level with Daisy's. She smoothed the girl's hair down, and lovingly cupped her cheek. "And I'll be …" She was at a loss for what to say.

"Can I call you mommy?" Daisy asked.

It didn't matter about tags and labels. Daisy was her daughter, and that was the end of that. Vanessa could try as hard as she wanted to be a thorn in their sides, but Ginny no longer cared about that. "Sure you can, sweetie. Sure, you can."

LIAM

"Have you heard the news?" Ford asked. They were waiting in the bar for Ryan to arrive.

"What news?"

"Ginny and Ryan got engaged. He proposed and she accepted."

Liam jolted, as if he'd been punched in the shoulder. "You serious?"

"It's true. Darcie told me this morning."

"Well. Sonofagun. He beat me to it."

Ford chortled. "Heck, at the rate you're going, son, *I'll* beat you to it."

"You're looking to get married?" Liam examined Ford's reaction. Seemed like everyone was ready to get married. He'd been so ready to pop the question to Elle but he'd messed it all up.

"I didn't say that. Marriage, no, it's not on the cards for me. I can't even think about it. Don't want to think about it," Ford replied, looking away.

"Too old, huh?" Liam forced a grin, trying to push down the sadness that scaled the walls of his chest. He tried to hold that plastic smile a little longer. Knew he'd lost his opportunity and worse, that he might never get another chance. "I'm happy for the guy, and those two make a nice couple."

"You and Eloise make a nice couple."

"Will you stop talking about me and Elle? There is no me and Elle." Though he'd been thinking about it. He'd been poised to call her so many times but she was so moody and vicious sometimes, with her tongue, and her words, and he didn't know what had come over her. He didn't want to take any more verbal hits from her. But he missed her. He missed her badly. He'd even set off to drive over to hers a couple of times, but each time he neared her place, he took a detour.

Couldn't do it.

Couldn't tell the woman he loved that he wanted to spend the rest of his life with her.

"You called her yet?"

He'd been wondering when Ford would get around to asking him. "No." He sucked in a breath.

Ryan walked into the bar just then. Ford elbowed him in the ribs. "You're not supposed to know. That's why Ryan arranged this, to tell us. Pretend to be surprised."

CHAPTER 37

ELOISE

She had to snap out of this. It wasn't doing her or the baby any good, her languishing in misery and feeling bad.

She was happy for Ginny. Happy that at last things had turned around for her younger sister, and that the beautiful future her sister deserved was finally hers to have, but Eloise's life was in flux. She placed a hand over her flat stomach, still shocked by the news of her pregnancy. Hard to believe that a life was growing inside her. A year from now, she would have a little baby reliant on her. How was she going to look after a baby when she couldn't even look after herself?

They had found one another; Ginny, Benjy, Ryan and Daisy. It was heartwarming to see. In contrast, her own situation seemed so dire, but now she had to make a decision. Liam hadn't picked up or called her back. He needed to know. He was obviously still in his silly mood, but she had to look beyond that. Maybe there was no way of getting back together —and she didn't want to, if he was going to be this whole other horrible person she no longer recognized.

But she couldn't keep this news secret any longer. She needed to tell people—Liam, her sisters and Beth. She had to forge ahead with her new role in life as a single mother.

How strange and bittersweet that Ginny had been in this position a year ago, and now things had turned around for her.

There was hope. The future need not be bleak, even though it seemed like it right now. Eloise was determined not to rely on a man to fix her problems. She would figure out how to take care of herself and the baby.

But first, she needed to go grocery shopping. She'd been so deep in her malaise that she'd let go of the usual everyday routines and chores. She'd neglected herself and the baby and she couldn't do that anymore. She was responsible for another life and she needed to take better care of herself or, as Ashleigh had said, she needed to 'woman up,'

She opened the door to leave, but jumped at the sight of Liam standing on the doorstep, ready to knock. She stumbled back a few steps. "You scared me," she cried.

Liam looked apologetic. "Sorry. I didn't mean to." He also looked a sight.

"I called you." She hurled the words at him like an accusation.

"You did? When?" He had the audacity to look surprised.

"A few days ago."

"You called me?" He sounded hopeful, even a little animated at the news as he fished out his phone.

"I did."

"I didn't know." He rifled through his cell phone frantically, then his face turned red. "Elle." His mouth fell open, he stared at her with big, sorry eyes. "I'm sorry. I ... I didn't realize."

"You didn't realize I'd called you?"

"I didn't hear it, and then later I obviously didn't check. The guys and I were on a big roofing job. I swear to you I didn't hear my phone ring, and usually I have it on silence anyway when we're working on a site. I must have just forgot."

Forgot? Just forgot?

Did he expect her to believe that? She'd been checking her phone constantly in case he'd texted or called her back. In case she'd missed anything from him. And he'd had his phone on silence. How completely different they were.

"It might be a guy thing. I tend not to rely on my cell phone too much." If this was his idea of an explanation, it was pathetic.

His words incensed her. "Why are you here now?" she snapped.

His gaze swept all over her face slowly. "I ... I wanted to see how you were. I heard about Ryan and Ginny, about their engagement. That's great news, for them. I wanted to make sure you were okay."

"Why wouldn't I be okay?"

"You're not okay." His voice was gentle. His eyes soft. "Can I come in?"

She didn't answer but moved back to let him in. He stepped inside, and looked around gingerly. It felt like a lifetime ago since he'd last been here. It seemed like they'd been other people in happier times back then.

"I'm sorry, Elle. I'm sorry for being such a jerk, for behaving the way I did at Griffin's party."

This was music to her ears. What had taken him so long? She folded her arms over her stomach protectively. "You waited all this time to apologize about that?"

He put his hands behind his back, then took of his ball cap, then put his hands and the ball cap behind his back. "I've been a mess without you, Elle. What took me so long? Fear. I just needed to be sure."

"Of what?"

"That you wanted me."

What was he talking about? She couldn't fathom his train of thought. "I don't understand you. I don't understand why you suddenly changed the way you felt about me."

He looked at her, his mouth open, as if words were dangling on the tip of his tongue. "Is there someone else?" she asked, in a voice that was weak.

"What?" His sharp retort was as strong as the look of confusion on his face. "Someone else? Are you kidding me?" He stepped towards her. "Are you being serious, Elle?"

She swallowed, then lifted a shoulder. "I don't know what to think. Look at us. Why are we even in this mess?"

"You tell me," he said softly. "You're the one who said we needed time apart."

"Because of the way you behaved and—"

"I know. I know. I messed up." He threw hands up in the air in exasperation, then lifted a hand towards her as if he were about to touch her arm. He shoved his hands behind his back again as if this was the only way he could stop himself from touching her. "I love you, Elle." His green eyes bore into hers as he blew out a loud breath and shrugged, as if the situation were hopeless.

He still loved her.

She stared back at him for what seemed like an eternity, letting the words sink in but saying nothing. Mulling them over in her mind, letting them imprint on her heart. He was back to being the man she'd fallen in love with.

"I love you, Elle. I do. I've been miserable without you. I've been a complete mess, and I need you." The words hit. They hit hard. It was more than love. He needed her. Yearning and desperation were palpable in his voice. She was about to say something, when he said, "My life without you is empty, and dull, and flat. It's grey. It's so bleak. I messed up but I hope it's not too late. Tell me it's not too late. I don't want to lose you. But I need you to know that I was scared of not measuring up. Of not being enough—"

"What?" She hadn't heard right. What did he mean about not being enough?

"You're my world, Elle, and I just needed to know that I was yours."

Her breath choked in her throat as she tried to make sense of what he was telling her. What had she missed? "But I've always told you I love you—" she started to say.

"You have. You love me, but I needed to be sure that *I was enough*, that *I* was the one you want to be with."

"It is, and you are. What made you think otherwise?"

"I needed to know we could last the distance."

He wasn't making sense. "We have lasted the distance, Liam. We love being together, at least, I thought we did. I cherish every day we're together."

"You do?" He sounded as if he were hearing this for the first time. This was all so unexpected and out of character for him that she wondered if he had a twin and that maybe she was talking to him instead. "I wasn't sure I was good enough."

His words shocked her. "You weren't good enough? For what?"

"For you."

"For me? Liam I don't understand why you would think that. I love you. I love you for being you, but you're scaring me now. Have you forgotten things about us, and how we are together?"

"I just wanted to make sure."

"Make sure of what?" she cried. "What in God's name happened to us?"

"I don't know, Elle. I don't know. It's a scary thing—"

"What's a scary thing?" He was scaring her now.

"Just …" He shrugged again. "When I saw Alex, at the party, I felt even more out of place."

She'd known it would be about that. "He's an ex-boyfriend, and we only spent a few days together. He's not important."

"But I saw Griffin, and his friends, and I was in that environment with them. I felt like the biggest loser."

"Why?" She was trying to put herself in his shoes, and to see with his eyes. She'd tried to do that anyway, but his reaction, and what he was telling her, unnerved her. She'd had no idea that it had affected him that much. Had he felt so out of place and miserable? Had that been the event that caused all this?

"Just. I did. They're so clever and rich and it's a whole other world, Elle. It's a world that maybe you belong in and—"

"It's not," she said firmly. "I want to belong in *our* world, here, just you and me." She bit her lip, reminding herself not to give in and let her secret out just yet. She quietly contemplated all that he'd told her. It still didn't make complete sense, but it gave her a window into his thoughts, and that was a start. But still, she had to tread carefully.

"I want to make it up to you," he declared.

She nodded in agreement. "I'd like us to talk, honestly and openly."

They'd both been irritated and annoyed by one another, each feeding off the negativity of the other, and it was no wonder they were here, in this situation, apart and lonely.

"You look like you haven't slept." He cupped her face with his hand, his warm palm lying flat against her cheek. She loved the feel of it, loved that he kept it there. She pressed her face against it. "I've had a tough few nights," she said, slowly. "You know how it gets for me, every month."

He nodded, understanding. "Want me to get you anything? Want me to take care of you, because, Elle, that's what I want to do."

"I'll .. I'll be okay." He was back. Her caring, wonderful man.

Tell him. Tell him now.

"Are we good?" she asked, needing it in lights, in writing, in a contract. Needing solid proof and confirmation.

"We're good. I'm good. Are you?" he asked.

She felt better. Like she could breathe again. As if the deadweight on her chest had lifted. She nodded.

"I've missed you, Elle. I miss you and love you and I don't want to spend another moment away from you."

His words melted the block of ice that had formed like a fissure around her heart. Her body softened, her shoulders sagging slightly, and her spine was no longer ramrod straight. Even her jaw relaxed. It was as if the sun was shining again and causing the hardness to thaw.

"I miss you." She wondered when it would be the right moment to tell him the news. "And I love you, too. I want to be with you forever." She held her breath as she assessed his reaction. Wondered if the old Liam was back. He moved to her and wrapped his arms around her. She slid her arms around his waist and vowed never to let go.

"I can stay a while, if you want," he offered. "We don't have to talk or do anything. I can just stay here a little while ..."

"I would like that."

"Hey," he said, and waited for her to lift her head. She stared up at him and he dropped a kiss on her lips. She mewled against his mouth, a shiver vibrating through her at the feel and touch of him.

They were deep in a kiss when she felt something vibrate between them. A humming noise, low and intrusive. He didn't seem to hear it, and kissed her again. She moaned, having missed his touch for so long. "Is that … is that your …" Her hand skated over the back pocket of his jeans, where she discovered his vibrating cell phone. "It's your phone, Liam!"

Now she understood how he'd missed her phone call.

He groaned loudly, one hand still around her, the other fishing out his phone. He answered it and she heard loud frantic voices. Then Liam's face turned white. "One of my guys just fell from the roof!" He rushed off without even saying goodbye.

CHAPTER 38

ASHLEIGH

Ashleigh grumbled with irritation.

Ginny had only come in for a few hours this morning, and Eloise had left an hour before, leaving Ashleigh to tidy up the shop at the close of the working day. She tidied up the desk, arranging her diary and papers neatly, when Patrick's business card fell out of her diary and onto the counter. She stared at it, picked it up and threw it into the bin.

That was one chapter of her life she would rather forget about. She chortled to herself. Not even a chapter. A sentence more like. It had been fun, trying something different, but it hadn't brought her any happiness. What did make her happy was seeing Ginny. Her sister's beaming face made Ashleigh happy.

There had been no talk of wedding dates yet. Ginny said she wanted a long engagement, and Ryan seemed content to go along with whatever Ginny wanted. Daisy loved Ginny as much as Benjy did, and this made Ashleigh's heart even fuller. From bleak days to leading a happy life—no one deserved this more than Ginny. Ashleigh recalled all the bad things that had plagued her youngest sister, and now welcomed the start of a new era for her.

As for Eloise, her younger sister seemed more like her usual self today. She was already at the shop and working when Ashleigh got in.

Ashleigh sighed with contentment. Change was in the air.

Her sisters were pulling their weight more, Ginny especially. Ryan putting a ring on her finger seemed to have given her an added burst of motivation. Ginny had mentioned to Ashleigh that when Benjy turned one, she was going to send him to home daycare run by a retired schoolteacher Kayla had recommended. It would only be for a few days a week, so that she could focus on the business without a baby in tow. She planned to come to work for a few hours, and she also mentioned that she'd been taking work home. Ashleigh had noticed. Ginny insisted that she could work from home, around Benjy, 'when he takes his naps.'

Ashleigh was okay with that. Something in her had also changed; she was letting go of control, giving up the reins, letting her sisters take more responsibility. Maybe the problem had been with her all along. She'd been in charge and hadn't been so great at delegating, possibly, misguidedly, believing that she could do it so much better and quicker than her sisters.

Picking up her jacket and bag, she sighed to herself, her eyes falling on the tagline of their business, and the words which she so hated:

Where dreams begin.

The gold writing on the cream colored wall often caught her eye, and she thought nothing of it. But in this very moment, she stopped and stared at it. Maybe there was some truth to it. They weren't in the business of selling wedding dresses. They were in the business of selling hopes and dreams. And even though her own life might not have a wedding dress related event in it, she was the mistress of her own destiny. She alone decided how she would live her life, on her terms.

Nodding at the epiphany, she headed towards the door when the broad figure of a man standing outside jolted her. Her heart almost leapfrogged out of her mouth in fright.

Until she saw him and relaxed.

Ford.

Silk butterfly wings skittered inside her belly.

She'd been fleetingly worried that it might be Patrick. As she stared in confusion at Ford's face peering at her from outside, she found herself wondering why she was so relieved that it wasn't Patrick. And why she was so glad it was Ford.

A smile spread across her face.

Friends were forever.

They could be friends if nothing else. She pushed the heavy thought away and opened the door. "Let me guess, you came to see Benjy?"

"Are you leaving?" he asked, a silly question given the time of day, and the fact that she had her jacket and bag in her hands.

"I'm trying to."

He marched straight past her and walked inside.

"What are you doing? Benjy's not here," she cried. "Ginny only comes in the mornings."

"I know."

If he knew, then what was he doing here? She asked him as much. Her elation at seeing him was now replaced by impatience. She wanted to go home. She and Darcie had a dinner reservation at the same restaurant Patrick had taken her to and she didn't want to be late.

"Nothing. I was just passing by."

She narrowed her eyes at him. "You're always passing by."

"I can't seem to keep away from you."

His words held her speechless.

What?

"Benjy's not here," she repeated.

"Yeah, you already told me. But *you're* here." Mischief twinkled in his eyes as he leaned against the counter, one foot crossed over the other. Looking effortlessly laid back. This man was up to something. Images of the past rushed back, all the times she'd tried to talk to him, wanting to resolve their differences. He hadn't given her the time of day, and now he had the audacity to think he could just breeze into her life and demand the same; expect her to give him her full attention. Indignation swirled around her like an angry hurricane.

"I have a date, if you don't mind. What do you want?" she asked, haughtily. That smug, comfortable look suddenly vanished from his face. The muscles along his jaw tensed, and flexed, popping a nerve along his neck.

"You … have another … *date*?"

He didn't like that the idea of that.

Oh, how she would have loved to run her hand across that rugged face of his. She tried not to gawk for too long at him, remembering a time when she would place her hands on those big, broad shoulders, while her heart would swoon and dive and rise again like an errant balloon, waiting for the kiss that would soon follow.

Once upon a long time ago.

"I do. We're going back to the Allendium, where Patrick and I had our first date." Ford's brows pushed together like angry caterpillars. There it was again. Another flex of the jawline. "You might want to take Kayla there," she suggested.

"What would I want to do that for?" he shot back.

She didn't understand his mood. Or why he was here, or why they were having this conversation.

Unless ... no.

It couldn't be.

He couldn't be ... jealous, could he?

"It's what people do when they want to spend quality time with people they love," she explained. Where he'd been leaning against the counter, all casual and cool, he now straightened up.

"You're going with Patrick?" he asked, looking perplexed. "Is it love?

"I don't know, is it?" she asked, answering his question with a question. He was talking in riddles. The first mention of Kayla seemed to have thrown him off. It was the most direct she'd ever been with him in respect to his relationship and he hadn't said anything in response. Instead, he seemed determined to dig up information on Patrick. He swiped a hand across his forehead. "I heard ... Ginny said, Ryan said ... that ... that it didn't work out."

Oh, so he knew things about her and Patrick. She made another attempt. "Don't worry about me, Ford. But maybe take Kayla to that restaurant. I'm sure you'll have a lovely time."

"Tell me it didn't work out," he said. "Tell me the truth, Ash. God knows there are enough rumors flying around this town."

"Tell you what? Why are you so obsessed about Patrick?"

"Wrong choice of words, Ash."

She chortled, enjoying see him in pain. He wanted the truth, did he? She almost rolled her eyes but stopped herself in time. There was nothing wrong in coming clean. She had nothing to hide. "Patrick and I, we never ... it was fun," she said, finally, after struggling to describe what it was they had together. "Something new to experience."

He sniffed. "Sounds like you're describing a spa experience."

"Careful, Ford. You're beginning to sound possessive."

"You're not going to dinner with him tonight?"

"He bought me flowers, and dinner, and we went our separate ways."

"He bought you flowers?" Ford almost spat the words out.

"Twice." She smiled at him, enjoying this more with each passing second.

"Pink, red and white, then different colors, purple, green and blue with glittery edges," he said, making her stand up straighter. He sounded like a stalker.

"How would you know?" she asked, shock making time slow to a halt.

"Because I sent the flowers." He hooked a thumb at his chest. "*Me*. Both times. I picked them out. I know what you like, I know they're your favorite, at least, the first bunch would have been. They were from me, Ash. *Me*."

Her shocked heart nosedived into a valley of surprise.

He'd sent her the flowers? The thought made her heart swoop up again, fuelled by burst of joy.

Her Ford.

It all made sense now.

Patrick had lied. He'd lied about them being from his PA. "Why that lying ..." She groaned loudly, unable to find the right words to describe him. Not only had he not sent them, but neither had his PA. She gritted her teeth feeling humiliated and silly. "That ... that ... that ... that man is a piece of work!"

Ford raised an eyebrow, looking amused. "He told you *he* sent them?"

She was grounding down so hard on her teeth, it took a while for her jaw to soften. "He said his PA sent them."

Ford roared with laughter. "His *PA?* The poor guy didn't even know whether his PA sent the flowers or not."

She felt like a fool. "You really sent them?"

He sobered up quickly. "Yes."

"Why?" Why on earth would he send her flowers? *Twice.* And say nothing about them? Why would he let her think someone else had sent them? She asked him these questions.

"Because I wanted to."

She dismissed his reply with a shake of her head. "Why?"

"Why?" he echoed back. "Isn't it obvious?"

"No, it's not. It's not obvious at all." She took a few steps back, excitement and nerves swirling around inside her like giddy dance partners. This was most disconcerting. She didn't want complications in her life. She didn't want this. What about Kayla? What game was Ford playing?

"Because I can, Ash." He walked towards her. "I can, so I did."

"Oh, really?" she snapped, her calm exterior disintegrating. She didn't need this. Or, maybe she did. A swirl of delicious happiness coiled inside her, warming her insides.

"Yes, really. I used to send you flowers before."

"That was then. Why now?"

"I sent them when I heard about some guy making moves on you. I didn't like it. I was jealous."

She blinked a couple of times, not quite believing her ears. "Jealous?" He had a nerve to be jealous.

"I didn't like the idea of another guy wanting you. I shouldn't have taken so long to come to my senses." He swiped a hand across his face. "But it's been ... heck. This year has been hard." He let out a harsh breath and stared at the floor, looking deep in thought.

"And Kayla?" What about the woman he'd led her to believe was his new love interest?

"Is a friend." He looked up, his gaze locking on her, trapping her with his azure blue eyes. "She's nothing but a friend."

"And yet the rumors would suggest otherwise."

"They did the job."

"You encouraged them?" She gasped loudly.

"I let people believe what they wanted. Kayla needed help and so did I. That's all that was about."

Her brow creased. "So, you two aren't together?"

"We're not, and have never been."

"But she likes you. It's so obvious to everyone."

His expression turned somber. "I don't feel the same way about her, and I hate that I had to let her down."

"Let her down?"

Something like guilt flickered across those blue eyes. "She ... she likes me and ... I told her I didn't feel the same way." He was hiding something, choosing not to share all the details. And it was okay. She got the drift of it. Ford was a gentleman above all. It should have come as no surprise that he wasn't telling her everything.

"It's you, Ash. I don't want to be with anyone else but you."

"I tried so many times to talk to you!" she yelled, the anger that had lain dormant now exploded.

"I'm sorry. It's not been a good year."

"It's not been great for me either."

"I know, and I'm sorry I haven't been around for you."

"You couldn't let me be happy with a new admirer?"

"I didn't interfere."

Her indignation spiked. "You sent me flowers you let me believe were from him!"

He pointed a finger at her. "I sent you flowers, but I had

nothing to do with him making you believe he sent them, or his PA. That's just unbelievable. How do you not know whether you sent someone flowers or not?"

"He thought his PA sent them."

"Even worse. What kind of man does that?"

She had no answer for him because she'd thought the same thing herself. "But why those colors?" she asked. Ford knew what she liked, and those were not the colors he would have chosen for her.

"I didn't want you to guess that it was me."

"Why send them anyway?" Ashleigh asked.

"Because I was jealous. Because I hated that someone else had muscled in and was making moves on you."

"And what about Kayla?

"What about her?" he asked.

"All that time I thought you and she were together."

"I let people think that. It served me at the time but I was wrong and I feel bad about it." He looked away. "I feel like maybe I led her on, but that wasn't my intention."

Her lips twisted. He was a catch. A great catch, and any woman in her right mind could see that. Why didn't he think that's what would happen? That Kayla might fall for him? But she already knew the answer to that. This man had no bigheaded ideas about himself.

"What if Patrick and I had worked out?" she asked.

"I wasn't going to break you up. Me sending you flowers was a knee-jerk reaction. Darcie told me and I couldn't sleep that night. I wanted to cause a minor disruption. I didn't think my plan would work out well and benefit Patrick—that you would think he sent them, and the guy would have the audacity to pretend the same."

"I think it was a genuine mistake. His PA handles a lot of

things, and he didn't know." She nodded to herself. "So, Darcie told you?"

"In passing one day."

"I know Darcie. I don't think it was a casual comment." Ashleigh's lips curved into a grin. That woman was a little minx. She always had Ashleigh's best interests at heart. "Why multi-colored with glitter? That's not your style."

"To throw you off the scent. I was having some fun."

He had thrown her off the scent. Not for a moment had she ever thought they might be from Ford. "What about Kayla?

"What about her?" he asked.

"All that time I thought you and she were together."

"I let people think that. It served me, I was wrong, and I feel bad about it, but she knows there's only one woman for me."

"Oh?"

"It's you, Ash. It's always been you. I don't want to be with anyone else."

Her insides went into free fall as he walked towards her and took her hands in his. "If you're single, and you'll forgive me, will you take me back?"

CHAPTER 39

GINNY

"Stop ... maybe don't stop just yet ..." murmured Ginny, sitting on the countertop with her legs wrapped around Ryan.

He willingly obliged and peppered her with more kisses before starting to pull away.

"Don't," she begged. Luckily he was still caged between her legs and couldn't quite get away. He pressed his mouth against hers again. "You're impossible to resist," he whispered. Their faces were so close. Most days it was rare to get precious time to themselves, but with Benjy asleep in the crib and Daisy reading a book somewhere, they'd grabbed it.

"We need to get started with dinner," she said, the logical part of her brain kicking in even though dinner was the last thing on her mind. Her body was on fire and when Ryan kissed her again she purred like a contented lioness.

She could not wait to marry this man, to be his wife, to

288

be a family with their respective children. But she was also in no rush. Ever since their life changing short break, ever since Ryan's had proposed, she'd been dizzy with delight. High on happiness. She smiled like a lunatic every time she looked at the ring on her finger. Ryan's proposal was all the security she needed. The rest would come in time. She didn't have the headspace to deal with wedding arrangements right now.

"They're kissing again!" Daisy shrieked, rushing in with Ryan's cell phone. "They're always kissing."

"Are they now?" They both froze at the sound of Vanessa's acid tone. Ryan groaned. Ginny's insides felt like she'd been tasered. Turning, she caught sight of Vanessa's big pouty lips on the phone; she looked even more odd because of the angle and the way Daisy held the phone.

She knew instinctively who was on the other end of that phone, and she was ready for her. Ryan's proposal, the ring he gave her, and the implicit promise of commitment that came with it, instilled in her the security that she was the one Ryan wanted. She was the woman he loved, and the woman he wanted to spend his life with.

"Look!" Daisy pointed the camera at them. Ginny gave the biggest, widest, happiest smile she could muster as she stared directly at Vanessa. "Hi, Vanessa!" she sang, gaily. She'd never been so glad to see the woman in her life. Judging from the look on the woman's face, Ginny was sure Daisy had spilled their news.

Ryan had said that he had no intention of announcing their engagement to Vanessa just yet. He was in no hurry and was more than happy for her to find out through Daisy. Between them, they were surprised it had taken Daisy a few days.

"You're getting married?" Vanessa might as well have been announcing a death.

Ginny held up her hand and showed her the ring. "We most certainly are!" she cried. She could not be happier.

"Ryan, you never said a word about this, you scheming devil."

Daisy was still holding the phone up at them, because neither Ginny nor Ryan were taking the phone from her.

Ryan looked at the phone. "I didn't."

"B-b-but," Vanessa blubbered, her eyes widened and her lips twisted as if she were going to say something, but clearly, she looked angry, fit to explode, and Ryan being calm and unaffected seemed to be making her temperament worse.

"But what?"

"I need to know! This affects my child!"

"Daisy loves Ginny."

At this, Daisy turned the phone to herself. "I get to call her mommy!" Daisy cried with complete innocence, looking deliriously happy as she made the announcement to her mom.

Even Ginny felt the hurt. Vanessa burst into tears and Daisy's looked distraught. "What's wrong Mommy?" she asked, her eyes filling with tears.

"Drama queen," Ryan muttered under his breath, still not taking the phone from Daisy. Finally, Ginny relented, and gently prised the phone away.

"I told her she could call me step-mom, but Daisy doesn't like the connotation of that word. I .... I didn't know what to say to her."

Vanessa didn't respond, but sniffled into her Kleenex. Ginny handed Ryan the phone. "Don't be upset, sweetie." Ginny bent down and wiped the little girl's tears away.

"You don't get to dictate what Daisy calls Ginny, butt out, Vanessa." Ryan's weariness was laced with anger.

"Mommy? She wants Daisy to call her Mommy?" Vanessa hissed. Ginny quickly pulled Daisy away and out of earshot.

"Sweetie, don't cry." She hugged the little girl firmly. No matter how hard she and Ryan tried to not let Vanessa impact their world, the woman always found a way to get through.

"Mommy's sad," Daisy whimpered, her lower wobbling. "I want to call you Mommy, too."

Ginny's lungs filled with too much air, too fast. Too many emotions to process. She hugged Daisy close to her, held her, then kissed her on the cheek as she pulled away.

"Sweetie, it's fine with us. You can call me whatever you want. Whatever you want. I love you with all my heart. I love you like I love Benjy, and you are my daughter, but ... I also understand why your mom might get upset, so .. maybe we just don't tell her all the little things in our life."

Ginny felt wretched for saying this, for telling Daisy to keep some things from her mother but with Daisy's sweet innocence and Vanessa's manipulative personality, they had to reach some sort of agreement. She smoothed Daisy's hair. "Want me to do those fish tail braids on you again?"

Daisy at once cheered up, nodding her head vehemently.

"Why don't you go and say 'bye' to your Mom, tell her you love her and tell her that she will always be your Mom, because she will be Dee, she will be. I'll also be your Mom, but your Mom is really your Mom." She stopped, feeling herself ramble on, but Daisy seemed supercharged and happier, and rushed out.

Ryan stomped in before Ginny managed to haul herself into a standing position.

"That woman. That blasted woman." Ryan swiped his hand across the back of his neck, his face red.

"Sssshh." Ginny wrapped her arms around him. "I understand that upsetting her. I'd be upset if the tables were turned and Benjy said something like that to me."

"You wouldn't milk it for dramatic effect." He wrapped his arms around her waist and kissed the top of her head. "You're not a drama queen, and you would understand. You wouldn't become theatrical, and you wouldn't do anything to hurt Benjy. That woman is a deceitful, manipulative, vindictive … " He stuttered and struggled to find a word. "*Shrew.*" For a split second there she thought he was going to use a different word.

She waited patiently, letting him vent his rage, but he suddenly turned all soft. His eyes shone as he looked at her. "I love you, Ginny. I. Love. *You.* Marrying you will be one of the best things I've ever done. Thank you for wanting to marry me."

His words made her take notice. She tilted her head up, and smiled. "Marrying you will be the greatest honor of my life, second only to giving birth to Benjy. I need you, Ryan. I need you like I need air to breathe, like I need air to survive. That's how much I need you and love you."

He shook his head. "You don't know how much *I* need *you,* my love."

She fell against his chest as they encircled arms around one another, holding each other as they kissed again. He was air, and water and sun. He was her everything.

"Ew!! They're kissing again, mommy!" Daisy appeared by their sides out of nowhere and pointed the phone at them again.

Ryan groaned, this time it was a growling sound low in his throat which only she heard.

"'Bye Vanessa," Ginny cried out, hoping that Daisy would take the hint.

"Mommy hung up," Daisy said, and handed the phone over to Ryan.

Ginny took Daisy's hand. "Let's get started with dinner. Will you help me?"

"Yes!"

CHAPTER 40

LIAM

He felt like Frodo, a man with a mission and a ring which was burning a hole in his pocket.

He'd been unable to sleep, and unable to concentrate at work, but he needed to be razor sharp given that they were two men down. Luckily Josh's fall hadn't been as bad as he'd initially thought. Another one of his guys had a wife who'd gone into labor a month early with their firstborn—so he'd told him to take some time off.

Now, after working a twelve-hour shift, he was exhausted but being bone tired and not thinking straight, helped. It meant he hadn't needed to think much about *this;* what he was doing now, the reason why he was here.

He knocked on Elle's door and when she opened it, their gazes held. He saw the uncertainty in hers. Could he blame her? No. He'd rushed off last time on hearing the news about Josh, but just before that he'd told her that he loved her. He'd told her a lot of things, about why he'd been so miserable lately, about the self-doubt that plagued him, about him not feeling like he was enough. But he hadn't told her *what* had caused all those feelings to surface. They had almost ended that conversation with a kiss and that would have cemented the fact that they were back together, but he'd had to rush off and now he wasn't sure exactly where they were. Things were slightly uneasy again. Were they friends, or lovers again?

To his surprise she smiled first. "Hey." Her voice was a friendly whisper, and he couldn't help but smile back. This was how it used to be before he'd ideas into his head and doubted her love for him.

"Hey. Feeling better today?" A sense of relief came over him. At least they weren't frosty with one another.

"Yes, thanks."

He reached into the pocket of his shirt and pulled out a couple of artisan protein bars he knew she loved. "I got these for you."

"For me?" She seemed surprised as she took them. "Thanks, Liam."

"I know they're your favorite. I'm sorry I should have checked in on you after I rushed off that last time but Josh fell and—"

"Oh, yes, he did. How is he?" She opened the door to let him in. He noticed the way her t-shirt seemed to hug her body more. She seemed a little fuller. Lush. He couldn't wait to get his hands on her and hold her.

"He'll live. It's just a broken leg."

"*Just* a broken leg?"

"I mean, I was expecting worse. Turns out he didn't fall from a high roof. Just a flat roof and he didn't fall far."

"Have you no heart? He still *fell*."

His heart thumped in his throat. He glanced at her sideways

to gauge her mood, not wanting to get off on the wrong foot. Thankfully she seemed relaxed. "I do have a heart. I meant it wasn't fatal, or anything bad. He's fine. He'll live."

"I'm glad he's okay." She smiled at him again, not the full wide smile of the past but something weaker, tentative. "You've got a big heart, Liam. It's the thing about you I love the most."

Her words gave him some comfort. The tension knotted in his shoulders now slowly unraveled. "I would have checked in on you but we're down a few men and there's a job that had to be finished otherwise the guy wasn't going to pay me the full amount."

"That's okay. I'm not holding it against you."

"You sure?" He wanted to make sure because lately, with her, he was never sure.

"Yes, I'm sure." She cocked her head, surveyed him more closely, her gaze trailing slowly from the waist up. Heat rushed all over his skin. He felt a tingle somewhere below and wished she wouldn't do that because he needed to have his wits about him. Clearing his throat, he willed himself to get into work mode. "I'm here to block up the hole," he announced, before marching into the living room.

Eloise looked at him dumbfounded. "What hole?"

"Sorry about the other day," he said, walking in unsure. Without answering her question, without thinking, without a plan. "Sorry I didn't call." He headed towards one of the walls and busied himself, examining the wall carefully. No hole or gap was visible, but he took out his tools—any tools—and pretended to check them. To see if they might be adequate for the so-called job.

"We just spoke about that. You okay?" she asked, peering at him with her brow creased. He was rambling because he was nervous. Talking too much.

"Yeah. I'm okay." Only, now that he was here, he had no

idea how to start. He'd spent hours, *days*, wondering how to go about it. Instead, here he was, crouched down and holding a wrench in his hands. Then he replaced it with a screwdriver. But he had no idea what he was going to do with it.

How would someone like Alex, or Griffin, or someone from *that* world do this? As usual he was overthinking it. The last few days, very late in the evening, he'd headed to the bar with the guys in his team, trying to formulate a plan in his head, while the others talked and joked. His mind was on other things. He didn't touch his beer, or engage in conversation. And now here he was, lost and bewildered.

Be yourself and just do it.

Enough was enough. He decided to wing it.

What hole?" she asked again.

"The one that field mouse must have got in through."

"You think he got in through a *hole?*" Elle cried, worry turned her eyes dark with fear. She didn't like mice, or creepy crawlies.

"I reckon so."

"You mean there could *already* be some mice in here, hiding out?"

"Could be, yeah."

"I haven't seen any evidence of it. No droppings or anything." Her voice dropped to a taper, and she looked scared, rubbing her arms. He was so tempted to put his arms around her, his lips on her and to kiss her, to get back what they had.

He needed to ask her, and he needed to know.

He'd find out soon enough. Either he was going to look like a fool, or not.

"I doubt any creatures have gotten in, but I just want to check and make sure it doesn't happen again. Don't worry, I'll fix it so that those pesky things can't get in even if they dared to try."

He had his back to her as he bent over the bag of tools and pretended to look for something. Next thing, he felt her hand on his shoulder. "Thanks, Liam." Then a deep sigh. "I don't know what I'd do without you."

A tightness gripped his chest, and something heavy settled in his belly. He wondered if he should go back home and get dressed, then take her out. Surely it would be better to kiss and make up properly, check that they were good again?

Ask her properly.

Make it be an event.

Get the gesture perfect.

Make it be unforgettable.

These thoughts paralyzed him. The overthinking tied him up in knots. Wouldn't it be better to ask Elle when they were outdoors, with the sun setting against the backdrop of a beautiful and dramatic landscape?

That's how these things were done. How Ryan had done it, probably.

How Alex would do it.

"Why would you need a wrench?" she asked, standing behind him and looking over his shoulder.

Fool.

He'd put the screwdriver down and picked up the wrench again. He stared up at her. His hand in his pocket, turning the soft velvet box over. "Huh?"

"You're nodding to yourself. Are you okay, Liam?" She looked concerned. Her face filled with worry.

No, he was not okay. He was about to spontaneously combust. Or walk out again.

Coward that he was.

Taking a huge breath, he swiveled around, still on the floor, and turned to face her. Except that he was still crouching on the floor while she stood. He bent his knee, straightened his spine, and looked up at her. Wanted to remember her face before he asked her.

"What are you doing, Liam? You're acting strangely." Her voice was breathless. Her eyes full of alarm.

He didn't want that. Didn't want to alarm her.

It was now or never.

Do or die.

He pulled the box out of his pocket, and prayed that she'd like the ring. He'd picked an oval sapphire flanked by three tiny diamonds on either side. She'd said something when looking through a magazine once, and he'd ripped out the page and kept it.

Now his hand was shaking and his fingers were wobbly and loose. If he wasn't careful he was going to drop the box and ruin the moment. With it lying on the flat of his palm, he watched for her reaction.

Elle's eyes widened like saucers. "Th-that's not a tool."

He looked at the box. Stupidly, he'd forgotten to open it. He flipped the lid open then turned it around so she could see. Her hand flew to her chest and she stumbled back, her eyes filling with tears. "Liam?"

"Will you marry me, Elle? Because I want nothing more than to spend the rest of my life with you."

Her face twisted with surprise and alarm, and she blinked furiously, her lips opening, then closing, then opening again. Then, a whoop of joy. Hands together, she covered her mouth, disbelief etched over her face. "Marry you?" She nodded. "Yes." And she burst out crying. What she said next, he couldn't make out because she collapsed into a heap along with him on the floor, sobbing, and telling him that she was fine, and happy, and surprised. That this was the last thing she expected, but 'oh my goodness, yes, yes, yes!', she wanted to marry him.

They kissed amid tears of joy, and then he stood up first and scooped her up in his arms, holding her close to him. They kissed again. She clung to him, and he saw the joy in her eyes. Saw how happy she was. "I'm sorry for being a jerk," he said. "I was scared I'd changed your plans."

"What plans?"

"You wanted to move to Boston."

"That was way before I met you."

"What if you have regrets?" This. This was the thing he wanted to be sure about.

"Regrets about what?"

"Trading down."

She shook her head. "I don't understand why you feel like this. As if you are somehow *less*. You are more in my eyes."

"I'm just a handyman."

"And a damn good one at that."

"I'm not in finance or oil or banking. I don't have private jets or mansions or millions."

"I don't want those things," she cried, aghast. "I want *you*, Liam. I want our home. I want *us*. I want to come home to you. Just you. I don't care about having wealth, or a big mansion in Cape Cod. Or a yacht, or the other things you think I want. They're not important to me. I knew that even before we got together. I want to settle down with my soulmate. And that's you, in case you're still wondering who I'm talking about." She poked him lightly in the chest.

"I could say the same about you. You're the one for me, Elle. If I feel less, it's no different to you when you obsess about your age relative to mine, about your weight, and your body, and the way you watch what you eat, and your worries about getting older—"

She put her hand up to stop him. "Okay, I get it. What's your point?"

"You can't even hear me say it all. Just like you have your

insecurities, I have mine. And mine Elle, are seeing the guy you were with, in his expensive tux—"

"You looked so handsome in your tux," she cried, not even letting him finish.

"His was expensive, and his watch, and just the way he was; polished and rich and moneyed."

"I don't want that." She peered at him, examining his face closely. "You sure checked him out carefully if you also noticed his watch."

"It was so big, it was hard to miss, but I was trying to look at him and see him as you might see him."

"But I didn't see him. I saw *you*."

They fell silent, with their arms around each other, staring at one another. Smiles dancing on their lips. "You make me so happy, Elle."

Her insides turned light. Strange, given that it was his child she carried in her belly. Liam's baby. Their baby. She would be a mom soon. She laughed, the happiness bubbling up from within. "I love you."

"And I have loved you since high school."

She breathed in deeply, letting those words settle around her heart. They kissed again, the yearning and desire that had been suppressed now coming to the fore.

"When?" she asked, after they pulled apart to take a breath and he set her down on the floor gently.

"When what?"

"When would you like to get married?"

He shrugged. It didn't matter to him. The sooner the better. "I'd marry you right now if I could."

And that was when she stepped away and said, "Good. Because I'd like it to be soon, if that's okay with you."

"Soon is good. I'd marry you in a heartbeat, Elle." He

moved towards her, confused by the distance she was putting between them, by the way she'd untangled herself from him.

"You're sure?" Something flashed in her eyes. Something that made his heart sink. Something that looked like worry. Or trouble. Something that haunted her.

"I'm two hundred per cent sure," he said, instantly on guard.

"I've got something to tell you."

He nodded, then braced himself for the news he was sure would break him. Taking her hands in his, he tried to guess what it might be.

ELOISE

This was the best ending she could have hope for. She and Liam were back together, and not only had they made up, but he'd asked her to marry him.

It was beyond wonderful.

Beyond her wildest dreams.

Beyond anything she could have dreamed up herself.

And she was happy that he'd asked her to marry him, before she broke the news to him.

If he'd proposed after, she would never know for certain if it was because of what she was about to tell him

But now she was plagued by another worry.

What if he didn't want the responsibility of a child?

What if the news for him wasn't good news?

"What is it, Elle? You're worrying me."

Each time she moved away from him, he moved closer. Each time she wrenched her hands away from his, he grabbed them again.

"It's ..." The wobble in her voice made him frown.

He caressed her face, tears forming in his own eyes. "Are you sick?"

She suddenly remembered about his ex-girlfriend, the one who'd gone too soon. She shook her head, then laugh-cried. It wasn't that kind of news. Thankfully. "I'm having our baby."

He jumped back, as if he'd been shocked by electricity. "You're ..." He looked down at her stomach, looked back up at her face. Eyes wide, welling with tears. He swiped the back of his hand over his mouth. "You're pregnant?"

She nodded.

"Oh, Elle!"

That was it. He scooped her up in his arms again and smothered her with kisses. Laughing and crying at the same time. "A baby?" he cried, needing her to confirm again.

"Our baby."

"And you're okay with it?" he asked. He'd known she wasn't too keen, once upon a time.

"I can't wait. Are you okay with it?"

He nodded so fast. "I always wanted children, but I was willing not to because you never sounded keen on them."

"Oh, Liam." A tear rolled down her cheek. "I'm sorry I was so selfish."

"No, no. Don't be. We're blessed. Look at what's happened."

They talked for hours, curled up on the couch, curled up together, and caught up on all that wasted time they'd spent apart.

It was only then that he told her he had planned to propose to her during those few days of vacation following Griffin's party. She finally understood why he'd been so aloof, and strange back then. How he'd wanted to be sure that she no longer yearned for the type of life Beth lived.

He'd needed to know, before he could propose. It all made sense.

She told him all about the baby, how she found out, and what she was afraid of; of being an older mom, an older wife, of being scared. He soothed her worries away with kisses and hugs and words of reassurance. "Do your sisters know?" he asked.

"No." She sat up. They didn't know. They didn't know any of it. "Let's go and break it to them now."

CHAPTER 41

ASHLEIGH

It was what she wanted. Having Ford back in her life. Getting back together with him.

They were sitting outside in her back yard, holding hands, admiring the view. Kissing every now and then. Reminiscing about old times and recent events.

Making up for that past they'd let slip by them. And to think he'd been the one behind the flowers.

She had called Darcie to cancel on her, but hadn't yet told her the reason why. She preferred to do that in person. Maybe tomorrow she and Ford would surprise her together. Darcie had taken her husband to the restaurant instead, so everything had worked out just fine.

She and Ford had come back to her place, and it was as if there hadn't been a split between them. Sitting outside on a balmy, hazy, warm August evening she felt at peace. The end of summer was in sight and the slightly cooler September days were on the horizon, as was the return to school, followed by Labor Day and Columbus Day. Not long after that Halloween, Thanksgiving and Christmas would follow.

Ford gave her hand a squeeze, and she made an appreciative noise. One of satisfaction and contentment. Ford was back, and that bleak, dreary future she had envisioned for herself quietly slipped away.

"What was that?" he asked.

"What?"

"That noise?" He leaned closer.

"Just." She gave a shrug.

"Just?"

"Just ... you know ... a squeal of delight."

"A squeal of delight?" he asked, in a mysterious voice. "I can elicit more of those in you."

Before she had a chance to say something, he moved in for another kiss. Her insides turned to jelly, and she gave in. Let him claim her mouth and cup her face.

This was divine.

And delicious.

To be loved and wanted. To have someone to share her moments with.

"Oh my goodness!"

She heard her sister's voice.

"Color me surprised." That sounded like Liam.

She and Ford quickly broke apart.

"What's this?" Eloise cried, wearing a massive grin. She sounded the happiest that Ashleigh had heard her in a while. She was holding hands with Liam. No wonder her sister sounded like her old self.

"I'll be damned." Liam stepped forward and flicked Ford

lightly with his ball cap. "How long has this been going on?" he asked, his gaze ping-ponging between Ashleigh and Ford.

Ashleigh sat up straighter. Ford cleared his throat, but didn't let go of her hand.

"How long has this been going on?" Ford nodded at Liam and Eloise.

Ashleigh examined her sister's face carefully. Eloise was glowing. She seemed to have blossomed overnight. She looked fuller, and happier, and she kept smiling as she looked at Liam. He couldn't keep his eyes off her, either. "We made up just now," she said, shyly, tucking a stray lock of hair behind her ear. That was when Ashleigh saw it.

She bolted up right out of her patio chair. "Is that a ring?" Her mouth fell open. It looked like an engagement ring. Eloise was wearing it on *that* finger.

"Yes!" Eloise screamed with joy. "It is. Liam proposed, just now."

They heard children laughing, and then Ryan and Ginny stepped into the garden. "Who proposed?" Ginny asked, holding Benjy in her arms.

"Liam proposed." Eloise proudly held up her hand for all to see.

Ginny's eyes widened and she moved to examine the ring. "He *proposed?*"

Chatter erupted at the news as everyone came to realize that Eloise and Liam had made up, and that Liam had proposed, just under an hour ago. Hugs and kisses were exchanged. The men shook hands. The air was filled with the sound of laughter and cries that were so infectious, that Daisy and Benjy joined in, even though they didn't fully understand why the grownups were so happy.

Congratulations were exchanged, and then more surprise

followed when Eloise and Ginny realized that Ashleigh and Ford were also back together.

Ryan laid out a picnic blanket on the ground, and set Benjy on it, with Daisy watching him.

"Well, this is quite a year," Ashleigh said, as the commotion died down. "Two engagements!"

Ford pulled out more patio chairs from the side and unfolded them. "Exciting, isn't it?" Eloise remarked, sitting down. Ashleigh still couldn't believe Eloise's announcement. It was such welcome news. Eloise and Liam were so good together and it had been painful seeing them be so miserable apart.

Just like she and Ford had been.

All that time she'd been thinking he and Kayla were an item, and it wasn't true at all.

"At this rate, we'll be busy working on *both* your dresses. The customers will have to take a back seat," she remarked, wondering what next year would bring.

"I don't want to get married just yet," Ginny said quickly. "I want to wait a while. I want to get to grips with the business and have Benjy be a little older."

"Is that okay with you, Ryan?" Ashleigh asked.

"I'm fine with whatever Ginny says. As long as I don't have to wait too long."

"That's good, because I don't want to wait at all," Eloise said.

"It's not a race," Ginny pointed out.

"No, it's not." Eloise looked at Liam, who leaned in and whispered something.

Ashleigh frowned and wondered what that was about. Eloise scratched the back of her neck. It was a tell. Ashleigh knew. Her sisters was nervous about something.

"Tell them," she heard Liam whisper.

Ashleigh looked from one to the other. "Tell us what?"

"We're having a baby," Eloise said, beaming at them. Silence fell for a few seconds and it took a while for the weight of the announcement to register.

"What? When?" she and Ginny cried at once. Then more excited cries filled the air.

In all the noise, it all fell into place. Eloise's moods and misery and all that crying. Ashleigh walked up to her sister and hugged her, then congratulated her and Liam, but not for long, because Ginny was waiting to do the same.

When everything had quietened down, they learned that Eloise's baby was due sometime towards the end of March. "But we want to get married quickly."

"What about you, Liam?" Ashleigh asked. "When do you want to get married?"

"I'd marry her today if I could." If Eloise smiled any more, she'd have a jaw ache.

"You need a dress!" Ashleigh cried.

"You need to make arrangements," Ginny added.

"I don't care much about the dress, or the arrangements," Eloise replied.

"But Liam might," Ashleigh retorted, not wanting Eloise to rush through this and do as she pleased. Liam lifted her hand and kissed it. "Like I said, I'd marry her now if I could."

Ryan and Ford guffawed at that.

Ashleigh sat back. There were so many questions. So much to think about and do.

The men were huddled together, talking, and Eloise and Ginny looked to be in deep conversation. Over by the rosebushes, Daisy was reading a book to Benjy. They had all found their way back to one another. Lively chatter was all around, and every now and then the sweet scent of the roses would wash over her.

This was so sublime. So perfect. She looked up, then at her garden with all its roses, and hoped their parents were looking down on them.

ASHLEIGH

"**Y**ou may now kiss the bride."

Ashleigh tried to hold back the tears as she watched Liam and Eloise kissing. Her younger sister looked so beautiful in her wedding gown, a simple yet sophisticated dress made from the finest silk, with a high neck and low strappy back.

Herb, Darcie's gardener, along with Liam and Ford had worked to make the garden ready to hold a small wedding. Eloise wanted to get married in the rose garden.

Secretly, Ashleigh was delighted. It was here that she felt the presence of her mother and father the most. Even though the garden had changed considerably over the years, she had the fondest memories of them all playing as children, of sunny days and family gatherings with her parents. Like the three of them, the garden had changed. It had transformed, evolving over time, becoming *more*.

"Awww." Ginny's sigh was loud enough to reach Ashleigh's ears. Ashleigh leaned forward over Daisy who sat between her and Ginny, and reached for her sister's hand. They both had tears in their eyes.

Everything had happened so fast. Eloise announcing her engagement to Liam, and then hitting them with the unexpected news that they were also expecting. Then, as if that wasn't enough, she'd hit them with a third announcement. "I want to get married, after the Labor Day weekend."

It gave them just over two weeks to plan and get everything ready. It had been madness, of course, what with trying to get her dress ready, and taking care of the catering, the cake and the flowers, but they had good contacts. It helped that they were in the business.

Remarkably and miraculously, they managed to get everything done in time. They had pulled it off.

And here they were. Things were changing in the Rose household. Eloise and Liam were married. A second baby would arrive in due course. Their family was growing and flourishing, just like the garden.

Who knew, maybe Ginny and Ryan would tie the knot next?

She sat back and felt Ford's hand slide around her waist. He kissed her just above the ear. "You okay?" he asked. She looked at him, found her comfort in those familiar blue eyes, and nodded.

She was okay. And so were Eloise and Ginny. Still deep in thought, she rose when everyone else did. The bride and groom had kissed and were now husband and wife. They walked back towards the house. Ryan and Herb had set up the patio table, which was beautifully decorated with a silk tablecloth and flowers. Champagne and beer bottles were in ice buckets and a collection of champagne flutes sparkled in the sunshine.

The sisters rushed to the table, wanting to be the first to congratulate the newlyweds.

"I'm so happy for you!" Ginny hugged her sister tightly. It was Ashleigh's turn next. She held onto her sister for more than a few seconds. "You were always meant to be together. I'm so happy for you both. And I'm so happy that you wanted to get married here where … " Her lower lip trembled and she couldn't finish the sentence. But there was no need to; Eloise understood. Ashleigh rested her hand against her sister's cheek before placing another kiss on her cheek. "I'm just so happy for you," she said, snifling, while trying hard to hold back her tears. She wasn't going to break down.

She wasn't.

Eloise looked at her and Ginny, and now her lower lip trembled, too. Her eyes filled with tears. Ashleigh blamed herself for getting her started. "Don't you dare cry," she hissed, shaking her head. "Your mascara will run."

"You don't want to get black streaks down your cheeks," Ginny agreed.

"I'm so lucky," Eloise whispered, holding back a sob. "I'm so lucky to have the *best* sisters in the world." They all hugged together, sharing a moment in time where the guests and the garden, the birdsong and the summer breeze, blurred into the background.

They had been through some tough times, from bad to worse, to tragic. Along the way they had argued and fought; had hated one another in moments of madness, yet loved each other unconditionally. They had laughed and cried, testing the bonds of sisterhood. And through it all, they had learned that they could withstand anything. They were bound by blood forever and they would never be alone. Now their family was growing, and they were doubly blessed with having the perfect life partners. Good men who would stand by them no matter what.

Ford and Ryan congratulated the couple next, and soon enough the rest of the guests slowly appeared. Liam uncorked a bottle of champagne before handing it to Ford to do the honors and make sure all the guests had a glass.

Then he made a toast where he talked about being the luckiest man alive and told the guests the story of how he'd first met his high school crush later in life and knew not long after that they were destined to be together. Eloise stood by his side radiating happiness.

The couple's baby secret wasn't common knowledge yet. It was known only by immediate family and friends like Darcie.

Even Beth didn't know. Eloise's friend hadn't been able to come to the wedding at such short notice because she and her husband were visiting the surrogate mother of their twins. Eloise planned to tell them in person when she and Liam honeymooned in Cape Cod and finished off the break they'd cut short.

Ashleigh grabbed Ford's hand and ushered Ginny and Ryan away, wanting to let Eloise and Liam talk to their friends.

"I suppose you're thinking of getting married here now?" Ryan asked Ginny.

"Is that what you think I'm thinking?" Ginny asked, sounding surprised. "I'm thinking we have a busy time ahead once the honeymooners leave."

Ashleigh and Ford exchanged glances. Ginny seemed to be wearing her business hat more and more, and Ashleigh, for one, was happy to let her.

"I'll help you," Ryan offered, holding her hand. "I'm good with accounts and tech. I could be good for something."

Ginny nodded. "That would be good. I've made a list of

things we should streamline." She glanced at Ashleigh. "I was going to run them by you and Eloise first."

Ashleigh nodded. "Sure. But now is not the time to talk about business, Ginny. Try to enjoy the day." If anyone had done a complete turn in their lives, it was Ginny.

"Where's Benjy?" Ginny cried, looking around for her son. "And Daisy?"

"They're with Kayla. Don't worry. They're in good hands." Ryan nodded towards the area where the nuptials had taken place. Sure enough there was Kayla with Benjy in her arms.

"Does she know Herb?" Ashleigh asked as she glanced in that direction.

Ford chuckled. "Seems to."

Ryan stared at Kayla in the distance. "Are you setting my sister up?" he asked Ford.

Ford shook his head. "I'm not doing a thing, buddy."

"Herb's a good guy," Darcie said. "I've known him for over a decade. He's nice and he's single. The poor man has been unlucky in love. I'm sure he feels out of place because he doesn't know many people here but—"

"It was only right we invited him. Eloise insisted on it." Ashleigh said. "He's done wonders with the rose garden and he's been great at helping us to get everything set up in the field. He even offered to oversee the tent being put up." They had decided to hold the wedding reception in a tent in the middle of the field between the main house and Eloise's house. The rose garden wouldn't have been big enough to host the extra guests expected to turn up later for the party. It had become quite a monumental task in the end, getting the tent ready, and Herb had been so helpful. He'd helped string lights both inside and outside the tent and by the time the helpers had finished setting up the tables and chairs and flowers and candles, it looked beautiful.

Ryan shrugged. "He doesn't sound too bad."

"He's not a serial killer, if you're worried about that." Darcie adjusted the brooch on her dress. Ashleigh glanced around their little group and marveled at how smart they all looked dressed in their best clothes.

It hadn't been so long ago when Ford and Eloise had turned up here, disrupting her peaceful Sunday lonesome yoga session. She never wanted to go back to that time; to being miserable and frustrated, believing that she had lost Ford, and drawn a short straw with Patrick. Thinking that she had lost her chance to find love and was destined to grow old and die alone.

Life was better now, and this group of people around her made it so.

"I need to freshen up," Eloise declared, turning up with Liam in tow.

"Where?" Ashleigh wondered if her sister was going to traipse across the field in her wedding dress and heels.

"Upstairs. I brought all my things over."

"I'll come with you," Liam offered. He was so attentive. So careful around Eloise. Ashleigh was sure her sister basked in all the extra attention. That man was going to make a great father. And Eloise would make a wonderful mother.

Not having any children of her own, and now too late to start a family, Ashleigh was at peace knowing that she at least had a nephew, and another nephew or niece on the way. That would be more than enough. She would shower so much love on those children, and treat them as if they were her own.

But for now, she was content to just be. To watch everything and everyone around her and to bask in joyous contentment.

"Happy?" Ford kissed the top of her head and hugged her to him. She sighed. She was ridiculously happy. "I wonder if this was meant to be," she whispered.

"What was meant to be?"

"This, everything coming together and happening here. Eloise getting married, Ginny getting engaged, you and me back together. Celebrating not just Eloise's wedding, but all of it, here, in this place, in this home my parents loved so much."

Ford hugged her closer still. "Could be," he said, after a while.

It truly felt as if her life had come full circle. The last few years had been the worst since her parents' death, but together, she and her sisters had weathered the bad times. The way close families do.

She was starting to realize that perhaps this was what life was. Ups and downs. Highs and lows. Endings and new beginnings. Tears and sadness followed by laughter and joy. The circle of life.

She looked forward to the future and was ready to embark on the next stage of her life.

Thank you for reading THE ROSE GARDEN. I hope you enjoyed reading about the sisters and their friends and family.

I have written TWO bonus epilogues for this story, and you can get them by signing up at the link below (if you're already a newsletter subscriber, you'll be sent these via email. No need to sign up again):

https://www.siennacarr.com/newsletter

Note: Please check the SPAM/JUNK/PROMOTIONS tabs of your email as my newsletters might end up in there.

Looking for something else to read? Check out WINTER'S KISS, the first book in a series of women's fiction romances set in a small town called Starling Bay. Read an excerpt from Winters Kiss Below

When widowed single mom Merry Nicholls visits Starling Bay, all she wants is some rest and relaxation during the Christmas holidays. But after her unruly Great Dane tramples through a gift shop, her connection with the store's handsome owner, Dylan Fraser, takes them both by surprise!

I appreciate your help in spreading the word, including telling a friend, and I would be grateful if you could leave a review on your favorite book site!

Thank you!
Sienna

"I hate Christmas," cried Merry, "and Starling Bay—why would I want to go *there*?"

Her mother liked to interfere, but this was taking things too far. Merry felt better now. She *was* better. Of course, she worked a little too hard, but she had it all under control.

"To spend some quality time with your daughter, for one thing. And to get some rest. You've never stopped, Meredith," her mother pointed out. "Not even after Brian—"

"Don't, Mom." She didn't want the constant reminders.

"The doctor signed you off. There's no point in you moping around at home. You need to get away."

"But to Starling Bay? If I wanted a real vacation I'd go overseas."

"Would you?" Her mother gave her *that* look.

Okay. Maybe not. She hadn't gotten on a plane ever since Brian's accident. What should have been an exhilarating experience, a trip in a light Cessna aircraft, had turned into her worst nightmare when the engine caught fire. The plane burst into flames as it hit the ground ten minutes after take-off, killing both Brian and the pilot. She'd bought him the flying experience as a joint birthday and Christmas gift. Ever since then, she hadn't stepped foot inside a plane.

"You don't need to fly. You can drive."

"With Spartacus?" Their beloved Great Dane wasn't going to like the long road trip.

"You loved it when we used to go."

"That was years ago, Mom. I was a teenager then."

"And Chloe's a teenager now."

"The place is dead!"

Her mother returned a smug smile. "Apparently, no. It's booming. It was always a pretty little coastal town, but it's growing. I don't think I would like it so much now. Hyacinth tells me that it has undergone a lot of changes, but she still lives there, so it can't be all that bad."

Hyacinth Fitzsimmons was her mother's friend. Rather, her mother had made friends with the matronly woman the first time they had visited Starling Bay.

"Besides, they'll be getting ready for Christmas," her mother continued, "and I know how pretty it looks around this time of year."

"God, no," Merry groaned. *I hate Christmas.* She hadn't always hated it, only since Brian had passed away. He had loved it, and she had too, but spending it without him, especially that first time, just weeks after his passing, had been the hardest. From that moment on, she no longer looked forward to it. Christmas was about family, and being together, and being thankful, it was about feeling joyous and happy, and without her husband, she felt none of those things. The following year she couldn't bring herself to put up the tree, or buy gifts, or decorate the house. Luckily, for Chloe's sake, her parents had taken care of things.

"Meredith, it's about time you started to think more about Chloe." She lifted her face at her mother's stern tone.

"I *do* think about my daughter," she retorted. "It's not easy being a single parent."

"You want for nothing, I get that. You work hard, we see that. But your father and I also see that your daughter needs you. She doesn't need her grandparents as much as she needs you. Use this time wisely and spend it with her. Her school will be winding down in a few weeks' time. Why not take this opportunity and go away for a few months?"

"A few *months?*" She was thinking about the disruption to her daughter's schooling.

"Isn't that what your boss suggested? Thanksgiving's over and if you're that worried about school, you can always homeschool Chloe for a while. Spend quality time with your daughter for a change as well as taking a well-earned break for yourself."

Merry shook her head. Homeschooling sounded like hard work. She loved Chloe, but she had a feeling that her surly tween daughter would have to be dragged kicking and screaming all the way to a place where she knew no one. A place she had never been to. A place Merry herself hadn't been to for over a decade.

The idea was ludicrous.

Merry folded her arms. She had thrown herself into work after Brian's accident, and after the promotion, she continued to work crazy hours. Being the marketing manager for Boyd & Meyer, one of Boston's upscale department stores, came with a lot of pressure and responsibility. She had worked hard to get where she was, and the pressure was always on her to prove that she was worthy of that position, especially when resumes were always coming in from people who were so much better qualified than her on paper. She might not have had the degrees to prove it, but she could get the results that mattered.

The department store's sales had been increasing in recent

years, and she liked to think that she had something to do with this. Dan Shepworth, her boss and CEO, seemed to agree. He had been good to her.

The run-up to Christmas was one of the busiest times of the year, but something had happened to her in recent months. At first she'd thought it was nothing, her bouts of dizziness, and feelings of anxiety, but when these things became physical, when her hands became so clammy that she'd messed up her presentation to the management team, and when her blood pressure spiked, and she'd suffered a nosebleed, her parents had forced her to go to the doctor.

The doctor had prescribed rest and taking things easy. He advised her to take time off because she seemed to be on the brink of a breakdown if she continued her long hours.

It wasn't the work, or the pressure. She knew what it was. The five-year anniversary of Brian's death might have had something to do with it, and her cute, sweet daughter turning twelve might have pushed things over the edge for her.

"I can't afford to lose you, Meredith," Dan had told her a few weeks ago. "Take a couple of months off. You haven't had a good long break. Take time off, and come back when you're fit and ready."

He hadn't given her a choice. He had signed her off the week before Thanksgiving. But her first week at home hadn't been easy, either.

"Hyacinth could do with your expertise," her mother continued. "She's offered you one of the houses by the bay, you know, one of those pretty little places overlooking the oceanfront."

"She offered? When did she offer it?" Merry smelled interference.

"Oh, sometime last week."

She let out an irritated breath. She loved her parents, but her mother could be an interfering little soul. Merry knew her recent health problems had scared her parents. It made them keep an even closer eye on her. They had moved all the way from California to Boston after Brian's death to be here for Merry and her daughter, and she was thankful for all they had done for her.

She also knew that her mother wasn't going to back down until she did what they suggested. "What am I going to do in one of those houses overlooking the ocean?" She would be bored out of her mind. Spartacus would be the only one who'd find any adventure in the move. She stared at the Great Dane who lay on his side, tongue lolling out, while she paced around the living room.

Her mother stepped in front of her, and gently took her by the shoulders. "This isn't just a difficult Christmas for you, it's hard on Chloe, too, seeing you looking down and not being well. She's so sensitive, given that she's on the brink of being a teenager."

"Don't I know it?" she muttered. Lately, her daughter had become more distant, preferring to stay in her room on her devices, or talking to friends on the phone. Merry knew it was her fault, that she had turned her back on her daughter in an attempt to come to terms with her grief. Brian's sudden passing had hit them like a train.

"I know it hasn't been easy for you, but don't think that it's been any easier for that girl. She was seven when Brian died."

"Don't, Mom." Merry looked away. Some Thanksgiving dinner this had turned out to be. Her father and Chloe were in the other room, her father asleep on the couch, and Chloe watching *Home Alone* for probably the tenth time.

It was time to take stock. Could she spend a few weeks, maybe even a month at Starling Bay? At least she'd get to spend Christmas away from Boston. That was an advantage worth considering. The malls and streets were already looking festive, and had been for the past month. She felt as if she'd stepped into Christmas the moment Halloween had ended.

"We want you back, Meredith," Dan Shepworth had told her. "I'm keeping this position open for you. Just get well, and come back." He reassured her that they would get by. She had a good team in place, and she would be in regular contact in case they needed her. Maybe a couple of months away would be good for her.

"Your boss might start thinking of replacing you, if you're not as sharp as you used to be." Her mother was oh-so-very clever. She had hit her right where it hurt.

Merry swallowed. Being considered not good enough by Mr. Shepworth, being replaced, would kill her.

"What do I have to do?" she asked, knowing full well that this casual conversation about Starling Bay was anything but casual. Her mother had a plan.

"Live in a beautiful home, enjoy Starling Bay, have quality time to yourself, get to know your daughter all over again. That's not too much to ask, is it?"

"What did you sign me up for, Mom? You said Hyacinth's letting me stay there for free. What's she expecting in return?"

"Nothing much."

"That doesn't sound like Hyacinth." She remembered her mother's friend as being a formidable woman who wore too much powder on her face.

"She could do with some of your marketing expertise, Meredith."

"*Marketing expertise*? I thought you wanted me to rest and take a break from the world of work."

"Oh, Meredith," her mother crooned. "Hyacinth is on the town committee, and she's leading the Christmas festivities. She only wants a few of your ideas and help."

"Ideas and help?" That job description was so vague as to be useless. But, compared to what her current workload would have been like at the department store, giving Hyacinth a few tips would be simple. She could do it with her eyes shut. "Okay. I'll go." At the very least it would get her mother off her back.

"Wonderful!" Her mother clapped her hands together and picked up the phone.

"What are you doing?"

"Calling Hyacinth to tell her that you're coming."

"When exactly does she expect me to come?" She hadn't thought about it, hadn't had time to get used to the idea.

"Next week, I expect. It's not long to go before Christmas."

Merry sucked in a breath, already regretting her hasty decision.

She hated Christmas.

WINTER'S KISS now available at all major retailers.

BOOKLIST

The Rose Sisters:
The Bridal Shop
The Summer House
The Winter Beach
The Rose Garden

Starling Bay books:
Whirlwind Kisses
Winter's Kiss
Maid for Him
Love Letters
Escape to Starling Bay (Books 1-3)
From Faking to Forever
Winter's Vow
Guarded Hearts
Table for Two
A Bouquet of Charm
Christmas Wish

ACKNOWLEDGMENTS

I would like to thank my amazing group of proofreaders who check my manuscript for errors, typos and inconsistencies.
I am eternally grateful for their help and support:

Marcia Chamberlain
Dena Pugh
Carole Tunstall

I would also like to thank Tatiana Vila of Vila Design for creating the awesome cover.

ABOUT THE AUTHOR

Sienna Carr has been writing romance since 2013. She lives in the UK with her husband, three children, and a parrot.

Connect with Me

I love hearing from you – so please don't be shy!
You can email me at: sienna@siennacarr.com

Goodreads | Bookbub | Website

BB bookbub.com/authors/sienna-carr

www.ingramcontent.com/pod-product-compliance
Lightning Source LLC
Chambersburg PA
CBHW021217220726
48287CB00015B/1575